WHISPERS IN THE DARK

Will awoke suddenly from a sleep so deep that his body panicked and his mind did the same, tripping back and forth, trying to figure out where he was, *when* he was.

Then he became aware of the whispers coming from beneath the bed, and knew that he was in his own house, in his own bed, at the blackest time of night, and that Michael was with him. Michael, dead and gone so many years, was back.

"You're dead," Will whispered. "You're dead."

Will, I'm here. Will, can you hear me? It's Michael.

Dreaming, Will told himself, *I'm only dreaming. I can wake myself up.*

Michael's voice continued to whisper, but he couldn't understand most of the words. *This is hypnogogia,* he told himself. *The voluntary muscles are paralyzed in this stage of sleep. This is when the boogeyman scares children and people see aliens coming to experiment on them. My boogeyman is Michael, and he's under the bed. I am taking charge by moving my dream arm and clicking on the light. The light will make the whispering stop. Michael will go away. He will rest in peace.*

Will continued the litany, refusing to listen to the constant whispers, paying attention only to his own voice.

It wasn't working. He heard Michael whisper, *You're already awake, Will. You're awake. And I'm here . . .*

Books by Tamara Thorne

HAUNTED

MOONFALL

ETERNITY

CANDLE BAY

BAD THINGS

THE FORGOTTEN

Published by Pinnacle Books

THE FORGOTTEN

Tamara Thorne

PINNACLE BOOKS
Kensington Publishing Corp.

http://www.kensingtonbooks.com

For Brian, the best son on earth.
You have your mother's eyes.
Now give them back!

ACKNOWLEDGMENTS

John Scognamiglio, you are living proof that chivalry isn't dead. For all the reasons you know, you have my undying devotion. And if I ever become undead, I will even eat brains for you. I wouldn't do that for just any old editor, you know . . .

Bill, who shoots straight and long
Q.L. Pearce, the woman who understands how to handle bananas
Quinn, essential
Dr. Mark, who puts the psycho in psychology
Dr. Jim, epitome of veterinarians
Dr. Susan, back cracker extraordinaire
Dr. Jacques, revealer of Secret Governments
Secret Governments, unending inspiration
Jeremy, Matthew, and Nathaniel, the real Orange Boys
Eric, Andy, Brett, Heather, Paula, Michele, Linda, Kay, Carol, Maryanne, Gilligan, the skipper too, but not the millionaire or his wife, for all sorts of things
And finally, special thanks to my darling devil man, Damien, because you always like to come last.

1

"It's awful, Doc. I can't get it to shut up." Daniel Hatch clasped his hands together, long fingers spidering around one another, pressing red and white polka dots into the flesh. "It just keeps talking to me. Talking and talking."

"How long has this been going on? I don't think you mentioned it during our last visit." Will Banning sat forward, studying his patient. Daniel Hatch was a wounded sparrow of a man who first came to him after completing three months on the wagon. Physically, he had handled the lack of alcohol fairly well, but his emotional problems—centering on timidity and fear of confrontation—remained, and he had sought out Will to help him find new ways to handle them. Progress since then had been slow but steady. Until now. This was something entirely new and unexpected.

"I've heard the voice for a while now."

"A week?" His last appointment had been two weeks ago.

"Well, maybe a month or two. But I didn't tell you because I thought I was imagining it." Hatch scratched his head. "And until last week it only talked a little, but now sometimes I can hear it talking right through my Jockeys, through my chinos." He touched his pant leg and lowered his voice, his nose and cheeks almost glowing with embarrassment. "I've got three pairs of briefs on under my pants."

"And you still hear it?" Will studied his patient. The afternoon sun came through the French doors behind Hatch and glowed angelically through his thin blond hair.

"Yes. It was working pretty well, you know, muffling the voice, but it's slowly getting louder and louder." He swallowed audibly. "I think pretty soon, other people will hear him all the time too."

"Can you give me an example of what you hear? Of what you're afraid other people may overhear?"

Hatch's eyes bugged incredulously. "It doesn't matter what he—it, I mean—says, my penis is *talking* to me!" He blushed and wouldn't meet his psychologist's eyes. "I'm sorry. I didn't mean to blow up at you."

"You didn't blow up. You made a valid point, but if you tell me what you seem to be hearing, it might give us some insight, Daniel." Seeing annoyance on Hatch's thin face, Will decided to stop speaking in Shrink and go along with Hatch's choice of words. "So what does your penis say to you?"

"Well, at the movies, it makes rude comments about actors and lewd ones about actresses."

"Does it tell you what movies to watch?"

"Yeah." Hatch blushed furiously and looked at his busy fingers. "It makes me watch porn." He glanced up, almost meeting Will's gaze, then looked back down at his knees. "He really likes lesbian orgy movies. I tell him it's bad, but he won't listen."

"It's not bad to like those movies," Will said gently, refusing to let himself smile. "In fact, I'm sure that's a pretty common trait among penises."

"Yeah. Well . . . Doctor, last night at a bar—I was just having a ginger ale, I swear—"

"I believe you. Go on."

"It talked to the woman on the barstool next to me. It asked if she . . ." He blushed deeply. "I can't say."

"You can say anything you want. It doesn't leave this room."

"Well, it told her he'd like to, uh, have relations with her. Only he, it, used a much cruder word."

"Did she hear it?"

"Yes. And she slapped *me* for what *he* said."

"Think hard. Did your penis say it or did you say it?"

"My dick. Penis, I mean. I told you that." Hatch ran a finger between his neck and collar then twined his fingers together again.

"I understand, but perhaps your penis is speaking *through* you." Will paused to study the man. Hatch might be in the midst of a psychotic episode or edging toward real schizophrenia. In the three years he'd counseled him, the man had never lost his grip on reality before. The rapid change was disturbing.

"Speaking *through* me?" Daniel's eyes widened. He began trembling and a fine sheen of sweat glossed his ruddy face. "That's it, Doctor! That's it! I'm being possessed. Possessed by my own penis!"

"Well, I wouldn't say—"

"Can you exorcize it, Doctor? The demon or whatever it is that's living in there talking to me?" Hatch crossed himself.

Will almost suggested he consult a priest, but changed his mind. Hatch had been born into a strict and religious family, but had said only enough to give Will the impression that maternal strictness was at the root of his problem, not the religion itself. *What if I was wrong? Damn!* "Your penis isn't harboring a demon, Daniel." He paused, then asked, "Do you believe in demonic possession?"

"I do now!" He slapped his hand to his forehead. "Why didn't I think of it myself? Of course. Possession. That's it, Doctor!"

Why did I ever use that word? "I know we discussed it years ago, but refresh my memory—do you still practice your religion?"

"Not really. I'm Catholic, I guess, because I went to Catholic school. Those nuns . . ." He licked his lips, not altogether anxiously. "They were strict. I still think about them sometimes."

Hatch's pupils enlarged, nudging memories of past sessions into Will's mind. Yes, he'd mentioned Catholic school, joked about the nuns, but nothing in his manner had suggested his patient's sexuality was excessively tied into religion. *How could I have missed that?* He had missed it, somehow. Hadn't he? He couldn't quite believe it. Maybe it had been buried beneath a slight but evident Oedipal complex. Or maybe it simply arose from a viewing of *The Exorcist* and combined with this new aberration. "But you don't attend church now?"

"No." Hatch smiled in small triumph. "No one can tell me what to do now. Heck, I don't even pray." Another smile. "My mother would disown me if she knew."

Will nodded. Mother was the problem they'd worked on since the beginning. "Do you believe in God?"

Hatch shrugged. "I never think about it." He rubbed his chin. "I guess I do though. If Satan's in my penis, then God must be real, too." He looked doubtful. "Unless demons have nothing to do with religion."

"Daniel, I doubt this problem with your penis is truly a religious issue."

"But it's trying to possess me," Hatch insisted. "The demon wants to take me over! Thank you! It's a relief to realize why I'm hearing the voice, Doctor. Possession."

Silently, Will cursed himself and tried another angle. "Daniel, listen to me. Do you think your subconscious might be trying to get loose long enough to tell you something? We've established that you've led a very repressed life, which makes it difficult to talk about some things. Or even think about them. Does that make sense?"

"Sure, but what's that got to do with my dick?"

Oh, just about everything. Tension banded Will's forehead. "Maybe you need to talk about something but just can't let yourself. Some people divide their personalities to solve the problem. You may be using your penis to personify the part of you that needs to talk. Notice that you're giving it a personality of its own when you refer to it as 'he' or as a demon."

Will's office, cool mauves and serene tans punctuated with greenery and tranquil Japanese ink and watercolor prints, suddenly felt like a hot little box. Will knew the hour was nearly up by the slant of the sunlight dappling the little courtyard beyond the glass doors behind Daniel's sofa. *Thank heaven.* His neck and back muscles were steel cords, ready to snap. As soon as Hatch left, he could lock his door and indulge in five minutes of tai chi before seeing his two o'clock patient, the last of the day.

There had been several requests for same-day appointments this morning, but nothing sounded particularly dire, and Will needed time off, even if he used it to catch up on paperwork, so he'd turned them down. Ever since the part-time therapist who had occupied the other office in his small building had left, he'd been mildly overworked. Lately, the workload had gotten heavier; he couldn't put off interviewing replacements much longer. Exhaustion lowered his psychic defenses, a bad situation for anyone constantly dealing with mentally disturbed people. One passive-aggressive patient would be enough to do him in today—fortunately, none were scheduled.

Will had given up his last two early Wednesdays, had worked three full Saturdays and half of last Sunday. He was bushed and it seemed like all his patients today (and recently) had more problems than usual. *Or maybe I just need a vacation.* Guiltily, he stared outside, wishing the doors were open to let in the breeze. His back hurt. Maybe Gabe would be willing to give it a quick crunch later. He could invite him and Kevin over for dinner in exchange. *I'll call Maggie, maybe she'd like to come.*

He returned his attention to Daniel, who was holding forth on demons in a way that sounded more Hollywood than Catholic. The man was processing information aloud, something he often did, and although Will approved, he could barely make himself listen now. How would he get through the interminable final patient? The outdoors beckoned. A small patio table and two chairs rested on a cement pad edged by an oval of lawn that ran twelve feet out to a border of fragrant striped petunias and marguerites, then trees in full summer leaf, all boxed in by a tall redwood fence. Some of his patients liked their sessions outdoors, but Daniel Hatch wasn't one of them. He was more of a small, enclosed space kind of guy, a connoisseur of recirculated central air conditioning. He had a thing about needing doors and windows shut and locked. Will suddenly felt like a martyr, giving up the ocean breeze for his patient. But it would be over soon. *Soon.* He realized Hatch was asking a question. He'd stopped talking about demons and was back to the personification of his genitalia.

"Doctor? Do you think I'm getting a split personality? Like in *The Three Faces of Eve?* Or *Sybil?*"

"No, not in that sense. In that case you wouldn't be aware of the division. This is a conscious separation, not so different from the public and private personas most of us slip into now and then."

He nodded. "So I'm not nuts?"

"You're not a split personality." He couldn't hazard a guess about the nuts situation, not yet. Hopefully, Daniel was experiencing a brief delusional disorder or a nonspecific psychosis that would subside as quickly as it appeared. But if it lasted, if it grew, they might be looking at schizophrenia or a schizoaffective disorder. Will hoped not. "Have you heard any other unusual voices?"

"Grackle spackle," Daniel said softly.

"What?"

"You heard it, didn't you?" He gazed at Will, eyes wide and hopeful.

"I thought I heard you say 'grackle spackle.' "

"He said it."

"What does it mean?"

"I don't know."

"What's a grackle?" Will asked, testing the waters.

"A bird."

He nodded, remembering that Maggie had mentioned she'd never seen a grackle along this stretch of the coast. Maggie noticed things like that. "Where did you grow up, Daniel?"

"Here. Well, Red Cay, but that's not far. Have you been there?"

"Sure, but not recently." Red Cay was a small fishing town maybe twenty-five miles south, just below Candle Bay. When he was a kid, his dad had taken him, Michael, and Pete fishing on the pier there now and then. It was supposed to be the best fishing in the area, but Will primarily remembered how Pete would point up to the old lighthouse and mansion across a narrow bay and try to scare him with stories of the ghosts lurking there. He remembered it well and fondly because it was one of the few times Pete had failed to get under his skin. Will was a born nonbeliever.

"There's a haunted house there. Body House. It's famous."

"Yes, I remember. Did you ever see or hear anything while you were there?"

"No. My friends and I dared each other to go in when we were kids—it was closed up then. But we never even got close."

Will nodded. Daniel wasn't the adventurous type. But more importantly, he hadn't hallucinated any sights or sounds, even near the haunted house, where it was likely no matter how normal you were. A good sign.

"That author lives in it now. David Masters. He's a novelist, but he's a ghost hunter too."

"He's a good writer." The idea that the man presented himself as a real-life ghost hunter took him down a notch in Will's mind. He hated charlatans. *Ghost hunter. Right.* He settled back in his chair, hiding his annoyance, then opened his mouth to speak.

Beyond the French doors, he saw a dark speck swoop down from the sky and disappear into the trees bordering the courtyard. In an instant it reappeared, an insane bird slamming into the glass so hard that it stuck, but before Daniel even turned to look, it slid down out of sight, leaving behind a bloody smear.

"Grackle spackle," Hatch repeated softly.

A precognizant talking penis. Will rose in slow motion, took a few steps, passing the sofa where Daniel still sat, and looked at the cement pad outside the doors. It might be a precognizant penis, he thought, but it didn't know birds. On the cement lay a crow, ruby blood rilling between the shiny jet feathers.

"Daniel?" Will asked. "How did you—"

"*He* knew. I didn't." Daniel stood and turned to look at the bird from behind the sofa. Visibly, he cringed then turned to Will. "He hopes those doors are shatterproof."

"He?"

"You know." Hatch peered down at his own crotch. "Don't make me say it again."

Will barely nodded, then turned to look at the bird, and saw two more balls of black streak through the trees. Ripped and tattered leaves rained from the trees even as the birds hit the glass. Hearing ferocious cawing in the distance, Will turned his gaze above the trees to see a large, growing inkblot in the otherwise clear blue sky. It grew and in mere seconds individual birds became visible within the flock, their harsh calls a din even through the thick glass. Will stepped behind the couch and pushed Daniel down onto the carpet, dropping next to him as the first of the main flock struck the building. The room dappled dark as more and more bodies hit the glass, tens, maybe hundreds, then with a crackling crunch, rays of sunlight filtered through breaking panes only to be extinguished by the birds and blood spattering into the room.

Flashing on a scene from some old war movie, soldiers flattened in trenches as the enemy fired and fired and fired, Will hunkered lower and covered Daniel's head with one arm, his own with the other.

He knew only seconds were passing, maybe a minute or two, but time crawled and birds continued to kill themselves. Under his arm Daniel was a stone trembling on a fault line. Will felt a bird hit his back, then it fell beside him, black eyes gleaming, pearls of scarlet dripping from its spasming beak. Throat tight, he stared at the poor broken, bloodied creature until it stilled. His eyes burned. A single hot tear ran down his cheek.

Michael.

2

"Dr. Banning?" Kevin banged on Will's office door. "Dr. Banning? Are you okay in there?"

Kevin Bass, snug in his glassed-in reception area where Abba songs softly filled the air, hadn't heard or seen anything until the patient in the waiting room, who had been quietly having a pleasant conversation with herself, suddenly stood and walked toward the building's entrance, out of his line of sight. A second passed, then she started screeching "The birds, the birds!" like Rosie O'Donnell aping Tippi Hedrin. Kevin nearly grinned—he couldn't stand old Marcia. Controlling himself, he noticed a growing cacophony of avian shrieks outside the building, so let himself out of the office—instantly, the shrieks increased in volume—and trotted up front to peer outside. Marcia, jaw gawping between cries of "the birds, the birds," stayed plastered to the glass.

He saw very little, but what he saw—black birds apparently going kamakaze at the other side of the building—shocked him. They were headed for the patio side. *Will's office.*

Marcia Gauss continued to blubber, so he made soothing noises and guided her back to a chair out of sight of the doors. Pointing out the coffee pot, he turned on the television, told her the birds did this every mating season, and promised to be right back. As soon as he was out of sight, he had run like hell to Will's closed door.

"Doc!" Kevin listened now, heard a tinkle of breaking glass behind raucous caws. Alarmed, he yelled, "I'm coming in!" and turned the knob.

Something slapped against the door. Three more thumps followed in rapid succession; a second, two, passed, then one more soft thunk came, like a late-blooming kernel of popcorn. He pushed, but the door opened only a crack, the movement accompanied by a few disheartened caws. Looking down, he saw black feathers moving as a wing spread beneath the door. "Holy guacamole," he murmured, nearly as stunned as the bird.

"Kevin?" Will Banning's voice.

Then mobility returned. "Will? Will? Are you okay?" He refused to think about what was blocking the door as he pushed again. Slowly, excruciatingly, it gave an inch, another. Something squawked. He paused. "Doc? Will?"

"We're okay."

Will's voice, though strained, was strong. Kevin put his eye to the opening and saw the doc, his arm protectively around Daniel Hatch, standing by the couch. Behind them, shattered glass was smeared with blood. Beneath them, the beige carpet was invisible beneath wiggling mounds of feathers.

"Four and twenty blackbirds," Kevin said.

"What?" Will looked at him.

"Baked in a pie." He pushed the door more and stepped forward. Something crunched under his foot. "Oh. Oh, dear God." He lifted his foot, shaking it like he'd stepped in dog crap.

"Kevin, is everything all right out there?"

"There aren't any birds, if that's what you mean."

"What about patients?"

"Just Mrs. Gauss. She's okay." The phone began ringing out front.

"Better get that, Kevin." Will paused, saying something calming to Daniel Hatch, then looked at the floor and began to push one foot forward through the birds, but stopped after an instant. "Bring me a small broom from the storeroom as soon as you can."

"Okay." Kevin escaped. Entering the reception area, he saw Mrs. Gauss staring at the TV, her lips moving. He wondered what she was talking about as he picked up the phone. "Dr. Banning's office. May I help you?"

"Kev? What's going on over there?" Gabe Rawlins, D.O., usually sounded rumbly and laid back like Barry White, but now his voice was clipped. His office was across the street from Will's. Will sent his patients to his old friend for medical tests and prescriptions. Gabe had talked Will into giving Kevin his job.

"You saw the birds?"

"Hell, yes!" Gabe spoke softly. Probably Nurse Boobies was nearby. Her ears were as big as her Amazonian breasts.

"Birds just crashed into Will's office. Everybody's fine, but the birds. They don't look too good. And Will's carpet's going to need cleaning like you wouldn't believe."

"Why?"

"It's covered with birds, silly. Why do you think?"

Gabe was silent a moment. "Why did they crash? Any idea?"

"Not a clue. Marcia Gauss is in the waiting room talking to herself. Maybe she's sending out telepathic messages, too. You know, to make sure the previous appointment didn't run over."

"Kevin, what are we going to do with you?" Gabe's voice resumed its normal ease.

"You'll think of something." He paused then added, "You remember what tonight is?"

"I remember. About the birds. Shall I call Maggie, let her know?"

"Well, yes, no, I don't know. No. Let me see what Will wants to do. I'll get back to you." He paused. "What time are you off tonight?"

"I'll be home by six."

"Good. I've got bourbon chicken marinating. Your favorite. We'll eat at six-thirty, okay?"

"Okay."

"Happy anniversary. Love you."

"Back at'cha. Bye."

Nurse Boobies was definitely listening. He hung up and there was Marcia Gauss's porcine face staring at him through the glass. She held her black handbag tightly against her plump body, which was encased in a pink flower-print dress that looked like a sausage casing.

"May I help you, Mrs. Gauss?"

Her little piggy nostrils flared and she narrowed her beady eyes. "My appointment. It's late. Where's the doctor? I'm not paying for time another patient is using."

Not a word about the birds. Just as well. "Of course you're not paying for anyone else's time." *You old bitch.* He studied the processed blond hair, big '80s hair, and the wet-looking lip gloss, clues to her problems, but he couldn't remember what they were, other than talking to herself. *Living in the past? An advanced case of pig-face?* "Doctor had a little emergency. Why don't you sit down and have some coffee while I check on things for you?" He smiled, nearly batted his eyelashes at the broom-butted hag, then caught himself. He let himself out of the glass office and picked up the coffee pot.

"I want tea."

"Fine." Quickly he switched pots, poured hot water, and inserted a teabag. "Sugar?"

"Iced tea."

"I'm sorry, Mrs. Gauss. We only have hot tea. We have cold water though." He gestured at the water fountain. "Do you want me to put some in a cup for you?"

She harumphed. "Tea. Two Equals. I have to watch my figure."

Watch it do what? He did as ordered then followed her back to her chair near the television and handed the tea to her. "Here you go. Now if you'll excuse me . . ."

"Change the station," she ordered.

"To what?" All he could think of was Will in that sea of birds, waiting for him.

"Something interesting."

"Be right back."

He felt her glare as he sprinted back into his office and reemerged with the remote. He forced a big smile. "There's no one else here, so why don't you just surf yourself?"

"Why don't *I* what?"

"Surf. You know, use the remote and check out what's on."

"Don't you have a *TV Guide?*"

"No. But the TV does." Practically dancing with

impatience, he stood beside her seat and clicked on the menu button. "See? Cable listings for everything. Just use the arrow keys to look up and down." He handed her the remote. Her fingernail polish was the same pink as her dress. Nice job. Too bad her hands were so puffy. "Now, if you'll excuse me." He started off.

"Wait. There's no description."

"Hit the info button or just surf, sweetie. Now, you'll have to excuse me while I go see what's keeping Doctor." She oinked something behind him, but he didn't stop to listen, just headed for the supply closet, where a broom and dustpan waited.

3

"Kevin's still cleaning up," Will told Gabe Rawlins. "Oh, yeah, that's the spot."

"Relax. Put your head back down," Gabe ordered. "That rib is out of place again."

Will, lying on the table, did as ordered, felt Gabe's big hands pressing a spot on his back. It took his breath away, but it was good.

"How's that?"

Will wiggled. "Much better."

"How much? Tell me where it hurts." Gabe's hands moved up his spine, always pausing in the right spots just before Will could tell him to. If only he could fix people as easily as Gabe could.

"Why's Kevin picking up the birds? Why not animal control?"

"More trouble than it's worth." The Caledonia shelter was a no-kill and unofficial one, run by an elderly couple a few miles north of town, funded by donations and Maggie's spare time, but that wasn't where the crows would go. The crows were dead. That meant a low-on-the-pole cop would come out in an old pickup, armed with a shovel and garbage bags. He could—probably should—call down to San Luis Obispo and do something official like report the incident—but they couldn't do anything Maggie couldn't do, except close his entire office down and cause a riot. "I phoned Maggie already. She'll autopsy a few birds, just to make sure they aren't sick."

"Maybe I ought to run some bloods on you and Kevin. And Mr. Hatch. I took his blood for the Risperdal script anyway. He's coming for a checkup day after tomorrow, by the way. As you ordered."

"Good. He told you about the birds?"

"Not a word. He was quieter than usual. Pretty pale."

Will was relieved, but he wasn't sure why. "Take some of my blood, you old vampire. Might as well be careful."

Gabe pushed something into place in his back. It was wonderful. "Risperdal for Hatch. That's new."

"Yes," Will said. "Precautionary. Kevin E-mailed you the info?"

"Yep." Gabe kept working him over. "You didn't supply much. Delusions? Auditory hallucinations? You think he's schizophrenic all of a sudden?"

"No, I wouldn't go that far. I'll watch him for a month. He's displaying symptoms though. Probably transitory. It came on too suddenly. His penis is talking to him."

"What?"

"Ouch!"

"Sorry. Tell me more."

Will filled him in while Gabe manipulated his spine.

"Wow. Sit up. Slowly. How's that feel?"

Will sat up and stretched, rotated his shoulders.

He felt like he'd had a workout, all good-sore instead of bad-sore. "Great."

"Don't do any heavy exercising or lifting today. Your spine was a train wreck. Come back next week. We need to do this again, most likely."

Will grinned as he put on his shirt. "No problem. You don't have to twist my arm."

Gabe rolled his eyes. "Do you know how many people say that to me?"

Another grin. "You mean somebody besides me thought of that?" Will felt great. He stood and started to twist his back.

"Knock it off, Banning. You can do some stretching exercises in twenty-four hours. Nothing strenuous for now." Gabe led him out of the exam room, into his office, which was nothing like Will's. Gabe was a traditionalist, with cordovan leather chairs and a mahogany desk topped by an old-fashioned blotter and a turquoise case glass lamp that Will secretly coveted. Small framed photos of his sister's family and of Kevin punctuated the books in the hutch behind the desk. The usual diplomas were on the walls and his computer and printer were discreetly hidden in a cabinet next to the desk.

Gabe grunted as he lowered himself into his chair. Will sat opposite. "So, what's Maggie think about the birds?"

"I barely spoke to her," Will admitted. "She's having a busy day, but she said that sometimes birds can lose their sense of direction. That can drive them buggy. Same with whales, dolphins."

"And other migrating species. It's the magnetite thing." Gabe folded his hands.

"Yeah. Something throws it off." Will paused. "Makes sense to me. Compared with birds, we have almost none of it in our brains, but once in a while,

I'll suddenly lose my sense of direction and it's a physical thing—I feel nauseous until my bearings come back."

"I've felt that too. Personally, I think it's a sense, just like sight and taste and so forth."

"The *real* sixth sense?"

"Or seventh or eighth." Gabe smiled. "I can see you getting ready to lecture me about E.S.P.—don't. Did Maggie say anything else?"

"Just that she'd have to run tests to rule out illness."

"Zoonoses."

"What?"

"Zoonoses. Diseases that pass from animals to humans. Let me have one of those birds, too. Just to be safe. If there's anything weird, we'll have to tell the authorities." He paused. "We really should anyway."

Will made a face.

"Don't worry. We probably won't find anything."

"What's interesting to me is what could possibly throw off the flock's sense of direction so badly that its members would commit mass suicide."

"Bird brains." Gabe shrugged. "Maybe we're going to have an earthquake."

Will felt a little shiver. "Christ, I hope you're wrong. Maggie was overrun with patients today. Animals know." He checked his watch. "I need to get home and finish up some paperwork. Can't really do it in my office, you know?"

"I know. Are you going to open tomorrow?"

"Sure. I'll use the extra office for now. My schedule's busier than usual, too. I have three first-timers tomorrow and two requests for extra sessions I don't feel I can refuse."

Gabe raised his eyebrows. "Sounds like a twelve-hour day."

"I hope not. Kevin did some rescheduling for me, so some of my hour sessions are half hours. Speaking of Kevin, do you two want to come for dinner tonight? I thought I'd ask Maggie, too."

"How about a rain check for Saturday? Tonight's an anniversary. You know how that is."

"It's August. I thought your commitment ceremony anniversary was in April."

Chuckling, Gabe stood. "That's right. This is a different anniversary. Ten years ago tonight was the first time we . . ." He smiled.

"Gotcha." Gabe and Kevin had ten years of romance and lust under their belts. He'd never had more than three anniversaries, and none of those included romance that lasted anywhere near that long. They were just legal dates, nothing more.

"Let me steal a little blood, and you can be on your way." Gabe came around the desk and patted Will's shoulder. "You'll find your match too, Will. You just have to open your eyes and look for someone who doesn't treat you like shit."

4

"Last night poor little Poopypie just started making pee-pee everywhere." Penny Spender scratched the curly white topknot on her coiffed and perfumed teacup poodle's head, then put her nose to the dog's. "Poopypie just doesn't do that, does he? No, he doesn't! He's such a good widdle Poopypie, isn't he?"

Maggie Maewood's assistant had already taken the poodle's temperature and a urine sample. Its eyes were clear, there was no dehydration, vomiting, or other obvious symptoms other than the fact that the poor little thing had been overbred, a likely product of a puppy mill. As usual, Maggie kept that opinion to herself. "It's probably nothing," she told Mrs. Spender after listening to the animal's heartbeat, which was rapid but normal. "These little guys are naturally nervous. He might have some kind of U.T.I., but there's no fever."

"U.T.I.?" Penny's eyes widened with concern. "What's that?"

"Urinary tract infection. Annette's checking now,

we'll know in a minute. Has anything changed around your house?"

"What do you mean?"

"Changes in routine can cause nervous reactions like inappropriate urination. Have you introduced a new animal into the house?"

"No. Poopypie likes to have me all to himself." Penny let the dog lick her lips. Maggie almost expected her to lick him back.

"Have you had any visitors? Moved any furniture?"

Penny considered. "Janet Vining came by, but she does every week. Poopypie loves her, don't you, sweetie pie? We have lunch, you know. Poopypie gets his own plate. He has his doggie food, while we have our people food." She paused. "Let's see. I paid the paperboy yesterday, but he didn't come in. A man from the cable company came by a few days ago. But he was only there a few minutes and didn't pay any attention to Poopypie. Dr. Maewood, maybe Poopy's upset because he *didn't* pet him?"

"I doubt it." Maggie turned over the dog's problem in her mind, her thoughts briefly going to Will's avian attack. What had upset those birds? And she'd seen several other apparently healthy but anxious animals herself today, too. Recently, she realized, she'd probably seen at least two every day—not an alarming number, certainly, but more than usual. From long experience, she knew that there were flurries of anxiety among animals, sometimes preceding an earthquake, but more often for reasons that never revealed themselves, though Maggie thought it was likely they had to do with natural disturbances undetectable by humans. Hopefully, that would be the case this time. No one needed an out-and-out earthquake.

"Doctor?" Annette Neal, her assistant, stuck her head through the doorway.

"Yes?"

"The urine's clear."

"Thanks. Well, Mrs. Spender, we can run some blood tests if you like, but, uh, Poopypie—*How could anyone give a helpless animal such an awful name?*—just had his annual checkup a few weeks ago, so I suggest we wait a day or two and see if the problem goes away by itself. I suspect it will."

"Oh, I hope so. Can I get some tranquilizers for him in case he can't sleep?"

"Sure, but please don't use them constantly. On the off-chance there's an illness, we don't want to mask the symptoms. Annette?" The young woman peeked in and Maggie gave her a prescription to fill then turned back to Penny Spender. "Take him home and if you go out without him, you might try turning on the radio—a talk station, or soft music. Nothing noisy. That always helps anxious pets. And check around your house—you may have used a new air freshener or cleaner. Even something like that could cause a problem." She paused. "You don't let him drink out of the toilet, do you?"

The woman gasped. "Of course not. He drinks bottled water. Just like I do. The water delivery man came by, too, but Poopypie was outside."

"I'm sure that wasn't a problem," Maggie soothed. "But what about you, Mrs. Spender? If you're upset about anything, your dog could be picking up on your emotions." Normally she called animals by their names, but Poopypie was one she just couldn't get out twice in one conversation.

"Oh, no, everything's fine." She hesitated. "I've been dreaming about my husband. He's dead, you know."

"I'm sorry."

"It's okay, he's been dead for five years."

"Does your dog sleep with you? If you're having nightmares, he may be sensing your fear."

Penny smiled. "They're not nightmares."

Frenzied barking in the waiting room reminded Maggie that time was getting away from her. "Call me in a few days and let me know how he's doing. We'll decide if we need to do anything else at that point." She led her to the door, followed her out into the waiting room, and left her at the counter.

It was four-thirty and she had a full house. Several birds, which was unusual and a little intimidating since her partner, who really knew birds, was on vacation, two people with cat carriers, three with leashed dogs, one of which was madly barking at Kevin Bass, who stood against a wall, looking as nervous as Poopypie. He held a white plastic grocery sack. The barking dog stared fixedly at it.

Maggie crossed to Kevin. "Is that the bird?" she asked softly.

"I brought you two," he murmured, grinning sickly. "I mean, we had plenty to spare."

She took the sack. "Thanks. Is Will still at the office?"

"No. He's working at home."

"Okay." She studied his pale face. "Pretty bad, huh?"

He nodded. "Disgusting. I'm going to go home and shower for an hour."

"Say hello to Gabe for me."

Kevin's smile was tentative but genuine. "I will."

"Do you want me to call you two after I check out the birds?"

"No. Just Will. Gabe and I are celebrating tonight."

"Of course." She smiled, too. "That's so romantic."

"Yeah. And really naughty. I bought a new DVD

just for tonight. You can borrow it later. You'll love it. The guys are so much better looking than in straight porn."

She stifled a laugh. "See you later, Kevin."

"Yeah. Saturday night."

"Saturday night?"

"Will's cooking. He didn't tell you yet?"

"Not yet. But he was a little preoccupied when we spoke."

"He'll ask. You say yes." Kevin looked concerned. "You don't have a date or anything?"

She smiled. "Me? Who'd have me?"

Kevin looked her up and down. "If I wasn't taken, I'd be all over you, babe." He made a tiger growl. "See you Saturday night. Wear something sexy."

"Why? Are you thinking of switch-hitting?"

"You know me better than that, lover. Give Will a thrill and leave your bra at home. Poor guy needs something nice to look at."

"Then invite Nurse Boobies." She spoke quickly, aware that her face was on fire. "You know I don't like you to joke about that."

Kevin's eyes locked on hers for a long moment. "Ever wonder why you don't like it, Maggie?" An impish eyebrow shot up as he added, "Maybe you should discuss it with a therapist."

Furiously blushing, she said, "See you," turned and took the bag into the lab and tossed it in a refrigerator, where it joined a few other items no one would ever want to eat. She washed up and returned to the exam room, then signaled Annette that she was ready for her next patient.

A moment later, a man with a caged cockatiel entered. "I think my bird is having palpitations."

It was going to be a long afternoon.

5

Will's office was his favorite room in the modest ranch house situated on a rolling hill on the western edge of town. The room was light and airy despite the walls of overloaded bookshelves, and his desk sat before a long picture window. From it, the Pacific Coast Highway remained out of sight, giving him an unsullied view of the narrow, forested coastal crescent of Caledonia, home to fragrant juniper and fir, squirrels, rabbits, deer, a rocky shore, and a few expensive restaurants and B&Bs, which were wonderfully invisible from Will's angle. Beyond the trees, he could even see a ribbon of ocean, and with the window open as it was now, feel the breeze and smell the salt sea. The blue sky wore wispy white clouds low on the horizon and as sunset approached, they would turn shades of salmon and lemon and lavender, and later, fiery reds and bruised purples. Will never tired of the view, day or night, but most of all he loved the sunsets.

He had watched them through good times and bad, and they had always seen him through. He bought this house only three and a half years ago, after the failure of his third—and final—attempt at marriage. It wasn't as big as his previous place (though the ocean view was far superior), nor was it in the same elegantly price-bloated neighborhood, but it was far more to his taste than the big old successful-psychologist showplace, that house of dead marriages. This home, *my home, all mine,* was less than 2000 square feet, which was still far more room than one man and three cats really needed. It contained no brocade draperies, no uncomfortable furniture, no meaningless modern art or ugly hunks of alleged sculptures. When he'd bought the place, he'd had the wall-to-wall carpeting removed, the wood floors stripped and stained and polished to a warm golden sheen, and the walls painted what Kevin, his volunteer decorating consultant, called "a pale shade of just-ripened apricots." He put up art of his own choosing for the first time since pubescence when he'd pinned up a Farrah poster. Although he still had a soft spot for his first pin-up girl, what he chose now ran toward serene sea- and landscapes, pictures of places that inspired tranquility, the kind of paintings that made you feel as if you could walk into them and escape the real world. The furniture was comfortable and overstuffed, warm earth-patterned colors that camouflaged cat fur, the tables solid oak, the lamps Mission-style. Kevin had tried to talk him into colorful Tiffany shades, but Will chose plain, mellow-yellowish glass shades. He actually liked the stained-glass stuff, but flowers and dragonflies were just too much for a straight male who had sworn off women.

In Will's home, you could put your feet on the coffee table, and the nubby woven drapes easily withstood the felines who occasionally mistook them for tree trunks. Maggie's housewarming gift, a catpost extravagantly built to resemble a tree with brown carpet trunk and branches and green carpet ovals of foliage, occupied space not far from the massive entertainment center. The cats liked to climb the post and leap onto the big armoire, draping themselves so that their feet and tails drooped down to brush the tops of the TV people's heads. Will smiled. None of his wives would have approved. *Screw you all!*

Back then, during all those various marital disasters, when he wanted an animal fix, he visited Maggie, and although their relationship was purely platonic— they'd known each other since the summer before kindergarten, for Christ's sake—those visits cost him one of his marriages. Barbara didn't believe Will was visiting Maggie's pussycats, just her pussy. Barbara's words, not his. He shook his head, amused, and wondered what might have been if he and Mags had met when they were adults, sexual organs all plumped up and ready for use. Maybe something, maybe nothing, but it was a moot point. They were best friends, like brother and sister only better, and that thought always made him shut off the wondering because it felt much too taboo. Maggie felt the same way. It was, after all, human nature.

In his office with its real-life escapist view, he needed no landscapes, but he had two other pieces of art. One was a print of M.C. Escher's hands drawing each other, an old present from Maggie that he'd kept in his home office even in the other house despite the fact that all three wives thought it was cheap and tacky. Will loved it, and loved Maggie for knowing that, for giving him things he wanted; the exes always presented him with gifts they wanted, or thought a man in his position should possess. The other artwork was an original Kevin Bass. When not greeting patients, Kevin painted, and he was one talented puppy. This painting, just to the right of the window, where he could easily look at it, was of Freud, Jung, and Rorschach, at about nine months of age, when they were part kitten, part cat.

A tall, less extravagant climbing post stood to the left of the desk. Jung was sleeping on his back on the middle platform, only a few feet from Will's face. The huge buff-orange puffball was splayed out, legs in the air, paws twitching with dreams, his head hanging over the edge, exposing his throat with the kind of trust that a king showed only his most beloved old nanny. Freud lay on the top shelf, alertly staring down at Will, waiting for eye contact. His tail swished. Will knew cat body language almost as well as human: It meant indecision. *Should I stay up here or jump on his keyboard? Or maybe his shoulder?* Eye contact would result in a leap of some sort.

Will refused to look at him, and turned back to the computer screen. Out of the corner of his eye, he saw Freud sit up and begin cleaning his ass. He smiled, wondering, as usual, what the feline's namesake would think of that ability. *He'd love it.* He turned a page of session notes and lifted his hands to the keyboard, but the phone rang, saving him from work in the nick of time. "Hello."

"Hey, Will! How are you, buddy?"

Will, Pavlovian as always, flinched at his older brother's voice, even though it held none of the old meanness—hadn't since Pete had returned to Caledonia after a long Navy stint. His brother had come home a new man, dressed for success, armed with a grin and a manner that melted old ladies and charmed most children. He'd charmed the pants right off Candy, Will's second badly chosen wife.

Funny thing was, though he didn't like his brother, he hadn't really blamed him for that because he instinctively knew Pete lacked the morals necessary to keep him from screwing his brother's wife—in fact, he probably was incapable of understanding them. Candy understood but didn't care. She'd been a high-end real estate broker, and by the time his brother came looking for house-hunting help, Will was already fairly sure she was polishing knobs to increase sales possibilities and sealing the deals with all the lips she possessed. Pete was just another sales conquest to her, more fun because he was even more forbidden than her usual fruit.

It was ancient history now, and these days, Pete Banning, successful businessman, was full of good cheer, and almost everybody bought it. Will, unconvinced, pushed back an inch or two from the desk and sat up straighter, phone to his ear. Rorschach, stretched out next to the computer, looked up, annoyed, and reached one big white-socked paw toward the keyboard. "Hello, Pete." Will nudged the keyboard out of the cat's reach. "I wasn't expecting to hear from you."

Behind Pete's hearty chuckle, Rorschach trilled, sure Will was talking to him. The cat yawned then began to rise in slow, slow motion.

"How's the shrink business, baby brother?"

There it was, the flaw in the mask, the sneer in the cheer. Some of Will's friends and acquaintances called him a shrink, but he never sensed any derision in it. It was shorthand, like cop for police officer. But with Pete, it was passive aggression. Malice oozed from beneath that candy coating.

Or did it? *Psychologist, heal thyself.* Maybe he was overreacting. All his training and natural talent for seeing into people's motives was pretty useless when it came to knowing himself. That was why shrinks had shrinks, but his advisor, a beloved old professor, had retired and headed for Florida two years before. Maybe it was time to find a new one.

Rorschach trilled again and head-butted Will's hand. He and his two brothers were good listeners, but a little short on advice. Still, Will didn't relish the idea of looking elsewhere, testing strangers with tales of his inner life. Maybe he should talk to Gabe, or just shoot the breeze with Kevin. Beneath his assistant's display of frivolity, he was a keen judge of character, lessons learned hard in late childhood when the boy refused to keep his gayer traits safely in the closet.

Maggie, his oldest, most trusted friend, would have been the logical choice—she'd seen him through the bad marriages and worse—but she hated Pete for reasons she never wanted to discuss. Old stuff, kid stuff, from when he was a bully, was what she always pleaded. She said he was just one of those people she simply didn't like. Maggie was long on loyalty, and whatever else was going on there, Will knew part of her abhorrence stemmed from the way Pete had treated him when they were little; Maggie had appointed herself his guard dog when they were ten years old. *After Michael died.*

"Willy?" Pete said again, using the name Will hated more than any other. "Cat got your tongue?"

He scratched behind Rorschach's ears. Pets lowered your blood pressure, that was medical fact. He scratched some more. "Business is fine."

"That's great, Willy. Just great."

Pete would have said that if Will told him he'd gone deaf and blind; the guy didn't care, it was all bullshit by rote. "Why do you ask, *Petey?*"

His brother chuckled. "Okay, *Will.* Still hate that

name, huh? Think there's some deep dark reason for that?"

Willy is slang for penis and you are fully aware of that. Will said nothing, wondering if he was being too suspicious.

"I know you're about to ask me about my business," Pete said as if he really believed it. "Caledonia Cable's doing great. You've seen the new ads?"

"Uh, yes, I think so." That was Pete's company, Caledonia Cable, a dozen years old and thriving. Having undercut the competition, he'd taken over television in Caledonia and was planning to extend feeder roots down into Candle Bay and Red Cay. If you wanted to watch TV and didn't have a satellite here in the hills, you had Pete Banning and his trusty cable box in your house. Will even had it—a comp from his brother he hadn't known how to refuse. When he brought up disconnecting in favor of a satellite dish to his friends, even Maggie thought it was a foolish idea. She suggested the free cable was some kind of penance for long ago cruelties.

"There are lots more stations available on our new digital cable," Pete bragged. "Just as many as a satellite system offers. We've run most of the new cable already, too."

"That's great." Will wondered how Pete, who never could save a dime as a kid, had managed to turn into a successful businessman. *Same way he turned from a sour creep into everbody's buddy, probably.* "I have a huge load of work to get back to, but thanks for telling me the good news, Pete. I'm happy for you."

"Wait, wait, baby brother. Don't hang up yet. Don't you know all that hard work will kill you?"

This from a man who never seemed to stop working, who was always pitching and schmoozing, who lived in Will's former high-status neighborhood, who owned a Mercedes SUV, a Jaguar, and a Harley? "It doesn't seem to be killing you."

"I thrive on it, you know that, little bro. Action's my middle name."

Asshole's your middle name.

"You're the sensitive type. Always have been. You need more downtime than I do."

He thinks I'm backsliding because I moved into a smaller house and drive an Outback. Will quelled the thought. *When you assume . . .* Rorschach stood on his hind legs, put his paws on Will's shoulders and shoved his nose against his, swiping one side, then the other. A cat kiss, marking him with friendly feline phermerones. He trilled again, the sound going up the scale like a question.

"What the hell was that?" Pete asked.

"Nothing. The computer." Will never mentioned the cats. They'd just be fuel for more "good-natured" ribbing. Men were supposed to have dogs: retrievers or pit bulls. Macho pets for macho men. Creatures that followed orders and gave unquestioning devotion. Will preferred the contrary, independent feline personality, but that was something beyond Pete's comprehension. His brother liked to give orders and he liked them followed to the letter. Will had a childhood wealth of experience with that.

"That's a sissy-sounding computer you've got there, Willy-boy—sorry . . . *Will*. So, like I was saying, we're going digital. Eventually, all our customers will be switched over. When would you like your new box?"

"New box?"

"New cable, new box. Your neighborhood is wired and ready to go."

"I don't need to upgrade. I don't watch that much television."

One of those annoying chuckles. "Everybody's being switched over—it's called modernization. You know, like who uses anything but a cell phone these days?"

"*I* don't use a cell phone."

"You're a Luddite? *My* brother? Still wear button fly pants, or are zippers allowed now?"

"I have a beeper," Will said, sorry he felt compelled to say anything.

"You're a shrink. How can you not have a cell? I mean, don't you have patients you have to talk out of committing suicide, things like that?"

Guilt. He probably should have a cell for that very reason, but the beeper itself was more intrusive than he liked after a long day of listening to other people's problems. At least it gave him a little distance. "My beeper is all I need."

"Suit yourself, buddy. I've got a man in your neighborhood today and tomorrow. Want to leave a key under the doormat in the morning? He'll be in and out in ten minutes. Doesn't steal, I give you my personal guarantee."

"No, I won't be leaving a key under the mat. I don't let anyone in the house when I'm not present."

"Same old Willy. Will, I mean." Another smarmy chuckle. "Doesn't trust anyone. Tell you what. I'll stop by and install it for you myself."

"Sorry, but no one comes in here when I'm not home."

The chuckle turned into laughter, a false "ho-ho-ho." "No, baby brother, I meant while you're home. I haven't seen you in months. I miss you, little buddy. And you haven't ever invited me over to see your new place. What's it been? Two, three years?"

"I'm very busy right now, Pete. I don't really have time for a visit."

"Hey, hey, no problem. You need to relax, you know?"

"I know." *But not with you.*

"Listen, let me check with my man and get back to you. Maybe he can come by when you get off work tomorrow. What time will you be home?"

Will opened his mouth to put him off, but Freud chose that moment to come crashing down onto his shoulder. Will grimaced as claws stuck through his shirt. The cat balanced, released his flesh quickly, then slid his cheek against his. Rorschach trilled, and back on the cat post, Jung made his peculiar grunt-meow.

"Hey, little buddy, what's going on? Got a woman in there with you?"

Will sighed. "I should be home after six-thirty tomorrow. I can't guarantee it, though," he added blandly. "See you later, Pete." He hung up before he had to listen to another chuckle and tilted forward so that Freud would get off his shoulder. Jung joined his brothers on the desk, sat down and began staring at Will with golden eyes that appeared to contain vast ageless intelligence. *Appearances can be deceiving.* "You guys looking for an early dinner?"

Tails went up, eyes opened wide, talking and trilling commenced. Whatever their intelligence, the triplets had easily learned at least thirty-five human words and "dinner" was one they never pretended to forget. Will pushed back from the desk and stood as the massive orange hairballs swooped dizzily past him, all pausing at the doorway to make sure he was following, before they led him, eeling around his tripping feet, to the kitchen. *No wonder Seeing Eye cats never caught on.*

6

Thinking she heard something, Lara Sweethome muted the evening news and listened intently. Yes, there it was again—the sound of footsteps on the stairs. Heart thudding, she willed herself to remain calm as she put her fork and Lean Cuisine teriyaki bowl down on the coffee table and silently slid off the sofa. She crouched low behind the arm and peered across the room at the staircase. It was empty, at least as far as she could see. But she could still hear footsteps. The seventh stair from the bottom squeaked in its unmistakable way, but there was no one there.

Covered with goosebumps, she waited. More steps, more squeaks. Something invisible was ascending the stairs—she recognized the distinctive crunch of the third step from the top.

There's nothing there. You know that!

She heard someone—*something*—walking around upstairs, moving toward her bedroom.

A door slammed. Her bedroom door.

You didn't hear anything. You're imagining things.

Trembling, she rose and walked into the small downstairs bathroom and took her plastic pill box from the vanity drawer. It held seven days worth of medication, and every week she faithfully filled it so that she wouldn't forget a dose. Now she flipped open today's segment and counted. She hadn't missed a dose of anything, including the mild antipsychotic that Dr. Banning had recommended and Dr. Rawlins had then prescribed.

Upstairs, the bedroom door slammed again and the footsteps started back toward the staircase. Dizzy, nauseated, Lara steadied herself. "You're hallucinating," she murmured. Her stomach churned. She hadn't hallucinated since she began the medication a year ago. Why now? Her life was fine, free of any real problems. In fact, she was happier now, since beginning the medication, than she'd ever been since puberty and the mental problems had hit, fifteen years ago. Much happier. Dr. Banning had diagnosed a mild form of something related to schizophrenia and given her the pills. All the things that haunted her, the things she had heard—and even seen once or twice—subsided almost completely soon after.

She heard the third stair from the top crunch again as the hallucination—*that's what it is, just an hallucination, it's not a ghost, it's not her!*—descended the stairs. *Go out there and look. Prove there's nothing there!*

Okay, she would. She fumbled the pill dispenser back into the drawer and opened the bathroom door just as the seventh step from the bottom squeaked. She almost pulled back, but thought of Dr. Banning, of how he told her she wasn't a coward, there was nothing real to fear, and made herself walk back into the living room, right toward the staircase.

Something squeaked. The floorboards at the bottom of the stairs. *There's nothing there.* Lara moved forward. *Nothing there.*

The lights seemed to dim the slightest bit, letting a gloomy darkness seep in around her. Then the air changed, grew suffocatingly still despite the steady stirring of the ceiling fan in the center of the room, despite the early evening breeze coming in the front windows. She felt like she was in a vacuum.

Or an airplane. Pressure grew on her eardrums until dizziness made her grab a sideboard to keep her balance. Her ears roared with the sound you heard when you put a big conch shell to your ear to hear the ocean, but despite that, she heard the floor squeak again, only a few feet away.

Suddenly it hit in a rush, a roar. Physically hit. The invisible thing rushed her, pushing her back until she fell to the floor as the force of it swept through her body, like a freezing electrical shock. Behind her, another door slammed, then it was gone. All gone. Except for the faint cloying smell of her dead mother's violet perfume.

7

Sunset commenced with rare and brilliant fury and Will attempted to watch it while working, but soon found his eyes stolen by beauty, his mind adrift, his heart alone. The cats, sated, had deserted him to curl up and snooze together in his favorite chair. Or perhaps he had deserted them, since they always welcomed his attempts to retake the chair and watch television or read a book.

By now, Kevin and Gabe would be celebrating, having dinner and then other pleasures. Thinking of their anniversary as he watched the late summer sun sink into the sea made him think of a very different kind of anniversary that was only days away. It would be twenty-six years ago Saturday that his oldest brother, his hero, Michael, had died. The accident itself was only a series of blurred images, but he clearly remembered sitting with Maggie on the rocky crescent shore after the funeral, numbly watching the sun set. They were only ten, he was still in shock, and

Maggie took his hand and held it in both her own. After a while, her touch broke through his defenses and he finally cried for his brother. She never said a word, just held him until he was done. The next day, he was embarrassed and began avoiding her, but she acted as if nothing had happened, and except for an increased tendency in her to guard him—just as she did any wounded creature—everything went back the way it was. They remained best buddies.

He swallowed hard, choking back the old sorrow, and thought of other things. Marcia Gauss, the patient he reluctantly saw after the bird invasion, was a neurotic control freak who had been showing signs of improvement until recently. A supremely annoying woman, today she did her level best to make him run screaming from the room by grilling him about her mental state, which was a source of endless pride and fascination to her. Marcia was probably torturing her husband or children now. He wondered if she sat them under a hot bright light while she pulled from them the details of their days.

Daniel Hatch—*poor Daniel!*—was probably having dinner conversation with his precognitive genitals. The thought, meant to amuse, distressed him more, and he let himself think of Maggie instead. She would still be at the clinic, probably dissecting a dead crow.

He wondered what she'd find, if anything. He wondered, suddenly hungry, if she'd eaten yet and started to reach for the phone, then stopped, knowing she'd call him when she was done with the autopsy. Unlike him, she was a prisoner of propriety when it came to ringing phones, and unless she was in surgery, she'd drop everything to pick up, even though she knew the voice mail would do it for her. On one hand, he admired her for it, and knew that, considering his profession, he should be just as vigilant. On the other, he knew he'd lose his own mind if he didn't use an answering machine, screen calls, and carry a beeper instead of a cell. He'd learned in childhood to drive Mags nuts by ignoring a doorbell or ringing phone whenever they were at his house. Sometimes she'd get so frustrated that she'd get up and answer it herself, always flipping her hand across the top of his head as she went by. Nowadays, she admitted she was sometimes jealous of his ability to ignore the world, though she still couldn't fathom how he did it.

The doorbell chimed, startling Will out of his reverie, sending stray thoughts of synchronicity dancing through his head. He sat there as it rang a second time, a third, then in honor of Maggie and because synchronicity shouldn't be ignored, got up to see who it was.

He arrived at the door, looked out the peephole and saw the back of a short man in green coveralls as he stepped off the porch. Between his shoulder blades was an embroidered label that said CALEDONIA CABLE. Pete had sent the guy over without bothering to phone first. Will ground his teeth. Another one of his brother's passive-aggressive tricks. Pete knew Will resented unannounced visitors.

Or does he? They'd barely spoken in years, so how could he know? Quickly, Will opened the door. "Hey!"

The man, retreating to a white Caledonia Cable minivan, turned and looked, then held up one finger in a just-a-minute gesture, opened his van, and grabbed a large open toolbox and trotted up the walk.

"My brother sent you?" Will squinted at the rat-faced little man. He saw carroty hair just beginning to gray. Light from the streetlamp lit prominent ears and the weight of the toolbox tilted him a little. Will knew him from somewhere; he was familiar.

"He sure did send me. Have a new cable box or two, if you want, just for you," the man said in a whispery voice reminiscent of Lon Chaney's. "He said you didn't want anyone in the house while you're at work, so I should come and set it up now. And tomorrow, if you don't mind my going in your backyard, I'll just come back and run the new cable from the pole to the house. You'll be all connected when you get home."

Will didn't want to be bothered, but the wiring really was quick and easy to run in this house, and the rat-man intrigued him. "Okay," he said and stood back to let the guy enter. As he passed, he saw the name embroidered on the man's left breast: Mickey.

Holy hell, it's Mickey Elfbones! "Straight ahead," he said. "The main set is in the living room. There's another in my bedroom."

Elfbones nodded and headed into the living room. The puddle of cats in the chair stirred as he entered. Jung and Rorschach leapt down and disappeared behind the chair. Freud, afraid of nothing and no one, just watched from the chair. In a minute or two, he'd probably jump on the guy's back and scare him half to death. *Maybe not. Freud's got good taste.* But the idea still made Will smile. Mickey Elfbones had been Pete's childhood lieutenant, a ferrety kid without the balls to be a bully, so he'd latched on to Pete as full-time lackey instead. He did whatever Pete wanted and, in return, had some prestige and protection from Pete's competition. And even though he was a runt, he was four years older than Will and always bigger than him.

"You used to beat me up," Will said.

Elfbones turned white. "I, uh, I had to, I mean I didn't want to, but—"

"But Pete made you do it."

Cringing slightly, Mickey nodded, then looked him up and down and tried on a smile. "You sure got tall. You're a lot taller than Pete now."

Will smiled, enjoying his old tormentor's discomfort.

"I, uh, I apologize for being mean to you, uh, Willy, uh, I mean—"

"Dr. Banning."

"Dr. Banning," Mickey repeated. "Wow. You're a doctor? Pete didn't say nothing about that."

Of course he didn't. "I'm a psychologist."

Elfbones tried smiling again. "Then you understand why I had to do that stuff, right?"

"I do." He could have explained it to him, could have ground the little creep down with a few well-chosen words, but while he still didn't like the guy, his anger was already fading. And, damn it, he really *did* understand why Mickey had done it. "Need any more help, Mickey?"

"No, but maybe when I'm done. This set's huge."

"I'll help you put it back."

"Thanks."

Will almost left the room, intending to get the bedroom set ready, but he didn't trust the guy, so he sat down in his chair. Jung and Rorschach were nowhere to be seen, but Freud, displaced, instantly hopped into Will's lap then set to staring daggers at Mickey.

Elfbones glanced back nervously. "That your cat?"

"Yes."

"What's he do?"

"He kills rats," Will said smoothly.

Mickey looked around, oblivious to irony. "You got rats in a nice place like this?"

"Just one, but he won't be around long."

"Poor stupid rat. I sure wouldn't want to get bit by a big-ass cat like that. He part mountain lion?"

"Could be." Will already felt guilty for playing with the poor idiot and was relieved when the phone rang.

It was Maggie. She had to wait for test results, but couldn't find anything wrong with the dead birds and thought nothing would show up. Will thanked her and invited her to dinner Saturday night. She accepted, and that was that. Will hung up and saw Mickey was finished. He rose and helped him slide the set back into place, watched him set the new black box on top, accepted a new remote and pamphlet of instructions.

"You try it tomorrow night. Lots more stations."

"Pete mentioned that. Are you ready to do the bedroom set?"

Mickey nodded.

"This way."

Will sat in a chair while Mickey went to work. As soon as Elfbones was occupied, Rorschach and Jung appeared from behind the drapes. They looked worried. Will could see Jung's tail swishing. Would they decide to stay or go?

A few seconds later, both felines stealth-trotted out of the room. They were cautious around strangers, but he'd never seen them this nervous before. And it was also peculiar that fearless Freud hadn't followed him into the bedroom. *The cats must have good taste.*

"So, Mickey, what've you been up to since Pete joined the Navy?"

"I joined with him, but got washed out. I worked at Phil Ford's auto shop until ten years ago. I've been working for Pete ever since."

Will had never seen him around town and briefly wondered if he was lying. Not that it mattered.

In a few minutes, Mickey Elfbones was finished setting up. Will saw him to the front door. "Your brother said to tell you to stop by the new shop sometime," the lackey told him. "It's real nice."

"I'll try." He felt a cat rub against one leg and followed Mickey's eyes down. Freud was plastered against him, but the ears were up, maybe even a little forward, showing aggression as he stared at Mickey.

"That's a scary-looking cat," Mickey said anxiously.

"He's harmless," Will told him, feeling sorry for him. Freud disagreed with a world-class hiss.

"Uh, I gotta go." Mickey got out the door then peeked back in. "Uh, Dr. Banning?'

"Yes, Mickey?"

"Your cat won't be outside tomorrow, will he?"

"No. He stays indoors."

"Good. See you later."

Will locked the door then looked down at Freud and put his hands out, palms up. "You're rude," he said pleasantly.

With a grunt, Freud accepted the invitation to leap into his arms. Will carried him back into the living room, sat down in his chair and picked up a Nelson DeMille novel. Freud tried to sit on it, but failed and settled for his lap, but Jung and Rorschach spent the rest of the evening looking nervous and sniffing everywhere Mickey Elfbones had walked.

8

"So, Will," Kevin said, a coconut shrimp poised on his fork. "What would Sigmund Freud say if he knew you named your pussycat after him?"

"He'd probably be complimented. After all, sometimes a pussycat is only a pussycat."

"And Jung?" he persisted. "What would he think of his namesake?"

Will sipped his ale. "He'd be pleased to be associated with such a noble creature, I'm sure."

"And Rorschach would say the same thing," Maggie said before Kevin could ask.

"Thank you, Mags." Will tipped his glass toward her and enjoyed her grin. "I wonder where the Terrible Trio is." He'd been trying to keep track of the cats. Ever since Elfbones's visit they'd been a little jumpy.

"They're down here," Gabe rumbled, looking at the floor between him and Kevin.

"Yeah," Kevin said. He bit a small shrimp in half

and dangled a piece in his fingers until a big orange paw came up and snagged it away.

"Good thing you have wood floors." He looked at his mate. "Stop feeding them, Kev."

"You're spoiling them," Maggie pointed out in her best veterinarian voice.

"Wait," Will said. "First give the other ones pieces, too." Kevin smiled and bit another shrimp, his attention back on the Orange Boys. Gabe and Maggie both looked at Will, making him feel like an overindulgent parent. Which he was. Sort of. "We have to be fair," he said, and cracked too much pepper over his rice. "Damn it." Sham dignity in place, he returned to his meal.

"I still don't know how you tell these three cats apart," Gabe said. "They're identical."

"Don't be silly," Kevin said. "As a straight man, Will knows pussy, Right, Will?"

Will chuckled, ashamed that Kevin's bouts of pussy jokes—they seemed to come on him every month of two, ever since the Boys were kittens—still amused him. "Freud has a long nose and is very kingly and royal, Jung's coat is slightly paler than the others', and Rorschach has that little white blaze on his nose. His face is a little flatter, too."

"Flatter?" Gabe laughed. "Long nose? On a *cat*?"

"Flatter," Maggie said. "A little more Persian. And Freud's long nose makes him look more like a lion. But all three of them look like Maine Coons. With a whiff of Angora."

"A whiff—" Kevin began.

"They're huge, luxurious felines," Will said quickly. "With similar but different personalities. You can even tell them apart by their body language. Rorschach likes to head butt, but Jung and Freud usually prefer touching noses."

Maggie nodded. "The ways they habitually hold their tails—"

"Stop!" Kevin cried, then glanced accusingly at Gabe. "See what you did? You turned on their parental things again."

"I did no such thing. They do it to each other," Gabe said, a twinkle in his eye. "You two need to have some kids."

"They already have them," Kevin said as a white-socked orange paw and fluffy head briefly appeared and neatly snagged a whole shrimp from his fingers. "And they're brats. Imagine what they'd do to human children?" He grinned like a mad elf.

Will felt himself blush, but it wasn't so bad because Maggie was at least as red as he felt. They made brief eye contact and glanced away quickly. "They're not brats," Will said pointedly, "except when Kevin encourages them."

Kev dropped two more shrimps, then picked up his wineglass. "Just being fair. So, these guys don't look very upset."

"No, they're fine tonight. Maggie? What were your patients like today?"

She considered. "I'm still seeing more stressed animals than usual. Birds, in particular."

Will shook his head. "That's just so weird. Most of my two-legged patients are edgier than normal, too. I can't help but think it's connected. But to what? Apparently, we're not going to have an earthquake. It would have happened by now."

"Military activity," Gabe suggested. "Airborne radars, things like that, are supposed to upset some animals. Why not humans?"

"The birds would be especially susceptible to something like that," Maggie said. "Something that upsets the magnetite in their brains." She looked at Will.

"I wonder if the sea life was affected. Fish have lots of magnetite, too."

"Interesting idea." Will drained his glass. "What about us, Gabe? Do humans have much?"

"Not like some animals. Until recently, it was believed we lacked it, but that never made a lot of sense to me. As I told Will the other day, I think direction is a sixth sense."

"Why?" Kevin asked.

"I don't know about any of you except you, Will, but when I lose my sense of direction, I feel something physical for an instant."

"Queasy?" Will asked.

"Yeah. You could call it that."

"Panic," Maggie said. "That's what I feel. In my stomach. It's like the world tilts. Sometimes it's strong, but other times, it's barely noticible. We already know the birds' radar, or whatever you want to call it, went south, so to speak. It's the only explanation we have now for that kind of behavior. An electric storm—"

"But the day was clear," Kevin said.

"Military equipment." Will pushed his plate back. "Do you think they've reactivated Fort Charles?" The fort, sixty-some miles north, was built in the thirties and had been closed down for seven or eight years.

"Makes sense," Maggie said.

"Even if it isn't active—and I haven't heard that it's in use again—there are plenty of other bases along the coast." Gabe's face turned solemn. "Certainly, they're patrolling more, and the power plant at Avila Beach isn't all that far away. They're really watching that. Lord only knows what kind of equipment they're using up there." He glanced skyward.

"Wasn't Pete in the Navy?" Kevin asked. "You could call him. Maybe he still has friends."

"Kevin!" Gabe's reprimand was quiet but the younger man stopped smiling instantly.

"Sorry, Will."

Whenever his brother's name was mentioned, Will felt one of those little twinges, not so different from the queasy feeling of disorientation they were talking about a moment before. *Pavlovian response.* It wasn't so hard to fend off anymore, though. Pete had been nothing but friendly to him for quite a while. Friendlier than Will ever felt toward him. "It's fine, Kev. A good suggestion, but he was in the Navy, and he's been out for quite a while—since before Fort Charles closed down." He glanced at Maggie, saw empathy, and smiled. "If he happens to call me, I'll ask him. But Kevin?"

"Yes?"

"You know how you like to play games on the computer when you think I won't notice?" He spoke gently, but Kevin reddened. Will enjoyed it.

"I don't—"

"Shhh. Tomorrow, when it's quiet, spend some time on the Internet instead and see what's up with the military bases around here."

"Will," Gabe said, his voice deep and easy again. "You know Kevin. If he does a military search, he's going to order gay soldier porn and have it sent to your office."

"Gabriel Hannibal Rawlins, you take that back!" Kevin put on his I'm-outraged-but-I'm-cute face.

Maggie laughed heartily. *"Hannibal?* Really, Gabe? That's your middle name?"

Gabe nodded and Kevin did a tiger growl. "He's a real maneater."

9

Caledonia Cable's satellite and attendant equipment sat within the chain-link confines, crowned in razor wire, on top of Felsher Hill, land of antennas, a little northeast of town. Pete Banning loved to look at his equipment. And more than that, he liked getting a blow job while he looked at his equipment. So, at this moment, he was in heaven. The only thing that might make it even better would be if the Boobsie Twins were on the dish doing each other like they did in *Cable Hookers #5*. God, he loved that series. In all the movies, the twins played cable installers who liked getting plugged by their customers, but *CH#5* had a long kinky scene involving just the twins, a roll of cable wire, and a remote control—that scene gave new meaning to the term "laying cable." The thought set him off and he grabbed his secretary's ears and hung on tight while he painted her tonsils.

"Man, just look at that system," he said, while she used a Wet Nap to clean him up before tucking him away and neatly zipping his fly. "Isn't she a beauty?"

"Mmmph," was her reply. Evidently, he'd given her a real soaking.

He grinned. Jennifer Labouche was the archetypal dumb blonde and he'd convinced her that swallowing sperm would make her tits grow. All he had to do these days to get a quick B.J. was tell her he wasn't positive, but he thought her tits might look just a *little* bigger.

While Jennifer continued to clean up, he walked around the dish, admiring the smooth lines, relishing the extra little bits of technology hidden here and there.

"Want to see something cool?" he asked Jennifer. She nodded. He unlocked a white cylinder beneath the dish and flipped a lever. "Watch."

Thirty seconds passed. "What—"

"Shhhh. Just wait."

Suddenly mockingbirds screeched and several appeared from different directions, landing on the dish. A few more came.

"How'd you do that?" Jennifer asked. "How'd you call the birdies?"

"Magic," he said. Shielding her view with his body, he pressed another button and a miniature keypad and screen slid out of the cylinder. Quickly, he called up the map he wanted, entered coordinates and bits and bytes of data. He hit enter then had the keypad slide back out of view. "Watch," he repeated, as he locked up the cylinder.

"Watch what?" She was putting gum in her mouth. *What goes in long, pink, and hard and comes out limp and sticky?*

"The birds. Watch the birds."

"Watch them do what?"

Ten mockingbirds took off suddenly, their little bird brains having received a strong suggestion to take a joyride on the night wind. They all headed southwest.

"Where they goin'? How'd you do that?"

"Why do good blow jobs and bad grammar inevitably go together?"

"Huh?"

"Never mind." He paused, then lied. "I don't know where they're going." Opening the gate, he gestured for her to exit the enclosure. Following, he locked up after casting one last loving glance at his equipment. "Come on, hurry up. My wife's keeping my dinner warm."

10

"I wish Gabe and Kevin would give it up," Maggie said after the couple had left.

Will opened the living room drapes, revealing another view of the sea. "Give up what?" He opened the white-paned windows and stood in the bracing breeze. A wind, actually, and brisk enough to carry a trace of salty mist. Below, on the horizon, he could see smooth blackness and a short strip of reflected moonlight that abruptly disappeared against the ragged black silhouette of the Crescent.

"Trying to fix us up," Mags said, coming to stand beside him. "They're not very subtle."

Will laughed. "They gave up subtlety a long time ago."

"I guess so." She chuckled. "They're such romantics. We must frustrate the hell out of them. Oh!" She grabbed his arm as a cat landed on her shoulder from behind, then she let go and reached up and touched the beast. "Bad cat! Which one is it?"

Will looked. "Rorschach."

"Well, lift him off, will you?"

Will complied.

"You know, Gabe's right. These cats really are spoiled."

"I taught them to jump."

She snorted. "No, you just taught them that if you give a signal, you're going to catch them when they jump." She took the cat from Will and hugged it close. Rorschach trilled and purred madly at the same time, which made him sound like a tribble from *Star Trek*. "They already knew how to jump."

"They're cats."

"That's my line." She put the cat on the floor.

"I know. It's a good line, so I stole it. It's useful at my job, too, you know. Now, when a patient tells me about other people's strange behavior, I just say, 'They're people. That'll be eighty dollars, please.' "

Comfortable, familiar silence filled the space between them. Will inhaled summer wind, cooled and moistened by the sea. The dinner party had been just what he needed; he had even forgotten, for a while, what day it was. *The anniversary*. Michael had died a day after his own seventeenth birthday, twenty-six years ago today, the victim of a stupid shooting accident.

Will remembered little of that day. It was a hot afternoon, even here on the coast, and he, Michael, and Pete had taken their shotguns and spent a couple hours plinking cans and bottles over on the backside of Crackle Hill. The hill was private property, but Old Lady Anthem and her mate, who lived in a little house on top of the hill, (most of the family lived in a spooky-looking Victorian three-quarters up the front of the hill) let them take target practice as long as they asked first, same as she'd let Will's father when he was a kid. Today, the old lady and her equally old companion were still alive and kicking, and were still alleged to be witches. If so, they were good witches.

Will, only ten, had a .410 gauge, but Pete, fourteen, had a 12, and Michael had their grandfather's 12 gauge. They were old side-by-side shotguns, lovingly kept. Their grandfather had shot rabbits with the .410, had brought down bigger game with the 12. He hunted for food, supplementing butcher-shop beef and pork and the home-grown chickens with wild game, even though Grandma, at the age when Will knew her, made the old man dress out the kills. She used to call him an "old throwback," in a fond but annoyed tone when he tried to foist off something on her that needed skinning or worse.

The other 12 gauge was newer, their father's own gun, a present from Grandpa. It was never used for hunting, just skeet and plinking, much to Grandpa's displeasure. Dad preferred to shoot his game with a camera. He'd died only a couple years after Michael's accident, and Will felt a hard pang of longing for him, too. *Goddamned cigarettes. Goddamned lung cancer.*

"Will?" Maggie asked softly.

"What?" Grateful for the interruption, he smiled gently at her. She was long and lean and still tomboyish with thick, wavy, golden brown hair bobbed in a way that made him think of the flapper era. The same bright green eyes that had captured him the first time they met, when they were four years old and her family moved in across the street, held his. A few light freckles left over from girlhood still sprinkled her cheeks, and her nose still wrinkled when she laughed.

"Do you want to take a walk? Work off dinner?"

"Sure."

11

"This is Coastal Eddie, coming to you from KNDL, Candle Bay, on the cool California coast. Well, not too cool, friends and neighbors. After all, it's a warm August night where I'm sitting, and if you're ten or twenty miles inland, it's a hot night. A dog day night. Here at the Candle Bay boardwalk, the fog is hiding from the heat, and the amusement park is going full-tilt boogie even as we approach the witching hour. The Caledonia Philharmonic is at our own ampitheater tonight playing Bach for our pleasure. I wonder if the horn section sweats more than the string. Or vice versa."

Will reached over to turn off the bedside radio then withdrew his hand when the deejay added, "Right now, I've got a caller on the line in Caledonia who wants to tell us about some avian antics. Danny, are you there?"

Danny? Not Hatch. Please not Daniel Hatch.

"I'm here, Eddie."

"Turn down your radio, Danny."

"Oh, oh yes. Sorry." Fumbling sounds. "Okay."

"So, Danny, you were attacked by some birds?"

"I sure was."

"Tell me about it. Was it like in Hitchcock's movie?"

"Yes. Kind of. I knew it was going to happen."

It's him. Damn. When no news reporters picked up on the crow attack, Will had been overjoyed at the notion of the story dying a quiet death.

"How's that?" persisted the deejay. "Did someone tell you it would happen?"

"Yes, well, no. Yes."

"Make up your mind."

"I'm not sure."

"Danny, did anything really happen or are you just trying to make up a story for me?"

"It happened!"

"Details, then Dan, or I'm going to have to hang up. For instance, who told you it would happen? Start with that."

"My, uh . . ."

Don't say it. Don't say it. Don't say it.

"My penis told me."

"You have a talking penis, do you, Danny?"

"Yes. It's pretty talkative."

It was like listening to a train wreck. Will didn't want to hear it, but he couldn't turn it off.

"You're putting me on, man," said the deejay in a buddy-buddy voice.

"Uh, no. It's true."

"Well, so what does he say? I assume it's a he?"

Yes! Will smiled to himself. You could count on human nature to be more interested in genitals than birds.

"Yes, uh, he's male," Daniel stuttered.

Eddie chuckled. "They usually are. So does he talk about the ladies?"

"Um, yes."

"What does he say about them?"

"Oh, uh, ah, things."

"Thank you, Danny from Caledonia, but we're out of time. Next time have your penis phone in—maybe he'll be more talkative! And now here's a word from Fur D'Grease, the easy way to clean your dog."

As Eddie extolled the virtues of fur cleaner for dogs, Beethoven's music played softly in the background. Will realized he was rolling his eyes at the tacky advertisement even though no one was there to see him do it. Wondering if eye-rolling was a learned or inborn response, he clicked off the radio and lay in the dark on one side of his king-sized bed. The cats, who had been indulging in a mutual grooming orgy on the foot of the bed, moved around his body, going for their usual positions. One near each hand, in case, he supposed, he had a terrible yen to pet them in his sleep. Freud, always dominant, curled up next to his left shoulder and nuzzled his head up against Will's cheek and ear. None of his wives had ever been so affectionate.

He reached up and gave the cat one long stroke, which was how you turned on the purr. Before Maggie brought him the Orange Boys three years ago, he'd never been a sound sleeper, but it wasn't long before he discovered that contented purring was the best tranquilizer ever invented. Even when the Boys were kittens, the little purrs affected him. The huge deep adult purrs worked like anesthetic.

But not tonight. Will lay sleepless, staring into empty darkness above him. Curtains shivered in the breeze from the windows, casting watery gray moonlight across the foot of the bed. Freud dropped into sleep three times as Will waited for his own sleep. The first two times, he stroked the cat to start the purr. The third, he didn't bother. Instead, he tried to concentrate on the low, constant sound of the ocean, on the cries of nightbirds wheeling in the sky.

He almost turned the radio back on, but a little Coastal Eddie went a long way and nothing else came in well at night on the cheap little radio. Then he considered the television. He hadn't even checked out the new stations he was supposed to have; all he'd watched was the local news the night before. *Might as well try it.* Tentatively, he reached for the nightstand and felt around for the remote control, but when he finally found it, he managed to knock it to the floor. Briefly, he considered retrieving it, but moving that much would take him even farther from sleep. Ditto, reading. He hadn't brought anything to bed and getting up would be counterproductive. With a sigh, he withdrew his hand and used it to pet Freud into a new bout of purring.

Still, his mind refused to shut down.

It was because of the walk. Because of Maggie. Because of the anniversary of Michael's death. He and Maggie had walked all the way down to the Crescent and sat on a large flat rock, their feet hanging down. If the tide had been in, the waves would have lapped almost up to their knees, but as it was, the water never even touched their feet.

The night of Michael's funeral, they'd gone there too. That was the thing. It was a place they'd often visited over the years, but never on the anniversary. Brief anger welled at Maggie for leading him there tonight, but he could have steered her in another direction. Hell, maybe he even helped set the direction; he couldn't be sure.

You really have to get over this. Everybody else has. Pete probably didn't even know it was the anniversary of Michael's death. Not that he had ever cared anyway. Michael had been the oldest, tall and handsome, with great grades, a golden boy. He played varsity football and baseball and girls adored him. When he died, he was about to enter his senior year, Pete his sophomore year, and Will was still just a kid. As such, he idolized Michael, but Pete lived in the older boy's shadow in every way. He had the same broad shoulders, but was short, so they just made him look wide and squat even though he wasn't overweight. His hair was dishwater blond, not golden like Michael's, his eyes were muddier, his grades lower. He couldn't make the football team, but didn't do too bad at wrestling. *Because he spent all his spare time practicing on me.*

Pete's jealousy burned hot and obvious, and he turned his rage on Will whenever he could. When he got caught in the act, especially if it was by Michael himself, he just beat Will harder the next time. Will had tried telling on him a couple times, but true to his promise, Pete exacted harsh revenge, so Will learned to keep quiet. Their parents refused to believe that Pete was as abusive as Will claimed—he knew where to hit for maximum effect and minimum bruising—so he gave up and tried not to attract Pete's attention.

They knew Pete was mean. They knew he was a bully. Why were they so blind? An old question with a simple answer. They were parents: They didn't want to see. They thought it was all the usual childhood rough and tumble. Kids will be kids, the way of the world. All that crap. And to some extent it was true. Back then, Will suspected Pete was rougher than the typical older brother. Now he was sure. If he'd known then, would it have mattered? Probably not.

But everything has a silver lining. Will understood

his abused patients a little better than many thera-
pists. He understood why battered wives took beatings
over and over, and because of that, he was better
able to help them see their way out of abusive relationships. At least, if they actually wanted out. Many
didn't. They thought, on some level, they deserved
the beatings.

Will had never felt that way. Even when he was
little, he knew why Pete picked on him. He knew he
was a substitute for Michael, whom Pete despised.
He'd been right, too. After Michael died, Pete was
marginally nicer to him, though by then fear of Pete
was so ingrained that he never trusted him, and
although the beatings and teasing subsided greatly,
his fear grew. Will wasn't sure why; memories about
that time were muddled, and his best guess was that
his father's subsequent death increased his fear of
Pete, who became the man of the house, at least in
his own eyes. (Mom was always in charge, but she
was as blind as ever.)

Will had nightmares about Pete's eyes staring at
him. Glaring, enraged, accusing. His own brother was
his boogeyman long after such fears should have been
put away. Maybe that was why ghost stories had never
scared him. The real thing was so much worse.

Will skipped a grade and he and Pete were in high
school together a short time. Pete pretended he
didn't exist, which was exactly what Will had hoped
for. Pete entered junior college when Will was in
tenth grade, and a year later, joined the Navy, which
was the second-best thing that could ever happen.
The best would have been his falling off a cliff, but
you couldn't have everything.

Although Will made it his business not to know
anything about Pete's doings after that, a few things
got through, either via Mom or Pete himself on a

rare holiday visit. He became an electronics tech, was eventually promoted to a first-class petty officer. (Will, always a civilian, found the term "petty officer" highly amusing and he and Mags had spent hours thinking up special jobs just for officers who were especially petty.) Finally, Pete became a chief and claimed he ran the whole shebang up at Fort Charles, where he may have spent most of his time. His stories varied. On the rare occasions he decided to visit, his importance and job assignment grew more interesting with every beer he drank. Inevitably, with a twinkle in his eye, he'd end his tales with "If I tell you more, I have to kill you." Mom and most anybody else listening would laugh at this, but Will never detected a trace of real humor in Pete, even then, when his formerly surly brother's newly born pleasant personality had taken center stage. Evidently, the Navy taught him more than how to clean a gun. *But then, he already knew how to do that.*

Freud stretched, one paw reaching all the way up to Will's forehead, as if telling him to stop thinking. The cat's motor started up on its own, rumbling soothingly. This time, it worked. Will slid into fitful sleep, haunted by the old dreams about Pete's eyes.

4:17 A.M. Will glanced at the glowing clock on the radio as he sat up, not knowing what had disturbed his sleep, but knowing something had. Only one cat was on the bed with him. Rorschach, by the position. Will could see nothing, but touch told him that the feline was sitting up, facing the door, and that his muscles were tensed.

Will heard something, but it wasn't in the room. Maybe out near the foyer. *The front door?* It was a soft sound, and the muted squawk of a bird followed.

Rorschach sprung off the bed and left the room to join the investigation. There was another small shriek, followed by a noise similar to the first one. *No. It can't be.*

Will reached under the bed and grabbed his old baseball bat, just in case, then rose and walked softly down the hall. He found the triplets sitting in the dimly lit foyer staring intently at the front door. Rorschach glanced his way and trilled. Freud, tail plumed straight up with avid interest, sniffed the doorjamb. These were not frightened animals. Will rested the bat against the wall and turned on the porch light before peering out the peephole. Nothing. "So what's up, guys?" he murmured as he unlocked the heavy wooden door. The cats crowded him, curiosity boundless, Rorschach trilling, the other two meowing in the tone they usually reserved for raw steak. He blocked them with his legs, muttering, "Knock it off." Finally, he pulled the door open and peered out through the ornate semi-security screen door. The first thing he saw was at eye-level. It looked like a thorn poking through one of the heavy gauge wire holes. He pushed on it and it dropped, his gaze following. It wasn't a thorn, but a beak. *Yep, again.* On his doormat lay a small pile of birds. Not crows, smaller creatures, more gray and white than black. Mockingbirds, maybe. His mother used to call them catbirds, but he didn't know why. Some appeared dead, most of them wounded, and a couple were sitting up, looking dazed. Stunned.

The cats went nuts, proving that humans weren't the only ones who possessed a version of Jung's universal unconsciousness. They knew exactly what they were looking at and they wanted them. Will wondered what these cats, who'd never hunted their own food, would do with birds. Probably not eat them. His own curiosity roused, but then he flashed on what the Orange Boys did with the little rabbit-fur mice he bought for them and instantly decided all the growling and tossing and batting wouldn't be nearly as cute with a living creature as it was with toys.

Ah, isn't that sweet? He remembered the next-door neighbor, Mrs. Locke, cooing those words as her big gray tabby, Bruiser, batted around a hapless gopher he'd caught. Will had watched, fascinated, while Bruiser tormented the creature for a good twenty minutes before administering a death bite and trotting off with the dead thing, maybe to eat, probably to show off his hunting prowess to Mrs. Locke or maybe some other cat. Back then, he'd been too young to understand what the cat was putting the rodent through, no matter how well-deserved the torment, but now he did understand. He looked at his own fluffy little killing machines. "Sorry, guys, you're civilized."

He continued to watch the birds. One flew away successfully after several false starts. Meanwhile, another sat up and more birds began moving. The screen had evidently been far less deadly to the mockingbirds than the glass to the crows. After a few more birds took off, Will decided to let nature take its twisted course and used his foot to push all the cats out of the doorway long enough to close the main door before he turned off the porch light. "I'm going back to bed," he told them. "What about you guys?"

They didn't even look at him. All three had already moved in and flattened themselves against the marble tile and were trying to see beneath the door, very much like they did when an auto race was on TV and they tried to figure out how to get at those little cars.

12

"Hey, baby brother."

I knew I should've let the machine pick up. "Hello, Pete. What's up?" Will hit save on the computer then stared out the window. As usual, the Crescent was spectacular. Out to sea, whitecaps rode the choppy waves.

"Business is what's up, bro." A patented hearty chuckle followed. "I just wondered how the new cable's working? Like it? Have you checked out those adult stations I tossed in?"

Oh good, porn from my brother. What'll he give me next? Electronic VD? "I haven't had time to watch anything yet," he said in the friendliest tone he could muster.

"So you don't know if it's hooked up correctly?"

"The local news came in fine."

"Good. The hook-up's probably correct, then. Give me a call if it isn't."

"Will do. I'll talk to you later—"

"Hang on there, pardner. You sure don't like talking on the phone, do you?"

"I'm just busy."

"Maybe I should make an appointment so we can talk for an hour sometime."

"Fifty minutes," Will said dryly. "I'm booked a month in advance."

"Willy boy, you have no sense of humor," said the man who didn't realize Will had just made a joke. "Sounds like business is booming."

"It's busy."

"Busier than usual?"

"Why?"

"Just wondered. I've heard people get crazier when it's hot out."

"Tempers are shortened," Will replied. "But my patients all live on the coast. Even when it's hot, we still have the ocean breeze."

"Then why are you so busy?"

"I don't know." Will hid his irritation. "Sunspots?"

"Hey, is that a joke?"

"I don't know. It might be."

"Sunspots, solar flares, all that stuff, can affect satellite transmissions. Why not people?"

"Why not?" Will paused, an idea coming to him. "Is there a lot of activity right now?"

"Seriously?" Pete sounded astounded that Will would ask him a real question. With good reason; Will was amazed he had, but maybe something like that could explain the deviant bird behavior, so it was worth asking. "You want to know about solar storms and so forth?"

"Yes."

"Sure. Things are pretty active right now. Magnetic storms produce solar flares. Those can interfere with radio waves. We'll be running warnings about digital breakup during especially high activity."

"I don't understand."

"Digital images will briefly break up, sort of pixilate, sometimes. It's not a big deal; in fact, it's a lot less annoying than traditional interference. But that's not what you're asking about. You're asking about people acting crazy and sunspots, right?"

"Well, no, not seriously."

"Don't people get nuttier during a full moon?" Pete persisted. "That's a fact, right? It's the same kind of thing."

Why did I get myself into this conversation? "That's supposed to be an old wives' tale. It's perpetuated because people expect it to happen. An especially bad accident that happens during the full moon is going to be remembered for that reason. Odds are that there are just as many accidents on other nights." Though he wasn't about to tell Pete, Will wasn't all that sure there was nothing to those old tales.

"Oh. Do you get crazier patients when the moon is full?"

"Not that I've noticed."

"What about that cat of yours? Does it get the full-moon crazies?"

"My cat? How did you know I have a cat?"

The chuckle. "Well to hear poor old Mickey Elf-bones tell it, it was more of a mountain lion. It about scared the piss out of him."

"Mickey's a big phobic, then. My cat is normal and harmless. Even during a full moon."

More chuckling. "Don't go on the defense, Willy. Will, sorry. I know Mickey's scared of cats. He's afraid of dogs, too. In fact, he's damn near terrified of anything that has fur and walks on four legs. Doesn't mind reptiles, though. Isn't that weird? He has a horned toad for a pet."

"It's unusual, but not unheard of. He must've had a bad experience with something furry and generalized the fear."

"You're smart, baby brother. Do you remember Shagrat and Gorbag?"

"The names are familiar. Names from a book."

"Well, yeah, the names were from Tolkien's Ring books, but what I'm talking about were a pair of bull mastiffs that belonged to Mickey's dad. Big ugly bastards. Remember now?"

A scarecrow man with red hair throwing a ball down the beach. Will saw him suddenly in his mind's eye as if it happened yesterday. It was low tide and he and Maggie had just walked around an outcropping that would flood later. They came right up behind the man, who had just thrown a ball. Giant pale dogs chased after it, but sensing the kids, suddenly turned and started back toward their master—and them— snarling and barking, drool flying. The man glanced back and told them to leave unless they wanted to be eaten. Will and Maggie ran like hell and the dogs didn't follow. That had to be Mickey's father. "I vaguely remember," he told Pete.

"Daddy Elfbones trained the dogs to knock people down and hold them. He used to sic them on Mickey."

"That's unforgivable."

The old Pete emerged in unabashed laughter. "It was hysterical. Poor old Mickey never got over it. The old man had those dogs guard his room so he couldn't come out when he was supposed to be doing homework. Those dogs were always up his ass."

"You think that's funny?" Will said it before he

could stop himself. Engaging Pete any further was not what he wanted to do.

"Of course it's funny. It's hilarious." A pause. "You're just too sensitive. You always were. I mean, that's what makes you a good shrink, right?"

Will didn't reply.

"Sorry, bro. Didn't mean to step on any toes. But you know what's really weird about Mickey? He's scared of birds, too. Why would he be scared of birds?"

"I don't know," Will said slowly. "Maybe he was attacked."

"By birds?" Pete sounded incredulous. "Birds don't attack except in the movies."

"They sometimes swoop people to protect their nests. They can get pretty aggressive under the right circumstances. Or he might have been walking through a flock of gulls milling around on the beach when they decided to take flight. That's not aggressive, but it can feel that way, especially to a kid."

"Have you ever seen birds go crazy, Will?"

"I remember watching *The Birds* on TV then feeling a little nervous walking among the gulls."

"So you've never actually seen them attack?"

What is he doing? Does he know about the crows? Or last night? How could he? "I've been swooped by a mockingbird a few times. It had a nest in the yard at my other house."

"Did it scare you?"

"It surprised me. It didn't frighten me. Why?"

"You just really sounded like you knew what you were talking about."

"I'm a shrink," Will said, dry as dust. "I've heard firsthand accounts of attacks on patients by all sorts of creatures."

That damned chuckle. "I'm an idiot. Of course

you have. Tell me, bro, what kind of animal attacks the most?"

"The human kind." Will waited a beat. Hot damn, he'd actually scored one on Pete. "I have to go now, Pete. Say hello to your wife for me."

He hung up before Pete could speak, sat back, pleased with himself. *I finally got the last word on him, Michael.* He smiled and stood up, ready now to make his pilgrimage to Michael's grave. The Orange Boys, draped on his desk and the post next to it, blinked sleepily at him. "No wild parties while I'm gone, guys."

13

Most mornings Mickey Elfbones dragged his sorry ass out of bed sometime after 8 A.M., but today was Sunday, so he did the dragging at noon. Sleeping in didn't help; no matter what time it was, or how much sleep he'd had, getting up was always torture and had been as far back as he could remember.

More than anything, he wanted to go flop back down on his soft, inviting bed, but he had to be at work at 2 P.M., so he turned off his thought processes and let his body autopilot itself to the can, where he took a whiz and brushed his teeth, before going on to the kitchen to make coffee. Sometime later, Mickey became vaguely aware of his immediate world as the anesthetic of sleep finally surrendered to hot black coffee, strong and sublimely bitter.

After the first cup, he plodded back to the bathroom to brush his teeth again—just a thing he did, a habit, a routine—then returned to the cluttered kitchen and opened a big bag of Hostess Donuts, the little mouth-sized jobs smothered in powdered sugar. Taking as many as his hand would hold—six—he twisted the bag shut with a slingshot twirl then flung it onto the counter.

He dropped the donuts, sugar flying like sweet cocaine, onto a hardly-used paper plate left on the counter, poured more coffee, and carried them both into the living room, where he placed them on the coffee table and himself on the couch. It was a shitty little room in a shitty little apartment, but it was good enough, he guessed. The furniture, bought cheap at estate sales from money-grubbing relatives of dead people, was a wildly mismatched collection of high-quality, comfortable stuff. A sky blue and pine green plaid recliner was separated from an olive green velvety couch by a delicate dark wood Frenchy-curly legged end table. The other end table, at the far end of the couch, was chrome and glass, and the coffee table was oversized honey oak traditional stuff. Across from the sofa, the entertainment center, with its showpiece thirty-five-inch television, spanned the entire wall. Unlike anything else in the place, except maybe for Mickey's teeth, the massive center gleamed. Behind cabinet doors were his CD, video, and DVD collections, his books about movies and trivia. Behind the upper, glass-fronted shelves stood state of the art peripherals, VCRs, a DVD player, stereo equipment, a TiVo. He was currently shopping for a good DVD burner to add to the collection.

He picked up the remote and brought the equipment to life, quickly surfing until he landed on *Sunset Boulevard*. It had an hour left to run, which was just right. He settled back with his coffee and donuts to watch Nora Desmond go batty.

Three donuts in, he thought he heard something. Somebody talking, and it wasn't Nora. He heard the voice again. A male voice, though he wasn't sure what it said. Annoyed, he got up and opened the apartment door. Nobody was around.

There it was again, louder. *He's aware of the situation.*

That's what it said. Mickey checked outside again then cruised all the windows in the little apartment. Nothing. Nobody.

He returned to the couch, to his donuts and coffee and Nora.

He's aware of the situation. We have to control him.

"Holy shit, who's there?" Mickey cried, spraying donut crumbs. He slopped coffee as he jumped up and went to check the door, the windows, the closets, under the fucking bed. Nothing. Zip.

Heart racing, he returned to the living room. Maybe something was interfering with reception. He wasn't quite sure how that would work, but it was possible, right? How many times had he heard truckers' radio babble before he ever had cable? Plenty, that's how many times. Maybe somebody's cell phone was bouncing a signal off the satellite, or maybe somebody was hacking the system. Or just the movie. That was probably it.

We must control him by any means possible.

You mean?

Another voice, male, a little higher pitched.

You know what I mean. Begin the process.

"Shit!" The voices sounded like they were in the room with him. Hell, they sounded like they were in his head. Quickly, he changed stations, found an old *Twilight Zone* rerun. No, not that. He moved on to *Bringing Up Baby*. Katharine Hepburn was cooing to her leopard. *Good.*

His name is Mickey Elfbones. He must be controlled.

The mug dropped from his fingers, splashing coffee across the table and threadbare carpet. The mug rolled halfway across the room. "Shit!" Mickey cried. "Who the hell are you? Where are you? What do you want?"

No reply came.

14

In northern California, there is a town called
Colma, where the dead far outnumber the living. It
is a small city of cemeteries, populated by former San
Franciscans and ex-denizens of many other cities in
the area. Cemeteries of every sort—for Jews, for Cath-
olics, for children, for rich, and for poor—are only
a few of the funereal parks found there. Most of the
businesses, other than the cemeteries and mortuaries
themselves, are cemetery supports: florists, stone
masons, caterers for those who prefer wakes to more
somber viewings.

Candle Bay was the central coast's Colma. It wasn't
a place entirely devoted to death—it was home to
the only big local radio station, KNDL, as well as a
fairly well-known resort. It boasted the only boardwalk
amusement park between Santa Monica and Santa
Cruz. There were a few tourist shops and a harbor
tour, even an amphitheater, but with the exception
of the cemeteries, the resort and, Will supposed, the

radio station, things opened and closed there with alarming regularity.

Candle Bay, despite its pretty name, was meant for death. The town itself was drab and usually fogbound, the locals who kept shops and restaurants were, for the most part, solemn and gray. People lived near the sea; the Candle Bay Hotel overlooked the rest from a nest halfway up the hill. Above that, the cemeteries began, spreading across the rolling hills, gray tombstone teeth standing in mown green grass as far as the eye could see.

Will had turned off Pacific Coast Highway at the Candle Bay exit and found his way to St. Martin's Cemetery, and even to the grave itself, without getting lost, no mean feat in the maze of parks, even after twenty-six years of visits. The day was warm and clear as he trudged toward the gravesite.

When Michael died, it had been a beautiful day, much like this one. Beyond the rolling green cemetery lawns, wild grasses like the grass Michael had collapsed into, gleamed gold in the afternoon sunshine and orange wildflowers dotted the landscape until the low-lying mist over the town hid them from vision. Orange, the herald of autumn. He could feel it coming. It was in the air, just a whiff, but already there, cool zephyrs riding warm breezes.

He passed a weeping angel and two marble orbs, then arrived at Michael's simpler rounded monument.

MICHAEL BANNING
AUGUST 20, 1959–AUGUST 21,1976
BELOVED SON AND BROTHER — SLEEP GENTLY
BEYOND THE MORTAL VALE
IN OUR HEARTS YOU ARE ALWAYS WITH US

Will Banning stared at his big brother's headstone, feeling the old pain. It had dulled with time, but always burst fresh and bright inside him when he visited the grave. Nausea and confusion, a little vertigo, muddied the heartbreak as he knelt and placed the pristine baseball over the flower cup. It fit as if made for it.

There was no trace of the previous year's ball. Of course, there never was, but Will thought Michael, who loved all sports, would like the idea of some kid who liked to play ball finding it, holding it in a worn leather mitt and slugging it in a game at the park or on the school field.

"I miss you," Will murmured, flicking a piece of yellow grass from the top of the gray polished granite stone. "I guess I'll always miss you."

Each year he told himself he would end the annual twenty-mile trip down from Caledonia to St. Martin's Cemetery in the coastal hills above Candle Bay by placing *the* baseball, Michael's own, yellow with age, stained with use, the red stitching frayed and faded, over the flower cup. It would be his farewell, his letting go. He kept the ball wrapped in tissue paper in the trunk of his car, in case he felt the urge on a day other than the anniversary. But it never happened. He still couldn't let go of it, not yet, and so each year he came again, always popping the trunk and unwrapping the ball, then wrapping it again. Each year, he'd tell himself that maybe, next year, he would remember what had happened that horrible day so long ago. If he could do that, he could let go for once and for all.

You did it! It was you! You killed him!

The thought struck him, hard and cold.

No, I couldn't have.

But he couldn't be sure. He couldn't remember.

Silent tears escaped, more for himself than for Michael, and he wondered if he would go to his own grave without ever knowing the truth.

Stop lying to yourself, you know the truth. It's your fault he died.

15

"Kevin, get done with your shower! We're going to be late." Gabe, dressed in light blue shorts and a navy polo shirt, kept one eye on the tube, where the Dodgers and Reds were engaged in laconic battle, and one eye on the clock. Just once, he'd like to be on time for something that he and Kevin were doing together.

"I'm almost done," Kevin called. "Eric and Barry are always late. Don't worry."

"No, they're always on time. They're always polite about *our* being late."

No reply, but a moment later, he heard the water turn off. *Thank heaven.* Maybe they'd only be a few minutes late getting to the tennis court; it depended now on how long it took Kevin to decide what to wear. Gabe sighed and sat back to watch the game. In rock-paper-scissors, Gabe was the rock, Kevin the paper, and forget the scissors. Paper was safe and paper always covered the rock. Gabe had resigned himself to Kevin's quirks and whims years ago.

Gabe and Kevin were an unlikely looking duo, but after ten years, they were still going strong. Stronger than ever, despite Kevin's youth—he was only twenty-nine now—Gabe had practically robbed the cradle; despite their bickering, which was probably no different from any other married couple's; and despite being opposites, at least on the surface. Gabe had a football player's build and people usually thought he was joking if he admitted to being gay. His rumbly voice was almost always soft and gentle, though his looming size and steady gaze—and probably the color of his skin—had scared off a few patients who had come in for spinal manipulation when he'd first established his medical practice here. He knew he looked like he could snap them in half. Eventually, word of his prowess at curing aching backs and necks brought him so many patients that it interfered with his general medical practice. He cured that by talking a promising young pediatrician into establishing her practice in Caledonia. She covered everybody under eighteen, he covered the adults, and they often covered for each other. Business was getting too brisk now; they had been scouting for another physician for months.

And the way things had gone over the last couple weeks, he'd had to lean on her to cover far more of his patients than was reasonable. People were coming in with mysterious symptoms and he'd sent some Will's way—and Will sent more to him to rule out physical problems and prescribe medication. Last week, Will sent four long time patients and seven—*seven!*—new ones for check ups and all but one, an overactive thyroid case, proved to be physically fit candidates for Will's suggested mental pharmacopia of neuroleptics, SSRIs, and tranquilizers. Poor Will. He needed another hand worse than Gabe did. Although there was a physician in Candle Bay, which was the nearest town, there was no therapist of any kind there, and only one farther south in Red Cay. You had to go all the way down to Pismo before running into any real medical community, and most Caledonians preferred their doctors in town. More than most places, he thought, Caledonia liked its privacy. With its largely upscale and artistic tendencies, its top-flight chefs in restaurants too expensive even for a doctor to visit very often, and bed and breakfasts you had to book a year in advance, Caledonia had delusions of exclusivity. *Don't judge, lest you be judged.* Gabe smiled. He liked it here, too, he had to admit. It beat the hell out of South Central. And he was just as bad about exclusivity as anyone else. Any doctor could open a practice there, but he wanted to handpick his colleagues if he could get away with it.

He glanced at his watch. They were supposed to be at the courts in five minutes. "Kevin? Are you ready to go?"

"Almost." Kevin appeared seconds later, dressed in white, carrying his racket. "What do you think?"

"You look great."

Kevin eyed Gabe. "You should wear your tennis whites."

"You know I feel ridiculous in a uniform."

Kevin posed, showing his off. "It's not a uniform." He grinned. "They're togs. You feel ridiculous wearing togs."

Gabe chuckled. "You just made my point for me. I can't even say that word with a straight face."

"What word? Togs?"

Gabe nodded.

"Come on, say it. Say togs. Without smiling."

"Kevin—"

"Come on, please? Say togs like it's a disease you're diagnosing."

"Okay." Gabe steeled himself and spoke deeply. "Togs." Then his lips disobeyed and turned up on the left side.

"Ha! You can't do it."

"I told you I couldn't." He stood up. "All ready?"

"I've got the racket if you've got the balls, big guy."

Gabe grinned. "I've got all the balls you need, my boy."

"I was counting on it." Kevin, slim but not short, still had to stand on his toes to brush six-foot-three Gabe's lips with his. In mid-kiss, he stepped back, eyes wide. "What the hell is *that*?"

"What?"

"*That!*" Kevin pointed at something behind him, his face draining of color, his expression causing Gabe's neck to prickle up in goosebumps. *"Look!"*

Gabe looked. A woman was there, a horribly bloody woman, her lower jaw ragged and askew, the top of her skull sticking up like shark teeth through a dark mat of hair and brains. His eyes traveled downward. She wore a gore-splotched yellow dress similar to the kind his mother wore when he was a kid. Loosely, she held a revolver, the muzzle pointed toward the floor. The floor that was at least six inches below her feet.

Gabe's world started to spin as he locked eyes with the monstrosity. Kevin grasped his arm, grounding him. But it didn't ground the zombie or ghost or whatever the hell it was. As he watched, it slowly floated upward and disappeared inch by inch into the ceiling.

"Did you see that?" Kevin murmured.

"Did you?"

"Yes."

"Me, too."

"Was it a ghost, do you think?"

"I don't know what the fuck it was, Kev. You want to go play tennis?"

"Yes!" Kevin practically dragged him out the door.

They were in the car in record time. Kevin put the key in the ignition.

"Wait a minute, Kev. I forgot the sportsbag. The balls are in it."

"You usually put it in the car before we leave. Are you sure you didn't?"

"I'm sure. It's still in the living room."

They looked at the house, then at each other. "Gabe, why don't we just buy a couple cans on the way?"

"Good idea."

They took off. Gabe looked back, half expecting to see the dead woman looming over the house.

"What's the matter?" Kev asked blithely. "You look like you've seen a ghost." A nervous giggle escaped.

"Very funny. I was thinking maybe she was on the roof, but she's not." He paused. "What if she's sitting on top of the car, right over our heads?"

"Gabe! Don't say things like that while I'm driving. It's not funny."

Gabe didn't tell him he was serious, or that he was still trembling. "We've been in our house for five years," he said finally. "I've never noticed anything weird, not one tiny thing. Have you?"

"Just that blue-flowered wallpaper that was in the bathroom." He glanced at his mate. "Did we really see something?"

"Yeah. But if we hadn't both seen it, I'd say no and go get my eyes checked."

"What are we doing after tennis?"

"Drinks with Eric and Barry? Maybe dinner out. That's what we usually do."

"I was thinking. Wouldn't it be fun to drive down to the Candle Bay Hotel and spend the night in one of those sexy theme rooms?"

"Yes. But we'd need to go home and get our deodorant and toothbrushes and clothes first."

"We can buy what we need, Gabe." His voice was light but pleading. "Let's be spontaneous, okay? And we don't need clothes. We won't go anywhere. We'll order in."

"Sure, okay. Let's do it. But we have to get home by seven tomorrow morning to get ready for work."

"I know. It'll be nice and sunny by then."

"I like the sound of that." Gabe tried to relax, but couldn't. "Kev, we can't stay at hotels every night—"

"Will or Maggie would put us up."

"You know we can't do that. It's bad enough we know we're cowards. Do you want everyone else to know too?"

Kevin *tsk-tsked* like a stereotypical gay man. "Well, what's the use of being fairies if we can't use it as an excuse to be cowards?"

"You know you don't mean that."

"I know." Kevin's voice lost the extra added lilt. "You almost lost it for a second there when it happened, didn't you? Admit it."

"I admit it. If you hadn't grabbed me when you did, I might have passed out. But you don't need to tell anyone else that."

"Our secret. But can we tell Eric and Barry about the ghost?"

Gabe shrugged. "Why not? They'll think it's a great story—but let's not go to great lengths to convince them it's more than that."

Kevin nodded. "I wonder what Will will think?"

"Crap. Do we have to tell Will?"

"You know my big mouth. I'll end up telling him even if I promise not to. What?" He snickered. "Are you worried he'll try to have us committed?"

"You know Will. He won't believe we saw a ghost. He'll say we imagined the entire thing."

"I know. And he'll try to come up with a rational reason for our imagining it. I'd kind of like that. Wouldn't you?"

Gabe laughed and finally relaxed a little. "I'd love it."

16

A pleasant warm Sunday afternoon gave way to a perfect evening in Caledonia, and people were relaxing in the final hours of the weekend. Felicia Banning dutifully stirred the beef stew she was keeping warm for her Pete, who was working late again, then wheeled out the trash cans for Monday pickup. After, she curled up in an easy chair with a Danielle Steel novel and read while an Elton John CD supplied background music. She was trying very hard not to think about the lipstick she'd found on his briefs while sorting laundry. It wasn't the first time either. Not by a long shot. She didn't care about the cheating; what infuriated her was the lack of respect he showed by letting her find it.

She'd confronted him once, but the beating she received in return had kept her in bed for a week. That had happened several times since then, and he knew what he was doing. He didn't leave marks and she never told anyone—she knew they wouldn't believe her. Everyone loved Pete. He gave to charities, helped old ladies across the street.

And he wasn't that bad, really not bad at all as long as she didn't give him a reason to be pissed off. Sure, he was distant, only paying attention to her when he wanted sex, but unless some knight in shining armor, some rich knight, came along to rescue her, she didn't really have any intentions of leaving him anymore. After all, she easily carried on her own private life. He gave her material things readily and generously, an enviable allowance for clothes and beauty salons, a new car every year or two. Once, she'd commented on a silver SUV, a Mercedes, she'd seen in town. Two weeks later, for her birthday, she found one just like it in the driveway, a big blue bow on top.

He even paid for a housekeeper to come in three times a week, which wasn't necessary, but why knock it? Anyway, if she told him she didn't appreciate the cleaning woman, he'd undoubtedly become enraged. She had a pretty nice life. Looking good on his arm and keeping him in a pleasant mood were really all he required of her in return for his generosity. What kind of idiot would leave a cushy life for nothing but a return to secretarial work? Sure, she could divorce him and sue for half of everything, but she wouldn't because she understood that something might happen to her that was worse than a beating.

The phone rang. "Banning residence," she said because that's what Pete told her to say.

A masculine voice, all business, one she'd heard before. "Mr. Banning, please."

"He's not home yet. May I take a message?"

"When will he be home?"

"I'm not sure. Do you have his office number?"

"Yes, and his cell, but he's not picking up."

"I'm sorry. If you'd like to leave a name and number—"

"Tell him Uncle Neddy's looking for him. He has the number."

"I didn't know he had an uncle—" She stopped talking, realizing the phone had already gone dead.

17

Jennifer Labouche was still licking her lips when Pete checked the voice mail on his cell phone. He'd turned off the ringer half an hour ago, when they arrived at Felsher Hill. "Shit," he muttered. There was a message from Nedders and another from Felicia telling him his uncle Neddy was looking for him. "Shit. Shit."

"Is something wrong, lover?" Jennifer, lips nicely swollen from all her hard work, was staring at him with those big baby blues.

"Nothing's wrong. You go wait in the car while I make a call and lock up."

"Okay."

"And Jennifer?"

She batted her eyelashes. "What?"

"Don't call me lover."

"Okay, Pete."

He stared at her. "No, I'm your boss. Call me Mr. Banning."

"When we're alone? You always let me call you Pete."

He crossed his arms. "New rule."

"Yes, Mr. Banning." She turned and wiggled away. He loved that she didn't dare ask why. It was good to be the boss. He'd done it because he could. Maybe next time he'd tell her to start calling him "Master" when they were alone.

Hearing the car door open and close, he phoned Nedders, his old team leader and still head of Project Tingler. He picked up on the first ring. "It's me," Pete said.

"Talk to me."

"The broadcast experiments at the dish worked. Set off two flocks of birds."

"You mentioned that before. Any human feedback yet?"

"Not that I know of. Recon starts tomorrow. I'm also trying to cozy up to my brother. I figure he'll start getting new customers. Probably, he already has."

"Idiot. If he's got ethics, he's not going to tell you shit even if you win him over."

"I can make him do anything."

"Stop your Goddamned swaggering. You've got a dick up your ass about that brother of yours. Forget about him and concentrate on the project. How are the installations coming along?"

"On target. Even worked one of my boys on installs today. That's overtime pay. More than seventy-five percent of the town subscribes, and we've upgraded almost a quarter of those already."

"Good. What about bugs? Those installed too?"

"Very few. I can't have my workers do that. I'm going to do it while paying personal house calls to thank my customers for their loyalty and extol the virtues of their new channel capabilities. That starts in earnest tomorrow. That way, I can see what's going on with them, know what I mean?"

Nedders barked a laugh. "You know how to grease up tongues, I'll give you that. Get them talking. Wear the wire."

"Of course."

"And step on it. You've installed twenty-five percent, but how many of those have been activated?"

"I don't know yet, but most people will have surfed through the new channels. Activation requires clicking on The Chuckles Channel. If they haven't activated it already, I'll be doing it for them when I give them their personal demonstration."

"Good. Report in tomorrow at twenty-one-hundred."

"Will do." Nedders clicked off and Pete slipped the phone into its holster. Captain Nedders had handpicked him years ago to be a member of what was then called Project ELF, as in Extra-Low Frequency electronic transmissions. The military had been working with electronic mind-control techniques since the fifties; the Russians and Americans had bombarded each other's embassies unmercifully for years. At one point during the Cold War, part of Washington State was inundated with so much power that mysterious illnesses, miscarriages, and birth defects began to draw unwanted civilian attention. The US responded in kind, but at ten times the rate, and the Soviets backed off. Both powers continued their experimentations more subtly. Other countries got into the act, and for decades, experimentation had continued with everything from implanted radio chips—some subjects remembered being abducted by aliens, which was exactly what the little chips broadcasting in their brains instructed them to remember. Most were unaware of any major changes, but they developed urges to do things they ordinarily wouldn't. Sometimes subjects would be used in Manchurian Candidate ways. Most of the time, messages sent into their brains directed them to develop a particular obsession or compulsion or other disorder.

Project ELF, now Project Tingler because the term ELF was widely known to the public these days, specialized in causing nonspecific mental aberrations in larger populaces. No implants necessary. Waves were broadcast, via satellite and dish, into individual homes (and from the dish itself, specialized waves could be sprayed directly into the air to upset local wildlife). Eventually, they intended to modify the dish controls so that, from that location, specific commands to specific cable boxes could be sent. For now, the waves sent into homes were set at a frequency meant to disrupt the functionings of the brain in generalized ways. Project Tingler was here to gather data on what specific effects would be most common in a population of a small American city.

Realizing he'd become tense, Pete stretched and twisted back and forth, enjoying the *pops* as he loosened his spine and relaxed his muscles. The process made him think of Willy Boy. Even as a kid, Baby Brother had stiff necks and backaches. He didn't know how to relax. He didn't have the willpower to do it. He was weak then and, undoubtedly, weak now. He couldn't wait to find out what the specialized microwaves would do to Will.

18

Caledonia readied itself for bed.

Will, exhausted mentally from visiting Michael's grave, had exhausted himself physically by hiking all over the hilly cemeteries, reading names and epitaphs now and then, but mostly just moving quickly, working his muscles until they felt sore and heavy. Then he'd driven home, had a pizza delivered, and turned on Fox, which was running one *Simpsons* rerun after another. There he sat, eating pepperoni, olive, and onion pizza out of the box, tearing off cat-size bites for the Orange Boys—why these creatures loved anything Italian, he didn't know, but if it had tomato sauce on it, they always stared him into submission. They sat on the coffee table to eat—Will chuckled when he thought of how Gabe would react to that. He had a dark beer, they had a mug of water. Cats, being cats, preferred people mugs or glasses to bowls. Maggie assured him it was a common feline fetish. Something to do with pride, probably. All in all, it was a pleasant evening. Will didn't even stay up for the ten o'clock news, but hit the shower, amused by the unusual presence of the cats. All three waited in the bathroom throughout his ablutions, then followed him into the bedroom and sat on the foot of the bed while he slipped on a fresh pair of shorts. In deference to the heat, he skipped the usual T-shirt.

He read for a while, and the cats got into their lights-out positions before the lights were out. That was unusual, too. Finally, Will put the book aside and quickly drifted off to sleep, lulled by Freud's purrs. Always, after the cemetery visit, he dreamed about Michael, disjointed nightmares about the shooting, full of blood and gore. But tonight his dreams were good dreams about playing ball, exploring tidepools, and camping out in the backyard. Unbeknownst to him, the three brother cats picked up on his sleeping pleasure and snuggled closer.

Kevin and Gabe, though not in Caledonia, were in bed even earlier than Will, but fell asleep much later, wringing every bit of fun they could from the Cave-man Room they'd rented at the Candle Bay Hotel. The walls were rocky, there was a round fireplace, and a Jacuzzi in the room, and the bed was a cave within the cave, a grotto built into the wall. Both would dream about the dead thing in their Caledonia home, but neither would tell the other.

At their own house, something flickered in and out of the living room several times. Something that had once been alive.

* * *

Maggie Maewood ate dinner with her partner and his wife. An older couple, they'd just returned from Reno and were full of stories that took Maggie out of her worry about nervous animals. After dinner, Rose, who was also a veterinary nurse, walked over to the clinic and made the rounds while Maggie filled Charlie in on the two bird attacks on Will—and on the big influx of anxious patients, particularly ones with wings. Later, she went home and settled in with her house pets—two cats and a dog—and watched TV until she fell asleep on the couch. Around 3 A.M., she woke up, turned off the tube, and dragged herself to bed.

Lara Sweethome slept fitfully, locked in her bathroom. Despite the blankets, the tub was hard and uncomfortable. She prayed for morning to come as she listened to the footsteps that walked up and down, up and down, up and down the stairs. A blue box of Morton's salt waited next to the doorjamb. She'd poured a thick line of the stuff across the opening because that was how you kept ghosts out. She hoped. She had an appointment with Dr. Banning in the morning—or she would have as soon as his office opened. He wouldn't turn her away. Not with Mother marching through the house.

19

"I think we'll increase your Risperidone dosage and give you something to help you relax, maybe a little Valium, until this passes. I think you're having a mild relapse. It's not uncommon." Will smiled at Lara Sweethome, who had come to him over a year ago with symptoms born of exhaustion, fear, and guilt. There were hallucinations involved, which could indicate psychosis, but he didn't think she was schizophrenic; there was too much emotion involved. Lara was convinced her house was haunted by her mother who had died months before. She had responded immediately to a medium-sized dose of a neuroleptic, and had gradually tapered off to a low dose. The hallucinations stopped, and psychotherapy helped the woman, who had spent her entire life taking care of her ailing mother, adjust to life alone, and to not feel guilty about enjoying it. She was, he'd thought, a shining success.

But now, Lara looked like hell, her complexion

sallow, eyes sunken, worse than she had the first time he'd seen her. "Doctor, I know you'll think I'm crazy."

"I won't think you're crazy. You can say whatever you want, Lara."

"I think it's real. I mean, it's not just me. It's Mother."

"Why? After all, you know this supposed haunting went away when we started medication."

She twisted a tissue in her hands, then looked up at him. "Almost went away."

"Almost? I thought you said—"

"I didn't say it was completely gone."

"Actually, you did," he said gently.

"Well, it was as good as gone. I wanted to please you—"

"That's not—"

"I know. Hear me out. The thing was that the haunting—the footsteps and everything—diminished tremendously. It was softer and far less frequent and, frankly, what sounds I heard just didn't bother me anymore."

"Even if it didn't bother you, you should have told me."

"Dr. Banning, you've eased me down to almost no drugs and until last week the haunting stayed diminished. If anything, the haunting continued to lessen all the time you were lowering my medication. I think it was real and that it was fading away." She searched his eyes. "And then it came back so suddenly. So strong. Stronger than it was when I first came to you." She hesitated. "Or maybe something made me more sensitive to it. I was reading about schizophrenia."

"I really don't think you're schizophrenic, Lara."

"But Risperidone is for schizophrenia."

"Among other things. If you were truly schizophrenic, it would have taken a much higher dose to control your problem."

"Please, Dr. Banning, I want to ask you something about schizophrenia, even if I don't have it, all right?"

"Go ahead."

"Okay. From what I've read, schizophrenics hear things other people don't?"

"Yes. It's not uncommon. Voices in their heads telling them to do things or plotting against them are stereotypical of that type of problem."

"But that's not all they hear."

"Different people hear different things."

"Like my hearing my mother's footsteps? And the doors opening and closing?"

"Yes, but in your case, these hallucinations are tied to your emotions. That makes it different."

"Please, let me finish."

"Sorry. Go on."

"What about smelling her perfume?"

"Olfactory hallucinations are rarer, but they do occur. There's also likely to be a perfectly logical explanation for the fragrance."

She nodded. "What if some—not all, just some—schizophrenics aren't really mentally ill, but are just ultra-sensitive to things most people don't sense? What if they really do hear voices? Hear or see ghosts? Or what about people like me? I lived my entire life with my mother. Wouldn't it make sense that I'd be sensitive to her spirit?"

Will sat back and rubbed his chin. It was going to be a long, long day. "The possibility of ultra-sensitivity in some schizophrenics has been suggested many times, sometimes by very reputable experts. I concede that it's possible, perhaps even probable in a few cases. Just think of our normal senses. For example, a minority of people taste bitterness in spinach and other greens that most people aren't even aware of. It's an inherited trait, perfectly explainable. And some people have better hearing than others. Allergies are ultra-sensitivities. One man's fragrant rose is another's uncontrollable sneezing fit." He paused. "But as for sensing spirits, I'm up against a wall here."

"Why? It all fits, everything you say fits with what I'm talking about."

"Lara, I simply don't believe in ghosts. They're not logical. There's no empirical evidence."

"You mean to tell me you've never seen or heard anything you can't explain?"

Will smiled. "Sometimes my cats stare at things I can't see. That's a little unnerving. But it doesn't mean they're sensing ghosts."

"How can you know that for sure?"

"I can't. The only thing I'm certain of is that nothing is certain. But I do know that cats have better eyesight, particularly in low light where I couldn't possibly see the spider up in a corner that's so fascinating to them. They can also see into the infrared spectrum. Or maybe they're simply listening to squirrels in the attic. Their hearing is tremendously better than ours. Same with dogs."

"You're not going to budge on this, are you, Doctor?"

"Tell you what. Let's get your dosage back up and see if that doesn't help. If it doesn't, I'll do some research and try to keep an open mind."

Lara's smile was small but genuine. "Dr. Banning? Do you taste the bitterness in spinach?"

"Yes." He made a face. "Awful stuff."

"It doesn't taste bitter to me."

"Our perceptions are dictated by physiology."

She nodded. "I hear ghosts. Maybe it's in my physiology, but it's not in yours, so you can't conceive of hearing them."

Will shrugged. "Perhaps."

"Don't humor me."

"I'm sorry. I didn't mean to imply anything."

"I know. But, Doctor, if the pills don't help, would you consider making a house call? To hear for yourself?"

"All right." He rose, as did Lara. "I'll phone Dr. Rawlins with your prescriptions."

"Thanks. Tell him to send them to the usual pharmacy." She headed for the door of the little bird-free office he was using this week. "Thanks for listening."

"You're welcome. Make an appointment for Friday or Monday, and call if you have more trouble." He paused. "Do you have a friend you can stay with for a day or two—or who can stay with you—until you feel a little steadier?"

"I might. I'll think about it."

Will nodded. Lara Sweethome was not a hysteric. She even made some sort of sense with her ghost talk. But it was ridiculous to even consider such a thing. She was relapsing, that's all there was to it.

20

"May I help you?" Kevin asked the heavyset guy at the reception window.

"Yeah. You Will Banning?"

"The doctor's in session right now. I'm his assistant, Kevin. All his appointment slots are filled today, but—"

"I'm not here for an appointment," the man grunted. He glanced back at the waiting room with that uneasy I-don't-belong-here expression common to many who entered a psychologist's office. "I'm Harrison Beech." He rested hirsute knuckles on the countertop.

"You certainly are."

"What?"

"Nothing, Mr. Beech. Why are you here?"

"I'm from Glass Act. I've got panes waiting out on my truck." He pulled a folded piece of paper from his breast pocket. "Will Banning ordered replacement glass for a French door."

Kevin smiled, then directed Beech to a back entrance. The man lumbered out, and Kevin followed, watching from the window until the man pulled his Glass Act pickup truck toward the rear. He turned and beamed at the nervous-looking crowd in the waiting room then hurried back past his office and up the hall to unlock the back door, but Will's door opened suddenly, barely missing him.

"Sorry," Will said. He was holding the door for Lara Sweethome, who was looking about as frazzled as she had when she came in.

"Uh, glass guy's here," Kevin told him. "He's at the back entrance."

Will nodded. "You take care of Miss Sweethome. I'll let him in."

"Great." Kevin smiled at the little lady and slipped her hand over his elbow. "Right this way, my dear."

21

She smiled. Will watched Kevin lead Lara Sweethome away. He hadn't seen one genuine smile the entire session—granted it was only twenty minutes, but still, not one—but let Kevin be Kevin and the woman lit up like she hadn't a care in the world. *I think I'm jealous.* But a smile was a smile and, as he let Harrison Beech in, he realized how pleased he was that Lara actually had a smile in her, poor woman.

"This way." Will led Beech and his box of glass to his regular office and unlocked the door. The glass man entered and placed the glass on the empty desktop in the shadowed room. The room smelled of cleaners and furniture polish. Will turned on the light.

Plywood covered the doors, and since the little courtyard had no outside entrance and hid the breakage from view, they had decided not to bother nailing the wood to the framing. Instead, they took everything out of the office but the desk and bookcases, and those had been cleaned, along with the rug and walls, by a service early this morning. Kevin had already had the upholstered sofa and chair hauled away, too. Will's pristine desk chair had accompanied him into the spare office.

Beech whistled, looking around. "I'd hate to see what that rug looked like before you had it shampooed."

Will looked down. Small dark bloodstains still dotted the carpet, an almost solid line of them marking where the back of sofa had been. The walls were clean, but scrubbed down to an old coat of paint in places. The inside of the wood door appeared to be in good shape, at least.

"Bloodstains are hard to get out," Beech said.

Will nodded.

"Birds?"

"How'd you know?"

"We've had a few calls about broken windows in the last week or two." He scratched his chin. "Usually, we get about one a year." He looked around again. "Usually it's a really clean picture window, the bird's intent on whatever its little birdy brain is telling it to do and it just"—he slammed his fist into his palm—*"Bam!* Right into the glass. The hell of it is, the thing's probably chasing its own reflection. Usually it just stuns or kills the bird. Sometimes, when it hits just right, we get some business."

"So it's usually just one bird?"

"Yeah. Sometimes two or three."

"The calls you've had recently," Will began, "were there more birds than usual?"

Beech scratched his jaw with gusto. "My beard grows too fast. I get these ingrown hairs. Anything I can do for that, Doc?"

"I'm not that kind of doctor. Sorry. About the birds."

"Yeah. Four seagulls creamed themselves down at one of the restaurants on Crescent Drive. But that was a big picture window and the sun would've been reflecting in it when they hit. Four's not that many, but those are big birds and they hit just right." He grinned. "Expensive. I did one of the others. It was just a small window on a house. Already had a crack in it, but there were half a dozen sparrows dead on the ground beneath it. The other call was nothing, just a single bird, but it packed a punch. Some sort of hawk." Beech scratched a little more then nodded at the broken doors. "Now this, this is just plain weird. Looks like you had a massacre in here. How many birds?"

"A flock. Crows. I don't know how many."

"That's one for the books. If these were clear sliders, it wouldn't be quite as strange, but with the white panes, it's just freaky."

Will glanced at his watch. "I have a patient waiting. If you need anything, go see Kevin at the reception desk."

"I might need to talk to you again."

"Not a problem. I'm running short sessions all day. I'll be free ten minutes out of every half hour."

Harrison Beech pushed stray locks from his forehead then whistled again. "That's a hell of a short hour. Don't the crazy people get an hour?"

"Many of my patients usually have longer sessions, but we're very busy today."

"Everybody's going nuts, huh?" Beech guffawed. "Maybe people are gonna start slamming into windows, too."

22

"Really?" Kevin's eyes widened as he leaned over the counter until he was only a foot from Lara Sweethome's face. "You have a ghost?" He handed her an appointment slip. "What's it look like?"

"I hear it," Lara said. "I've never seen it, but it's my mother. I smell her perfume, too."

"Your mother? That's nice!"

"No, it isn't nice."

"Oh, she was an old meanie?"

"Not exactly. She was irritable. She had reason to be because she'd been an invalid since I was thirteen. She wouldn't leave the house."

Visions of Norman Bates's mom danced in Kevin's head. "Wouldn't or couldn't?"

"Wouldn't. She lost both her arms and she didn't want anybody to see her, so she called herself an invalid for years and years before she actually became ill and died. Before that, she walked and walked, but only in the house." She leaned even closer. "Do you know what she could do?"

"What?" whispered Kevin.

"She could feed herself with her feet. She could hold a spoon in her toes and have soup. Or use a knife and fork to cut a steak."

Kevin couldn't help it, he started to tremble with contained laughter. "I'm sorry," he muttered.

But Lara giggled too. "It's okay. I guess it's good she wouldn't go out. Can you imagine if she'd wanted to go to a restaurant?"

They both tittered. "Why didn't she get prosthetic arms?"

"She didn't believe in them. She said she lost her arms because she'd sinned and was being punished."

"My God. What did she do?"

"I'm not really sure." The smile returned. "There were so many things. She was going to become a nun, but got kicked out for having relations with a priest."

Kevin touched her hand in mock shock. "A *straight* priest?"

Lara smiled. "Then she became a Playtime Pussycat, but got kicked out for doing club patrons."

"Doing them? What do you mean?"

Lara blushed. "Once, when she was drunk, she told me about it. She specialized in, well, uh, masturbating men right in the restaurant or the club room, wherever she was working. She said she did it hundreds of times before she finally got caught and canned."

"You mean she gave them hand jobs?"

"Yes."

"Then that's the sin. A hand for a hand."

Lara smiled. "I never thought of that. Well, I never wanted to think about her doing that, so of course I didn't."

Kevin wanted to ask how Mommie Dearest lost her arms, but quelled the urge. "Tell me about the haunt. What does she say?"

"I've never heard her talk, thank heaven for small favors. She walks. She slams doors and opens them, and sometimes her perfume just suddenly overwhelms me, it's so strong. But mostly, it's the walking. She pushed me over last night."

"And it's scary?"

"Very. You believe me, don't you?"

"Yes. Does the doc still say it's your imagination? Don't answer that. Of course he does."

"Have you heard a ghost, too?" Lara asked softly.

"No. But I've seen one and, honey, it's a doozy."

"Where did you see it?"

"In our house. Yesterday. It was so scary that we stayed in a hotel last night."

"Did you tell the doctor?"

"Not yet, but I will when things calm down a little."

"He won't believe you."

"He'll have to believe something because my partner saw it, too."

"A witness! You're lucky. I asked Dr. Banning to make a house call if the meds don't get rid of my 'imagined' ghost. I don't know if he will or not." Lara's expression grew somber. "Kevin?"

"Yes?"

"What are you going to do about yours—your ghost?"

"Well, I guess I'm going to hope it was a one-time-only thing. And if it is, we'll chalk it up to bad clams or something."

"What if it comes back?"

"Honestly, sweetie, I don't know. Move, maybe. I mean, our ghost is *that* ugly!" He made a face. "What about you?"

"I can't afford to move. I've been reading up on getting rid of ghosts, but I don't know very much yet. My book says they can't cross salt."

"Salt." Two phone lines began ringing. "Oh, darn. When it rains, it pours. I'll see you in a few days, Lara. We'll talk then."

She waved and left, then Kevin fielded a rash of calls from people wanting last-minute appointments. He told them to call back tomorrow or to seek other help. It was all he could do since he didn't double-book in advance. (He filled the usual emergency half-hours, though. So much for Will getting a lunch hour. Or for himself.)

"How's it going?" Will asked. His patient, all paid up, nodded at Kevin and swept by.

"Well, you've got five people out there waiting."

"Five?"

"At last count."

"They have appointments?"

"Yes. Doc, I've turned away four walk-ins, and eight calls for same-days. Unless you want to work evening hours."

"If I thought I could hack it, I would. Our last appointment is when?"

"Six-thirty."

He shook his head. "If there's an honest-to-God emergency, I'll take one beyond that, but that's it. I've been here since eight A.M. and I'm exhausted already. How many med checkups do we have today?"

Kevin consulted the computer. "Four."

"Get hold of them and reschedule, tell them to call Gabe, that their prescriptions will be filled now, but that they must keep the new appointments. Might as well do the same thing for tomorrow, too. Use your judgment."

"No refills for potential abusers?"

Will sighed. "You know what's up. If the patient is a problem, don't put off the appointment. Ones with potential problems, well, tell them they'll get enough to tide them over until the rescheduled appointment—try to make it next week. I'm sorry to put so much on you."

"No problem."

"Thanks. Call Gabe and coordinate things with him, okay?"

"Will do."

"Is Gabe busy today?"

"Swamped."

Will nodded. "Tell him I won't send him anyone I absolutely don't have to. Are you seeing him for lunch?"

"And leave you here alone with patients up front? I don't think so."

"Kevin, you're wonderful."

Kevin twinkled. "Tell Gabe."

"I will, if you'll do one more thing for me."

"I'm at your command."

"Whatever you order for lunch for yourself, get the same for me? Charge it all to the office." He paused. "We do have a few minutes off, don't we?"

"We didn't, but now we have twenty minutes. One of those med patients was scheduled for noon. I'll call him right away."

"Twenty minutes, huh? Today that sounds positively hedonistic—so order up something good. We'll eat and talk about something fun."

"I know just the topic. Gabe and I spent last night in the Caveman Room at the Candle Bay Hotel."

"The Caveman Room?"

"Well, they have a prettier name for it, but believe me, it was the Caveman Room last night."

Will looked skyward, then at Kevin. "I don't think I want to hear too much about that."

"Okay," Kevin said blithely. "Then I'll tell you about our ghost."

"Don't mess with me, Kev."

"I'm not. Our house is haunted."

"Who's next?" Will asked abruptly.

"Huh?"

"Who's my next patient?"

Kevin glanced down. "Adam Goddson."

"Is he out there?" Will nodded toward the waiting room.

"Yes."

"I'll get him."

"No, Doc. Go back to your office. I'll bring him. The natives are restless out there. If they see you, they'll mob you."

"It can't be that bad." He eyed Kevin. "Can it?"

"Let's put it this way. You have five patients. Three of them arrived in the last hour even though they aren't scheduled until after lunch. They want to see you."

"I bow to your judgment," Will said quietly. "I'll be in my office."

23

Except for the Crescent, the little city of Caledonia was located across Pacific Coast Highway from the ocean. The town was long and narrow, built like a vagina, according to the wisdom of Pete Banning. Main Street was the slit, the center of town, down in the valley. The lips—that's what Pete used to call the twin sets of low hills rising on either side—cradled the slit. The inmost ones had been well built-up for years, but the outer hills had seen real construction only in the last two decades. Pete's brother, Will, lived on top of the outer lip that bordered by the highway. Quite a few people lived there now. But when Mickey Elfbones was a kid hanging out with Pete, a trail had run for several miles along the hill above the highway.

It was still there in places, just a worn dirt track that had ceased to be of interest once you couldn't hike it without running into homes. When Mickey was a kid, it was vaguely off-limits because of lack of fencing, but the hill was wide, and though parents told kids not to hike up there, they'd done the same when they were kids, and nobody much cared, as long as you were on your feet. Just your feet. No bikes. Even then there were metal NO BICYCLING signs posted, and if you did it and got caught, the cops could write you a real ticket.

Of course, kids did, though not as much as you'd expect, and Pete, who was all for breaking laws, happened to like that one a lot because it pissed him off when asshole kids would fly by while he and Mickey were on patrol. They did that a lot when they were nine, ten, eleven years old. Pete loved to patrol. They pretended they were soldiers, and they'd scrutinize the town and the highway with cheap binoculars as they walked.

But there was this one kid, Andy Faircloud, a grade older than them, and a lot bigger, who loved to honk this stupid horn and race between them on his bike, which usually had a card snapping in the spokes. Pete tried to knock him over, but couldn't, and he wouldn't even entertain Mickey's suggestion that they rat him out to the cops or his parents. That was chickenshit, Pete said.

So one day, around Halloween, they hiked up the hill and hid behind some bushes. There, they opened their backpacks and put on Grim Reaper robes and painted up each other's faces to look like skeletons. Mickey had wanted to use masks, but Pete said those weren't scary enough. After the makeup, they put on black gloves on which Pete had painted white skeleton hands. It was really pretty cool.

They walked a short distance to a broad-trunked live oak and sat behind it. It was located at a curve in the trail, a nice wide space. They waited, and pretty soon, they heard the snapping card as Andy Faircloud approached. Mickey waited until Pete gave the high sign, and they leapt out from behind the tree onto the trail, not eight feet in front of Andy. Andy screamed and lost control of his bike, the front end wig-wagging madly for a second or two, and then Pete screeched and lunged at him, even though it was obvious the kid was about to crash right next to them. But Pete's action made Andy turn white, it made his screams go silent—and the kid tried to avoid the Grim Reaper with a hard left. Mickey thought the kid probably didn't even realize what he was doing, he was so scared. The bicycle, Andy still hanging on, flew off the hill and disappeared. It took only a second or two, but it felt like forever. Pete grabbed Mickey and propelled him toward the edge just in time to see the bicycle, the boy holding on with a rictus grip, tumble end over end before it hit Highway 1.

A semi, a double, came around the curve at the same time. The horn blared, brakes squealed, but there was no way it could stop. Mickey saw Andy Faircloud's eyes on him before the truck squashed him flat.

"Idiot," Pete said, yanking him back by the shroud. "We gotta get out of here." Mickey was numb. He ran with Pete to the shrubs where their backpacks were hidden. They stowed the shrouds and gloves into their packs, then Pete pulled out a bottle of lotion and some rags. It took about ten minutes to erase all the makeup.

After everything was stowed away, they stayed hidden for a while just in case anybody else came up to check out the sirens that followed not long after the huge truck jack-knifed all over Andy's body, spreading him like strawberry jam across the highway. After fifteen minutes passed—that along with the fifteen minutes they'd spent cleaning up seemed like a reasonable amount of time to hike up the hill after the accident—they returned to the oak, not even having to bother smudging out footprints because the afternoon wind had come up and was doing it for them. They sat down and watched the show.

Immediately, Mickey threw up. Pete cursed him and made him bury it. Mickey complied, then told himself it was a television show he was looking at, that it wasn't real. The truck blocked most of the highway and local cops were down there setting out flares and directing the small amount of traffic around the accident, letting north- and southbound traffic take turns using the southbound lane closest to the ocean. There were fire trucks but no fires, and there were boxes and boxes of Tide detergent spilling from one of the trailers. Pete loved that. Mickey was grateful that the bright oranges, yellows, and reds of the boxes helped hide the gore.

An ambulance took away the driver about the same time that a TV crew started filming. Another ambulance crew was picking its way around the wreckage. They wore gloves and were carrying big black bags. Every now and then they'd put something in a bag and Mickey would feel his stomach lurch while Pete would comment, "Parts is parts," and snicker.

"This is great," Pete said, and licked his lips. "Hey, you want to go down there and get interviewed by the news? Be on TV?"

"What? You mean confess?"

Pete punched him in the ribs so hard it brought tears to Mickey's eyes. "Asshole. Confess to what? We didn't see it happen. We came up here to see what was going on. We're just concerned." He stopped talking and looked at Mickey like he was a piece of bad pork. "Forget it. You can't act."

Tow trucks came and one of the trailers was righted just as twilight began to fall. Mickey saw a piece of bicycle, a bent handlebar. A hand and part of an arm were attached to it. "It's late. My parents are going to kill me if I don't get home," Mickey said, trying to sound like everything was okay.

"Man, look at that." Pete looked at him, eyes bright, a creepy smile on his lips. "We made all that happen. Just you and me, pal. And we take it to our graves."

"To our graves."

They rose and walked to their homes, had their dinners, saw the accident reported on the evening news, and were reminded by their mothers never to ride their bikes on the trails. They went to bed. Pete slept like a baby.

Mickey didn't sleep at all that night. He had seen the face of fear, the real face, the eyes, and it would haunt his dreams, along with the strawberry gore and the shadowy glimpse of the arm ripped from its body. He felt fear of a kind worse than his father's dogs could ever instill. And he carried it with him forever, even though his adulation of Pete, brave and bold, grew. He loved his hero and he also feared him.

Now, standing in the home of Colonel Wallis Tilton, Retired, Mickey felt some of that old fear return. He remembered Tilton from his short stint in the military. He was a square-jawed man with a white mustache and piercing blue eyes and you could feel his presence, like a powerful force. He led men because he was obviously born for just that purpose, and if there was a God, Mickey knew he looked like Wallis Tilton. Even now, with Tilton in a polo shirt and jeans, tilted back in a La-Z-Boy, sipping lemonade brought to them both by his doting wife, Tilton seemed to be looking right through him. Seemed to be seeing into Mickey's soul.

He knows about us.

"What's wrong?" Tilton asked.

Mickey turned. "Nothing."

"You look like you've seen a ghost, son. You about jumped out of your skin. Have your lemonade and tell me why."

"I, uh, touched a live wire, sir. Just gave myself a little shock." He stepped away from the television and flicked the remote, clicking onto The Chuckles Channel, which Pete had told him to start doing, who knew why, then a few other new ones. "I think you'll be pleased with your new selection." Then he handed the remote to Colonel Tilton.

We're going to have to do something about Elfbones. He's becoming a problem.

"No," whispered Mickey.

"Are you talking to that ghost, son? Because you look like you just saw it again."

"I'm sorry. I thought I heard something. It was just the television."

"The sound is muted." So saying, Tilton unmuted it.

Oprah was being interviewed by a woman. He'd heard a man's voice, the same one as the night before. He looked at Tilton and shrugged. "Maybe I picked up a radio signal on a filling."

"Then judging by the look on your face, you'd better go see your dentist."

"I think I will." He felt naked.

He's trying to eavesdrop on us right now.

Quickly, he gulped the lemonade, then gathered his tools, gave Tilton a pamphlet about his new cable box, and got the hell out of there.

Outside, he still felt like he was being watched, but at least it wasn't by Tilton, a.k.a. God.

Before starting the van, he did his paperwork and tilted his head back and closed his eyes. *Is this what it feels like to go insane?*

24

Will's last patient before lunch was Mia Hunt Hartz, a woman who was at least as pretentious as her name. He saw her once a month, and it was all her idea. Everyone who was civilized had a therapist. She had suggested on more than one occasion that it was a pity there wasn't a psychiatrist in Caledonia and she had to make do with a mere psychologist. A few months ago, he had suggested she drive down to San Luis Obispo for better service. She hadn't complained again. Will couldn't stand the woman, who was merely a bully in a female body.

She didn't have any real problems, except for being a vapid, shallow bitch, but that wasn't a problem either, not for her, at any rate. A rich daddy's girl, she also ran a thriving real estate office, and was a former neighbor of Will's when he'd lived in the Heights, Caledonia's version of Beverly Hills. Occasionally, she fucked rich older men who gave her presents. The woman was a living, breathing cliché.

But today, there was more. The cliché's world had been rattled. There were children in her yard, she told him, awful little children, three of them, running through her gardens, trampling her prized Venus flytraps (well, she actually said Dutch irises, but Will thought flytraps were more fitting), and climbing a century-old oak tree that had been allowed to live when the house was built. The children—she wasn't sure, but thought there were two of one sex and one of the other—giggled and shrieked with laughter. Mia Hunt Hartz, upstairs, opened her bedroom window and yelled at them to get out or be arrested.

They didn't even look at her, just kept playing. She yelled again, but they acted, she said, like she didn't exist, the little monstrosities. Not monsters. That was too common for Mia. Only monstrosities would dare enter her world.

Mia exited the room and found her maid, directed her to go down and detain them while she contacted the authorities. She returned to the window, her phone in her hand. The children still played. That was when she noticed them race over her prize koi pond, which was ten feet in diameter, impossible for the invaders to jump. But they must have, she said, because they crossed straight through the center without splashing, without even rippling the water. Unable to get a clear signal on her cell phone, she moved away from the window to call the authorities, and had just completed the call when her maid used the intercom to report that the children were gone.

Mia didn't cancel the call, of course. After all, she paid those people's salaries! When a nice young officer arrived, she accompanied him into the backyard to show him the damage, and she was mortified—absolutely mortified—to find not a leaf out of place, not a footprint in sight.

Will had to work to keep from smiling, to do the job he was there to do. He tried counseling first. She merely looked down her nose at him when he attempted to reassure her that sometimes things just work that way. Then he suggested what he believed really happened—that since she saw them from her bedroom, where she had gone to take a twenty-minute nap in her easy chair, that she may have experienced a certain type of dream that happened only in the hypnogogic state. He started to explain, but she cut him off; Mia didn't even want to know what "hypnogogic" meant—no one could hypnotize her, she announced, revealing a flaw in her alleged Stanford education. *Valedictorian, my ass!*

Hiding his amusement, he gave her what she really wanted: a stronger Valium prescription. Since she really liked her tranquilizers, he gave her a sample pack and told her she could pick them up at the pharmacy tomorrow, and that the number would be whatever Dr. Rawlins recommended. He wanted to talk to Gabe personally about this one—he had a feeling she might have several prescriptions going at once.

Mia Hunt Hartz wouldn't leave his private office without his escort. She wasn't afraid of being alone or getting lost, she was just a pretentious society bitch. Once she asked him why he didn't employ a valet to park his patients' cars. Amazed—the lot was directly adjacent to the entrance, for Christ's sake—he'd told her no one had ever asked. She sniffed at that. She sniffed at almost everything with her long, narrow, pointy nose.

She waited while he opened the door. He routinely opened the office door for his patients, both sexes, and never thought twice about it, but with her, it made his blood boil. More precisely, it made his neck muscles tighten. He hid it, and walked out to the reception desk with her. He could smell the luscious aroma of food from Chen's Iron Wok before he saw the uniformed cop setting brown paper bags of food on the desk in front of Kevin.

"Well, Officer Hoyle," said Mia Hunt Hartz, looking the handsome young man up and down disapprovingly. "No wonder you couldn't find any trace of those horrible children who trespassed the other day. It must be difficult to enforce the law and hold a part-time job as a delivery boy."

"Ooooooh." That was Kevin, almost inaudible, but highly amused.

The cop, whom Will had met but couldn't quite place, finished setting down the bags then turned his square-jawed, blue-eyed Nordic face to Mia. He stared at her. She stared back defiantly. It was a staring contest. He wished Conan O'Brien was there to send his masturbating bear in to stand behind the officer and cause Mia to lose the battle.

Seconds passed slowly. Food was cooling down. Will's stomach growled. Neither starer would give in. Fortunately, there was Kevin.

He came out from his glass office and stood beside the cop. "Will Banning, Eric Hoyle, you two met at our Halloween party last year. Remember? Eric was dressed as a policeman because he was technically on duty and Will—Dr. Banning—and Maggie Maewood came as Hades and Persephone."

"How charming," drawled Mia Hunt Hartz. "That's our country girl veterinarian, I believe? A little old to be playing the virgin bride."

Kevin read in Will's eyes what others could only guess at—Kevin was like that—and he whisked up to Mia and took her arm, a big false smile plastered on his face. "Dear, you're all paid up and Doctor needs his lunch, so let me see you to your car." He propelled her to the front door, craning his neck once to make a face.

"You just spent an hour with that woman?" Eric Hoyle asked, shaking his head.

"Twenty minutes. But it seemed like an hour."

"That's how long I was with her. It seemed more like two days." Eric grinned. "I take it you heard about her invisible trespassers."

"Yes."

Eric glanced around. "Seeing her here explains a lot."

"No," Will said. "She doesn't need to see me. It's purely a status thing. She must have a personal housekeeper, investment banker, therapist."

"She's not nuts, then?"

"Who's not nuts?" Kevin asked, joining them. "Mia Cunt Hurts?"

"Shhh. Kevin, there are people in the waiting room."

"There were. I told them we were closing until one o'clock and sent them to lunch. We're all alone, just the three of us."

"I hope you don't mind my joining you, Dr. Banning. I called Kevin about lunch and he asked me to pick up an order he'd leave at Chen's and eat with both of you."

"Call me Will. Of course I don't mind."

"There's more," Kevin said.

"Wait, Kev. Will? About Ms. Hartz—"

"You mean Mia Cunt Farts."

"Be quiet, Kevin."

Kevin raised his eyebrows and covered his mouth.

Eric shook his head, half-smiling. "She's not a nut case?"

Will paused. "I can't discuss her, but I think it's okay for me to say she's of sound mind."

Eric looked a little disappointed. "So you think there really were kids in her yard? I swear, there wasn't a blade of grass out of place."

"I can't break confidentiality, but the fact that she was taking a nap when they *apparently* woke her isn't confidential, I think."

"You think she dreamed it?"

Will shrugged. "I can't say. But people who are between true sleep and wakefulness, are rarely aware of the hypnogogic hallucinations that precede true dreams. When they do become aware of them, they're often shocking in their reality. It's pretty common. In fact, I think a whole industry has grown up around hypnogogic dreams."

"Will thinks alien abductees dream it all. It's very Jungian."

Eric nodded, looking a little overwhelmed. "Okay, Will. That makes sense. I've had a couple dreams that I was positive weren't dreams."

"But remember," Kevin said. "Sometimes a penis is only a penis."

"Kevin—"

"The doctor's not a Freudian," Kevin explained.

"What the hell are you talking about?"

Will answered before Kevin could pour more murk in the waters. "Freud was known for believing that nearly everything had a sexual connotation. If a patient told him he dreamed of a tower erupting in flame, Freud interpreted this as a penis ejaculating. If a patient entered a tunnel, he was in a vagina."

Eric nodded. "But you disagree?"

"Like Kevin said, sometimes a penis is only a penis. And often a tower is only a tower. Lots of times, climbing a tower is a dream metaphor for struggling to attain a goal, but only the dreamer really knows what a dream means."

"Come on," Kevin said, carrying the bags toward the group therapy room. Eric and Will followed.

"That is so cool!" Eric said, all boy, despite the uniform. "Maybe I could make an appointment sometime and you could tell me what a recurring dream I have means."

Will chuckled. "I can't tell you. I can only ask you questions that will help you figure it out for yourself."

They sat down at the round table. Kevin got paper plates and extra napkins from a cupboard and joined them. "Do us a favor, Eric. Don't make any appointments until things calm down. We're taking it up the ass here."

"Kevin!"

Kevin *tsked* at him. "Obviously, you don't remember Eric too well."

"We said hello at your party, Kev. I don't *know* anything."

"You didn't meet Barry? Eric, what was he wearing?"

"You know Barry. He wore a black suit. He won't dress up more than that."

"So he was either a mortician or an MIB? Do you remember him, Will?"

"No."

"Well, it doesn't matter. The thing is, Officer Eric is one of *us.*"

"*You're* gay, too? Really?" Eric stared at Will. "I don't believe it."

"Will's honorary gay," Kevin said. "Pass the Kung Pao chicken."

"That's a relief. I thought I was slipping." He passed a soda to Will, then started spooning Szechuan beef onto his plate.

"Eric always gets his men," Kevin said. "Chopsticks all round?"

"Why do you always ask that? To torment me?"

"Yes." Kevin handed him a plastic fork.

"Dr. Maewood's great. We've been taking our hounds to her forever," Eric said. Like Kevin, he was an expert with chopsticks.

"She is," Kevin said. "She and Will are perfect for each other. Neither of them can work the sticks. They're forkers."

Eric suppressed a laugh. "So she's your girlfriend?"

"No. She's my best friend."

"He's going to tell you how they met when they were four years old, yada, yada, yada. Sum it up: They do everything together but make love." Kevin pointed a chopstick at Will. "He doesn't know it because he's straight, but they're meant for each other. She doesn't know it either."

"Really?"

"Kevin . . ." Will was glad he was eating Kung Pao. It gave him an excuse to be red in the face.

"She's a woman, she must suspect it. Will probably does too. Will? Do you ever interpret your own dreams? Bet'cha she's in there."

"Kevin, we've known each other too long—"

"To mess up your friendship." Kevin rolled his eyes. "She saw him through three bad marriages. Will, don't feel bad. Most gay guys are as bad at picking the right partner as straight guys are." He looked at Eric. "It's so romantic. You should see them look at each other. They don't even know they're doing it. Not yet. It's the oldest story in the book, you know?"

"Kevin," Eric said. "You're embarrassing Will. And me. Do you talk about Barry and me like this?"

"No, sorry."

"How do you put up with him?" Eric asked.

"I'm not sure. It has something to do with my inability to stay mad at him for more than five minutes."

"I hear you."

"Tick tock. Tick tock." Kevin rapped his chopsticks. "Eric, time to sing for your supper. You said you had something to tell me about our haunted house."

"Oh, Lord, Kevin," Will moaned. "No more haunted houses. Please!"

Eric looked at him sharply. "Are you hearing about hauntings?"

"Just one or two."

"We're getting way more intruder calls than usual. Normal people, scared to death, phoning from their beds or in their closets. They think they've got a burglar or worse in their houses. We get there and there's no sign of forced entry." He paused. "We get those kind of calls pretty often, but they've doubled lately."

"Are people calling in about ghosts?" Will asked.

"No." The cop grinned. "I guess the ones who think they've got ghosts all come to you. As far as I know. You want me to check with Sergeant Thursday? He's in charge of graveyard right now. He might have some stories."

"Sergeant Thursday?" Will laughed. "You're kidding."

"He's not kidding. Sergeant Jeff Thursday. Dah-da-da-dah!" Kevin laughed. "He's a cutie, too. Too bad he's straight." Kevin turned serious. "Now, tell us what you found out about the house."

Will tried rolling his eyes, but it did no good.

25

The voices wouldn't stop. Well, they would—Mickey was only hearing them once or twice an hour, but he sure as hell couldn't stop thinking about them. He was being watched like a lab rat by men, at least two, and official, probably military by the sound of them.

Pete was military for a long time and even though he was civilian now, he'd worked black ops and intelligence. Sometimes, after a couple beers, he'd tell Mickey stories about missions, how he'd assassinate people. Great stories, though sometimes they sure sounded a lot like movies Mickey had seen. Like when he'd told him the story of his trek up a Colombian river to find and terminate a crazy Army general who had founded some sort of weird empire and liked to cut off people's heads. That was *Apocalypse Now.*

Does he really think I'm that stupid? Sometimes Pete really pissed him off when he tried passing off a movie as his own tale. He even ripped off the camel race from *Lawrence of Arabia*. Mickey always forgave him, though, because he only said that shit when he was a little drunk. And some of the stories were true, probably.

A few times, after a sixer, he hinted at different kinds of adventures. Once, they'd watched *The Manchurian Candidate*, which was about the military creating assassins through mind control, hypnosis. Pete loved that movie. He said the stuff in the movie was all true, that he knew lots more about it but was sworn to secrecy. He'd say that there were way more sophisticated ways of controlling men, but that if he told him, he'd have to kill him.

Pete was always saying that. It was his favorite line. "How many more installs we got today, Pete?" "Well, I could tell you, Mickey Rat, but if I did, I'd have to kill you." "Pete, you ever meet a president?" "Well, Mickey Rat, I could tell you, but I'd have to kill you." Pete thought it was funny. He never got tired of it.

Sometimes Mickey got real tired of it.

When Pete said that stuff about mind control, which wasn't often, and wasn't detailed, Mickey always got the shivers. He wondered if Pete still knew those guys from when he did that stuff. He wondered if the voices had something to do with it.

Maybe they're watching Pete through me. Maybe they want to kill him! He almost hoped they did, in a way, but he was pretty sure they were after Mickey himself because he knew too much. He shivered. He needed to do something to keep the invisible men out of his mind, whether they were after him or Pete or both of them. He couldn't have them finding out the stuff he and Pete had done over the years, like how they'd scared Andy Faircloud to death. *Maybe they already know.*

But they were still talking about him. They maybe

knew a lot, but not everything, and as long as he had secrets—even if he wasn't sure what they were—he'd stay alive.

He picked up his clipboard to double-check the address of the next install. It was down off Main Street, in his old neighborhood. He didn't recognize the name, and he prayed to Holy Shit that there wouldn't be any animals around, especially dogs. Pete knew he was nervous around animals, but he didn't know how nervous. He could barely move. Even that fluffy cat at Pete's shrink-brother's house threw a scare into him like it was a grizzly bear or something. Pete would probably fire him if he knew how scared he was. He'd laugh at him, too.

He turned off Main and navigated the maze of streets, going out of his way to avoid seeing the house he grew up in. If he saw it, he'd have nightmares about Daddy's mastiffs. He wondered if Will the Shrink would say he was nuts. Maybe there was medicine now to stop phobias. He was pretty sure that's what he had. Shrinks were doctors, they didn't tell if you visited them. The shrink lady on *The Sopranos* was as good as a priest that way. Better, probably. He didn't have to tell Will the Shrink about the voices— he'd put him in a nuthouse for sure—but maybe he could ask about the animal thing. He was a nice guy. Nicer than Pete.

Mickey couldn't believe what he was thinking of doing. If he told Pete, Pete would have to kill him.

Really. He probably would kill him. He'd be afraid of what he might tell him. But he wouldn't tell him anything but about his thing about animals. Instead, he would get some medicine or something to help him hide it.

He pulled up in front of a modest two-story Cape Cod, an old house with a nice fresh coat of paint—

gray with blue trim. A white picket fence surrounded it. He got out of the van and got his toolbox, then went to the gate and almost fainted when he heard a dog bark. "Save me, save me, save me," he whispered, and looked down. It was a wiener dog, littler than Will Banning's cat. Its tail was up and wagging. It was friendly, dancing on its stubby legs in anticipation.

It might as well have been a wolf. Mickey took a step backwards and just stood there, not knowing what to do. Pete would fire him for being such a coward. He couldn't leave. Finally, he looked up, saw that the main door of the house was open, the entrance covered only by a screen door. "Hello?" he called. The dog wagged and barked again. "Hello? Caledonia Cable. Hello?" He looked at the order sheet. "Mr. McCobb? Mrs. McCobb?"

A woman appeared in the doorway. "The gate's not locked. Come on in."

"I'm allergic to dogs, Mrs. McCobb."

"Oh, I'm sorry." She came out, a pleasant woman in her late sixties. She scooped up the dog. "I'll put him in our bedroom. You just come on in." She turned and disappeared into the house, taking the miniature wolf with her.

Mickey followed. *Scared of a wiener dog.* He decided he would go see the shrink. Then he made himself decide not to, in case the men—the voices—were listening. He'd have to block them from his head before thinking anything but doodly-crap for now. Maybe he'd find out how on the Internet. You could find anything there. *Okay, but I'm not really going to find out.* He thought that thought really hard, then made himself think about doing his job.

26

"I did a little digging," Officer Eric Hoyle said as he deftly manipulated his chopsticks. He looked at Will. "Something wrong?"

"I just don't know how anyone can eat rice with those things."

"It's sticky rice," Kevin said dismissively. "So what did you dig up, Eric?"

"In 1966, a family named Cockburn lived in your house." Eric paused so that Kevin could snicker. "Got that out of your system?"

"For the moment."

"Jason and Carrie Cockburn had been married eight years. They had two kids, but both died of crib death."

"Ooooh," Kevin murmured. "That sounds suspicious."

"SIDS?" Will asked. "Sudden infant death syndrome twice in the same family?"

"Yeah. There were cursory investigations, but the

coronor said crib death in the reports—I guess that was before they called it SIDS. Considering what happened later, maybe they weren't accidents."

"So we might have baby ghosts, too."

Will shot him a look. "You don't have any ghosts, Kev."

"If you'd let me tell you about it, you'd believe me."

"After Eric tells his story, you can tell me what you think you saw." Will knew they were nearly out of time already, so Kevin wouldn't be able to go on and on if he had to wait his turn.

"Hurry up, Eric. What happened?"

"We got several calls each year about their loud fights. Jason beat up Carrie, but she never pressed charges. Back then, cops couldn't arrest an abuser on their own unless the wife wanted to press charges. She always said she ran into the door or tripped or fell off a ladder."

"Go on," Kevin urged. "What happened?"

"Murder-suicide. She shot him with a .44 Magnum, then put the gun in her mouth and blew her brains out."

"She died in the living room, right?"

"How'd you know?"

"I saw the ghost. But, crap, I didn't know there were two of them. Where'd she shoot him?"

"In the face."

Kevin cringed. "I mean in what room?"

"Oh, sorry. I believe it was in the living area as well." Eric stood and retrieved his jacket from a hook on the door. "I copied a couple photos." He pulled folded papers from the jacket pocket. "Want to see them?"

Kevin's upper lip twitched. "I guess. Wait. Show

the woman to Will first. Will, I'm going to tell you what she looks like. That'll prove I saw her ghost."

"No, it won't." Will accepted the copy.

"Well, it'd prove it to anyone else. It'll make you wonder."

Will unfolded the page, which had two reduced photos on it, one a body shot and one just the head. His stomach lurched.

"Yellow dress," began Kevin.

"This is black and white."

"He's right. In the report it says she had on a yellow dress."

Kevin looked pleased. "The dress is just sodden with blood. Her jaw's hanging off, she has dark hair, the bullet blew a big hole and there are pointed pieces of bones sticking out of the hair on the top of her head. Brains all over the place. Her eyes were kind of little and deeply set. Brown, I think. Piercing."

"Her eyes are closed."

"She looked at me, Will. Eric, what's the report say?"

"Dark brown hair, brown eyes."

Triumphantly, Kevin put his hand out to Will. "Give."

"Gladly." He handed it over and when Kevin saw it, the look of recognition on his face convinced Will that he had indeed seen something.

"You want to see Jason Cockburn too?" Eric held out the other page.

"No," Kevin said. "If I look, I'll have nightmares. If he shows up on his own, and I've seen the photo, Will won't believe me, right, Will?"

Will tried to smile. It was a failure.

Eric tried to hand the page to Will, but he shook his head. "I've seen enough."

"This bothers you? You're a doctor."

"Not that kind of doctor." He could feel Chen's fine cooking getting ready to leave his body the same way it came in. Akwardly, he pushed back his chair and stumbled to his feet. "If you'll excuse me."

"Are you all right, Doc?" Eric started to take his arm.

"I'm fine. My brother died from a shotgun blast when I was a kid. This is a little close to home. Excuse me."

"Jesus, Will," Kevin said as he was going out the door. "I'm sorry. I didn't know you saw him!"

Will didn't stop to reply.

27

"What was all that about?" Eric asked. "He looked like he was going to lose his lunch."

"Yeah, I think he was. At least it's not digested yet, so it won't taste bad coming up."

"Kevin, that's disgusting."

"Not as disgusting as it would be in an hour." Kevin looked at Eric. "He was the youngest of three brothers. His oldest brother, Michael, was some kind of god to him, I guess. His middle brother is Pete Banning, owner of the cable company."

"Oh yeah, nice guy. He called and wants to stop by personally tonight to show Barry and me how the new cable box works."

"It's a cable box. What's to know? It's the same as the old one, but you get more stations and a new remote. He probably just wants to hit you up to buy more systems or something."

"You don't like him?"

"No. I think he's a sleaze. He screwed one of Will's wives."

"One of his wives?"

"Three-time loser. He picks ice queens. Gold diggers. Well, he did. He's sworn off women now. Which means he's finally ready to realize what he really wants is right under his nose."

"You mean Dr. Maewood?"

"Who else? He's afraid to make a move because it could ruin their friendship."

Eric shrugged his eyebrows. "It could."

"Trust the Love Fairy, Eric. It won't ruin anything. He's just a big dope. So's she." He saw the time. "Crap. I have to go open up. Anyway, if anybody knows anything about Michael's death, it'd be Maggie. Will doesn't talk about it. All I really know is that the three brothers were out shooting and there was some kind of accident. Michael's gun went off somehow and it was really ugly."

"You want me to look up the police report?"

"No. It was just an accident anyway."

"There'd be a report since a gun was involved."

"No. There's nothing more to it and frankly, I'd feel like I was peeping on him. It wouldn't be right."

"Yeah. But what about Pete Banning? You really think he's a scumbag?"

"Yeah. You know, he's the kind of guy who wouldn't think twice about selling a crappy used car to a poor old lady. He's a salesman through and through." He paused. "And Will can't stand him, so out of loyalty, I can't either."

"Oh? He hates his own brother?"

"Stop being such a cop. Pete was a bully and he picked on Will like crazy."

Eric nodded. "I can see the bully thing. He seems really nice, but he's pushy, too. Thanks for the warning. Barry and I won't let him sell us anything." He put on his jacket.

"Hey, let me have that other copy after all."

"Really?" Eric handed it over and Kevin slipped it into his own pocket. "It won't destroy your credibility?"

"I'm not going to look at it unless I see another ghost. Then I'll check it out. Hey, you're a cop. Why are you so open-minded about this?"

"Stuff happens. You know that old B&B out on Peneverde Road?"

"Giardia's Inn? I thought that closed down last winter. Did you ever stay there? The food was awful!"

"It *is* closed, for renovations, but the owners still live there. We've had several intruder calls there since it's been closed to the public. It's a big old house, so the K-9 units take the calls. The dogs wouldn't go upstairs. Neither of them. They whimpered. It happened every time. Old Lady Giardia said it was because of the ghosts." Eric paused. "I met up with one of the K-9 units there once. That dog was scared to death. I went upstairs—nobody was up there, but I didn't like it much. So I don't know. Ghosts sound like a good reason. Nothing bothers those dogs ordinarily. I didn't notice anything spooky, but it didn't have that nice cozy atmosphere, you know?"

Kevin walked Eric to the front door and unlocked it. Five people, looking annoyed, poured in as Eric stepped out.

"My appointment was supposed to start ten minutes ago," complained prissy nerd Daniel Hatch.

"I'm sorry. Doctor had an emergency. You sit down, he'll see you very soon." He looked around at the other patients. "Would you all like me to turn on the television?"

They started arguing about what to watch.

"People, you know the rules. You have to watch

what I put on. That's why the TV's way up there by the ceiling and I have the remote."

Dirty glares from a couple of them, the others looked bored.

"Okay." He trotted back to his office, glanced at the listings, and got the remote then tuned in one of the old movie channels. It was showing *Gone With the Wind*. That was safe. You had to be careful about what you put on in this waiting room, especially if there were several people present. He'd tried E! repeatedly, thinking everybody liked gossip, but the noise drove some people out of their trees. Which was pretty easy to do around here. He'd tried the Game Show Network, but that one drove *him* out of his tree. The home improvement networks were his next choice, but half the time there were artsy-craftsy shows on and men hated those. Soaps didn't work either—sometimes they made people weird. Old movies were the best.

"I was a confederate soldier in my last life," announced one of the patients.

Crap.

But the other patients ignored the guy and he shut up. Kevin retreated to his office and buzzed Will's office.

It took a minute, but Will answered, sounding a little shaky. "I'm here."

"You okay, big guy?"

"I've been better."

"Sorry about the picture."

"Forget it."

"Daniel Hatch is sitting out there complaining to himself. Ready for him?"

"Ready as I'll ever be. Give me three minutes, then send him in."

28

Pete Banning cruised by Colonel Wallis Tilton's house, knowing that Mickey had installed a box earlier in the day. There was no way he would try to get himself invited into Tilton's house—the old shitbird would go on guard instantly. They had developed a mutual understanding back when they were both at Fort Charles: They hated each others' guts. Tilton was Army, but high on the muckety-muck scale, treated more like royalty than a mere colonel. They called him the Silver Eagle, like he was some sort of superhero or something.

Tilton was a hero with a white hat who was always sticking his nose into places it didn't belong. He didn't approve of Project Tingler or any other ops that dealt in mind control, and he must've been the beloved of somebody in D.C., because he was always there, a big thorn in the ass. Pete was pretty sure he didn't know much detail about any of the experiments, but he did know basics. Captain Nedders once told him that Tilton was ballast, likening him to a Republican congress keeping a Democratic president from getting too free with everybody's money. Whenever anything was entirely in the hands of one party, things went in one dumper or the other. You had to have some ballast. Pete didn't agree, but he respected Nedders's opinion.

That, and the almost sure fact that Tilton had friends in high places had kept Pete from engineering an accident for the old silver bird. In rank, Pete had only been a chief and Tilton a colonel, but there was way more to both of them, and they both knew it.

Pete considered another drive-by, but it was obvious somebody was home, so he cruised toward Felsher Hill instead. "I wonder what you're going to see, Silver Shitbird. Or what you'll hear, or taste, or smell."

Maybe he should have had Mickey install the bug, but Mickey was just a faithful old mutt who didn't know his ass from a hole in the ground. And Pete really wanted to see the Tilton's, too, no way could Mickey be trusted to put in a camera. No, if he wanted it done, he had to do it himself, when the Tiltons were away from home. But should he even try? That was the question. Tilton played the true-hearted innocent, but if he was that innocent, he wouldn't have lasted. Chances were good his place was fully protected with alarms and cameras. Maybe the old man even swept his place for bugs.

Never let your lust loose. That's how you'll fuck yourself up. He could practically hear Nedders's voice spouting the words. He'd said that a lot over the years. Lust was Pete's personal Achilles heel, and though he hated hearing it, he listened because he knew Nedders was right.

He reached the hill and parked then walked past lesser electronic receivers and unlocked the cage surrounding the Caledonia Cable dish. Within, he walked around it, touching it, admiring it, getting turned on as hell. He worked a little animal magic at the hidden keypad, set it for delay, then walked around the dish, sparkling white, huge, powerful, beautiful, again. Finally, he started to reach for his cell to call Jennifer Labouche for a little breast enlargement session, but realized that was just the sort of lust Nedders was talking about. He'd thoroughly disapprove of his calling his assistant away from the phones during office hours. It wasn't professional. *What the fuck.* He climbed the short ladder and stood on the smooth white dish, then unzipped and took care of his lust himself, white on white. Then, carefully, he used a white linen handkerchief to wipe up the evidence, which was, as always, enough to strain a scumbag. He folded the monogrammed kerchief and took it with him back to the truck, knowing how much he'd enjoy watching Jennifer massage the congealing contents into her breasts.

29

You realize Elfbones has never had sex with a woman who wasn't drunk or charging him for it.

You've checked the records on this item?

Yes, sir. At the age of thirteen, having shown an ability for gymnastics, he went through a phase of autofellatio.

Mickey, putting the finishing touches on the McCobbs' cable setup, cringed. Autofellatio was a fancy word, but he could figure it out; whoever was watching him knew that he used to like to rub off on the backseat of his parents' car. It horrified and humiliated him to know they knew about that. At least, when he was really limber and did the other *really* twisted thing a few times, he'd locked himself in his bedroom closet and done it in the dark. They wouldn't know about that. Nobody did.

Have we been keeping track of his movements this month?

Yes, sir. Every movement has been recorded.

Have you reviewed the tapes?

Yes, sir.

Anything more suspicious than usual?

No sir. Movements remain normal, but thought processes are becoming more and more suspect.

We may not be able to trust him much longer. It may be time to take action.

Shit. They knew he was thinking of talking to the shrink. *I'M NOT GOING TO TALK TO THE SHRINK!* He thought it long, loud, and hard.

"Are you all right?" Mrs. McCobb asked.

He spun and stared at her. "Yes."

"You were still as a statue." She gazed at his embroidered name. "Mickey, would you like to have a little drink with me?" She held out a greenish glass full of red stuff.

"I'm sorry, ma'am, but I can't drink on the job."

The elderly woman laughed. "Dear, it's just V-8 juice with a little cayenne to give it bite. There's no vodka in it. Go on, take it. It's good for you. It'll put a little color in your cheeks, and if you don't mind my saying so, I think that's just what you need." She sipped from an identical glass. "Mmmm."

"Well, okay. Thanks." He picked up the remote and followed her to the sofa. She sat down and patted the cushion next to her. "Have your V-8 and show me how to work this new remote."

Mickey obeyed and explained all the buttons. "It's really a lot like the old one, but you get lots more channels on your new cable box," he finished, and clicked through a few channels. "Here's The Chuckles Channel. My boss is really proud of getting this one. It's like Comedy Central but more family oriented."

Mrs. McCobb raised an eyebrow. "You mean this channel doesn't show anything like *South Park?* Nothing vulgar?"

Mickey smiled. "Exactly. Most of our more mature

customers are very happy with this channel. They have clean stand-up comedians, and run some old shows like *The Honeymooners* and *Red Skelton.*"

"That's a pity," Mrs. McCobb said, looked sour. "Dan and I love *South Park. Red Skelton* bored me when I was young, and still bores me. I know most old farts like shows like that, but we don't. And I don't know what anybody sees in *The Honeymooners.* Oh, they could get away with all that abuse Gleason's oafish character heaped on his wife back then, and think it was funny, I understand that, but why it's still revered in this day and age, I'll never know. Any man who treats his wife like that deserves to have his balls cut off and fed to him!" She winked and added, "With fava beans and a nice Chianti."

"Uh, well, you still get Comedy Central, ma'am."

She smiled, looking like a sweet little grandma again. "I should hope so. What else have you got there?"

"Well, you get more feeds of HBO—"

Our operative is examining him now. She'll report to us later.

"Are you sure you're all right, dear? Would you like another glass of juice?"

"Uh, no, ma'am. Thanks." The old lady was one of them. He couldn't let on he knew. By rote, he talked about the new channels and gave her the pamphlet, surreptitiously glancing around. At first sight, the interior of the house seemed as nice and normal as the outside, but when he looked at the paintings and knick-knacks, they were pretty suspicious, not what old people should have. Some of it was naked art. Not porn, but naked. There was a reclining naked lady that looked a little like the nude drawing of young Rose in *Titanic,* and a moderny sculpture of a man and woman holding each other. There was a framed drawing of a grinning lady skeleton wearing a flower-laden hat. It wasn't the kind of thing somebody's granny should have out when the grandkids came to visit.

"Do you like that, Mickey?"

"What?"

"You're looking at Florita. That's what I call her."

"It's, uh, different."

"It's a famous *El Dia de los Muertos* drawing. A copy of it, anyway. Dan and I found it in Santa Fe. Isn't she wonderful? So dead, but so full of life!"

The subject is becoming confused.

Yes sir, that's exactly as we expected. If he doesn't bolt, she'll take him to the bedroom to show him the erotic art. Then she'll let the dog out and we can watch his reaction.

Mickey stood instantly. "Mrs. McCobb, I'm late for my next appointment. The booklet I gave you will tell you anything else you need to know. Or you can call the office for help anytime."

"Thank you, dear. Come again."

He could feel her eyes on him all the way down the walk.

30

"You sure you don't want to come over for dinner tonight, Will?" Kevin locked the front doors of the office.

"No, thanks. I'm bushed. I'm just going to the drive-through at CharPalace and eat junk food in front of the TV and go to bed." Will took a deep breath of ocean air. It was past seven and a pleasant coolness infused the breeze. "It seems like it should be dark out by now."

"Give it another month." Kevin looked at him. "Come on, follow me back to our place. You can't live on burgers and fries and Lord knows what else you put in there. That stuff will kill you. We're having salad and grilled chicken."

"Thanks, but I'm in the mood for comfort food, not anything that's good for me." He smiled tiredly. "And you just want me to come over and see your ghost. You must be almost as tired as I am."

"Well, I'm ten years younger than you."

"Eight."

"Nine."

"Not ten."

"Will Banning, straight men aren't supposed to care about their age."

"Wait'll forty's looking at you. You'll care."

"Thirty's looking at me and I hate it. But at least Gabe is older than both of us!"

Will laughed. "At least we have something to be thankful for. Is he home already? Or did you come in together?"

"Together. Do you think I'd go back to the house by myself and risk seeing that *thing?*"

"I knew it. You want me there to tell you there isn't a ghost. Well, there isn't."

"You haven't talked to Gabe. Won't you believe it if you hear it from him?"

"Look, I believe *you.* I know you two experienced something. I just don't believe in ghosts."

"You will once you see it."

"Let's hope it's all gone. You want me to drive you across the street?"

Kevin rolled his eyes. *"Drive* me across the street? And you're porking out on greasy burgers? Will, honey, you've got to change your ways before you grow love handles or stroke out."

"I'll think about it. See you at eight."

Kevin groaned. "Another day like today coming up."

"We'll get through it."

Will climbed in his car and pulled out after Kevin crossed the street. He was ravenous—there'd been nothing around to snack on after he lost his lunch— so he headed straight for CharPalace. The thought of food was the only thing that kept him going.

31

Freud, Rorschach, and Jung danced impatiently around the bulging white CharPalace bag Will had placed on the coffee table while he changed clothes and grabbed three small paper plates and two bottles of icy dark beer from kitchen. When he reentered the living room, the trilling and chirpy question-like little meows began in earnest. Freud looked him in the eye and brushed his cheek against the rolled closed top of the sack. "No touching," Will said, giving the cat the evil eye. Freud knew the words and backed off an inch, talking his head off, not his natural rather demanding nasal meows, but mimicking the adorable trills and chirps of his brothers. Freud was the smartest of the bunch, an Einstein of a cat, and he knew what Will could and couldn't resist.

He grabbed the remote, flicked the system on and sat down on the sofa behind the bag. The cats gathered, sat at attention, six golden eyes staring, three tongues daintily licking cat lips, salivary glands activated by the scent of hamburger. Pavlov had dogs. Will had cats. "Okay, you guys, let's find something to watch."

Golden eyes pleaded, and it would have given Will perverse pleasure to cruise the stations while making them wait, but he was too hungry and immediately switched on the news. Then decided he didn't want to hear any news and put on a *Simpsons* rerun. *Much better. Hamburgers. Mmmm . . .*

He opened the bag, telling the cats to back off. Reluctantly, they did, eyeing the three plain kid's burgers Will unwrapped. Normally, the cats ate cat food, and merely hoped for a treat or two when he ate, but not when it was CharPalace. As he tore up little patties, one on each paper plate, he wondered if it was the smell of the burgers or the sight of the plates that clued them in. Probably the latter reinforced the former. *Doesn't matter.* He placed a little plate in front of each cat and they went to work, not waiting for him to unwrap his own double deluxe cheeseburger or dig out his fries. That was okay.

Opening a beer, he settled down and stuffed himself, shamelessly scooping catsup onto his fries, picking melted cheese off the paper wrapper, and drinking the second beer before he was through. The cats finished up and nosed Will's leavings. Freud ate half a French fry, and Jung chewed on the edge of one of the buns shucked from the baby burgers, then all three joined him on the couch and began the bathing frenzy that always preceded sleeping off their food. Will thought about getting up and tossing the trash, but only got as far as stuffing it into the bag and balling it up. He left the buns out for later tearing and tossing—when he went to CharPalace, even the birds got a meal.

He sat back and put his feet on the table, not bothering to surf for something else to watch. What a day. Daniel Hatch was worse; evidently, his penis was now singing songs. Its favorite was "It's a Small World After All," which was a menace to mental stability in the best of times. Daniel kept asking if Will could hear it. Fortunately, he couldn't, but he still had to make an effort to keep the tune from starting up in his own head.

Other longtime patients ranged from normal (whatever normal was for each individual) to severe worsening of symptoms and displays of utterly new ones. At lunch, when Will told the cop he'd heard only a couple ghost stories—meaning Lara Sweethome's and Kevin's—that had been true. By the end of the day, he'd heard two more. One of his paranoid schizophrenic patients, who had been in remission, spent half his session telling voices in his head to go away, go away. Another, a depressive, was now hearing voices for the first time. A histrionic who'd been in good shape spent her time babbling about dead bodies under the house, something about ancient Indian burial grounds, and a hellmouth in her garage. His diagnosis, which he didn't voice was: Too much *Buffy*. He suggested she lay off the horror novels and movies and try some lighter stuff.

The entire day had been like that, and from what Kevin had told him about calls for appointments, tomorrow would be no different.

Freud had stealth-invaded his lap and Will idly scratched behind his ears. The purring commenced and Will dozed off.

32

Lara Sweethome spent the afternoon and evening in a delightful Valium daze, using music to help control her mood. She chose beautiful movie scores, sweeping, swelling romantic music from *Doctor Zhivago, Gone With the Wind, Lawrence of Arabia, Titanic,* and others. CDs were one of the few special luxuries she indulged in, and her player held six hours' worth. In the evening, she watched a video, *City of Angels,* a romance with Meg Ryan and Nicolas Cage. Cage usually looked rodenty to her, but in *Angels,* he looked beatific. She loved to watch the angels standing on the beach at sunset, or on skyscrapers. It moved her and somehow made her feel safe. She hoped she had a guardian angel that would help keep her mother's spirit at bay.

Once or twice, she heard footsteps on the stairs, and once, the sound of the bedroom door closing, but the sounds were mild and muffled and she felt safe enough to go upstairs and sleep in her bedroom that night. *Bless you and your pills, Dr. Banning.*

33

"Age before beauty," was what Kevin told Gabe when they'd arrived home. Big bad Gabe took the hint and went in first, not showing any fear except for the frantic way he slapped on the foyer light.

The place was quiet, deserted, just like it had been that morning, but both of them started turning on lights all over the house. To hell with the electric bill. Without talking about it, they decided not to discuss yesterday's phantom visitor, and went about almost normally. Gabe was pooped, and usually he'd collapse on the couch and find some sports to watch on TV while Kevin made dinner, but tonight, he stayed in the kitchen and made salad. They ate at the tiny breakfast table there instead of in the dining room that opened into the dreaded living room.

After the dishes were washed and put away—Gabe always helped with that, but tonight he took his time and didn't bitch—Kevin reluctantly said, "Want to watch television?"

Gabe tried to look unconcerned about going into the living room. "You know, we've got that nice big tub with the jets in the bathroom. What do you say to a good soak and maybe a massage afterward? I'm stiff and sore."

"I'm just stiff," Kevin said. "I'll massage all of you if you'll massage just a little of me."

"Not so little." Gabe smiled and more relieved than aroused, they headed away from the living room. "We watch too much television anyway."

"Yeah."

Safely in the tub, Gabe finally broached the subject. "Did you tell Will?"

"Yeah. He says it's not a you-know-what."

"What is it, then?"

"He promised to come and tell us if we ever see it again. Eric came by with a load of info, but it's not important. I'll tell you tomorrow, on the way down to work."

"Good. Turn up the jets, will you?"

Kevin made the water bubble faster. Then, since they were facing each other across the water, they relaxed and gave each other foot massages. It was bliss.

34

Mickey Elfbones normally spent all his at-home time parked in front of the television, but tonight he left it dark in favor of surfing the Internet to try to find a way to keep people from reading his mind or planting things in it or whatever the hell they were doing.

Finally, he hit pay dirt. He found a site completely devoted to making hats out of aluminum foil. There were detailed directions, drawings, and exact measurements. If he didn't know from personal experience that the voices existed, he might have thought it was all a joke, but it wasn't. It was deadly serious. So, after printing out everything on the site, he gathered a roll of heavy-duty foil, a few pieces of cardboard, glue, and some thin-gauge copper wire and started cutting, folding, and shaping. Within half an hour, he was wearing his first hat.

By bedtime, he had three spares, each more handsome than the last. The design was deceptively simple.

It looked something like a folded wax paper boat a kid would make to float in puddles, but it was head-sized. The cardboard was a stabilizer, and also helped hold the intricate pattern of wires in place.

All evening, the voices remained silent. Just to be safe, Mickey wore his hat to bed.

35

Will woke up rumpled and sore-necked and covered with cats just after the local news began on Fox. That made it just after ten. The cats tried to keep him in place—they weren't ready to get up—but there were advantages to being the alpha male, as Maggie would say. Reproachful stares were given to him as he pushed them off, stretching and yawning.

He came out from behind the coffee table and stood, doing stretching exercises for a couple of minutes, moving his shoulders, arching his back, and rotating his neck around and around. The cats found the last move endlessly fascinating. He always wondered what they thought he was doing; for all the stretching felines indulged in, he'd never seen one flop its head around in a circular fashion. But then, he never did the ass-in-the-air stretch that they favored. "Different strokes, huh, guys?"

Rorschach, always the most forgiving, trilled at him. He gathered the trash and took it into the kitchen, cats on his heels just in case something good magically fell out of the refrigerator. They watched as he tossed the leavings in the garbage pail then placed the empty bottles in a recycle bin under the sink.

He could feel their eyes on him. He always could. He turned and stared back. "No way."

Immediately, the trills and chirps began. Freud rumbled a purr and nearly knocked him over with a sudden headbutt and rub against his legs. "It's not going to work."

More shameless noises, more purring. More petting. Adult cats who weren't affectionate with their owners rarely vocalized beyond an occasional meow, but the pampered ones often kept up the kitten language throughout their lives. He was forever the parent, and they didn't have to grow up. Instead they talked to him the same way they'd communicated with their mother, in kitten language—and kittens, no matter how overgrown, were hard to resist. Still, he did. "You had your dinner." *Damn it.*

They danced around his feet, all rubbing and chatting. Cats always walked on their toes, but when they heard the magic word—*dinner*—they seemed to tiptoe even higher, almost prancing. "That wasn't fair. You made me say the word."

Now he had to give them something more. He opened a can of overpriced turkey cat food with every amino acid and vitamin a cat needed, and put it all on one plate. They gathered around it and ignored him.

Still sleepy, he turned off the television and walked down the hall toward the bedroom, undressing on the way. He took a long shower and when he stepped out, found the boys arrayed around the bathroom, bathing themselves and waiting for him.

"You guys sure are clingy lately."

They didn't reply, but they padded after him to the bedroom, followed him onto the bed, and resumed grooming.

As soon as his head hit the pillow, Will wasn't sleepy anymore. He thought about reading, but it sounded like too much work, so he grabbed the remote and turned on the bedroom set. He added the other bed pillow to the one he was using already and propped himself up so he could see the screen better.

"Let's see what we've got here." He started surfing through the channels, pausing here and there to check things out. There were more Discovery Channels, which pleased him, a second humor channel, but it appeared to be family oriented, considering the lightweight clean-cut movie it was showing this late at night. He moved on, delighting in extra feeds of all the premiums, finally settling on the last hour of *Memento*. Within fifteen minutes, he dropped off, leaving the television to talk to itself.

36

Midnight. Caledonia slept. Far from the big city, the sky loomed dark and clear and full of twinkling stars. Orion, Leo, and the other summer constellations were brilliant in the moonless night. Jupiter glowed steadily and the Milky Way banded the sky. A plane, traveling from Los Angeles to San Francisco, moved silently over Caledonia. From 30,000 feet, the town looked like a small serene constellation itself, a strip of Main Street lamps sided by a few more glowing lights here and there among the hills.

Up on Felsher Hill, Pete Banning's time-delay low-frequency transmission activated, and would remain active for the next twelve hours.

Instead of inundating the area birds with an umbrella-shaped plume of micro-microwaves, this one was directed seaward and had been set at a slightly different frequency. It would be Pete's first experiment in directional programming, and the results would be easy to spot. It began almost immediately, affecting the inner compasses of several small seals and a school of fish.

Daniel Hatch slept fitfully in his narrow bed in his half of the narrow duplex owned by his mother. He had left the television on—it was blaring infomercials now—in an effort to drown out the voice of his genitalia. Dr. Banning had increased his new medication and given him something to help him relax and get to sleep, but he could still hear the voice, singing and taunting. It was beginning to sound like Mother, and when your dick sounded like your mother, you were getting into real trouble.

Restless, he turned on his side. Coming into partial wakefulness, he wondered again if his mother might be behind the whole thing, pulling a trick to somehow make it seem like Dick was talking. He had mentioned this to Dr. Banning, who appeared concerned. He probably thought Daniel was around the bend now, and he was probably right.

But Hatch still thought Mother might be the real culprit. After all, she had spent an inordinate amount of his childhood grilling him about his habits and warning him about the evils of masturbation. Ever since he'd moved out of her house and begun paying her rent for the separate unit, she'd harped about the evils of cheap women, lecturing him on how they carried venereal disease. She called it "the drip."

She'd done it again tonight when he'd gone over for dinner. "Daniel, how was work? Did you make time to study the new tax laws today? If you want to get ahead, even when you're just a C.P.A., you have to study, you know. And what about that woman, Mr.

Queefer's secretary? Did she speak to you again? Did she ask you out again? Only cheap sluts ask men out.'' Daniel told her he'd studied and that Miss Moyle, a.k.a. the cheap slut, was a nice young woman who went to church (he didn't mention she was Jewish), and wore no makeup or low-cut blouses. She actually wore a little lipstick, and beneath her modest clothes, her figure was an hourglass that his penis frequently made lustful remarks about.

He had made up the story about her asking him out just to rile Mother one evening not long ago. He said they'd had coffee and conversation, then let her blat on about how expensive Starbucks was—he never said Starbucks, Mother assumed—instead of admitting they'd merely taken a coffee break at work, and that it was the only good thing that had happened that day.

When she finally shut up about Starbucks, she asked if he'd seen that worthless Dr. Banning again. He said yes, she asked why, and he wanted to scream, "Because of you!" but he merely said he helped him manage stress. She wanted to know, for the millionth time, what could possibly stress out a C.P.A., and when he didn't tell her, she told him Banning was a charlatan, all headshrinkers were charlatans.

All he could think about now was that his dick was nagging almost as much as Mother, but that she was his real problem. Dr. Banning knew she was a problem, but he was too embarrassed to tell him just how bad she'd become. That he put up with her was even more embarrassing than his talking dick.

As he drifted back to sleep, Dick slyly suggested Daniel get rid of her, right away. And that, he agreed, was a damn fine idea.

He clicked the remote and the television stopped babbling about carrot curlers and onion choppers.

His penis crooned a lullaby, just like Father used to do.

Lara Sweethome woke from sleep, thinking she heard the door to her bedroom open and close. She drew the sheet up around her neck and nervously listened for footsteps. Had her mother's ghost been in the room with her, or had it just entered?

Neither. You were dreaming. It was just a dream.

The room, the house, was filled with silence. It really had been a dream. Turning on her reading lamp, she glanced at the alarm clock. It was long past midnight and her Valium had worn off. The bottle was on the bedstand, but she'd forgotten to bring in a glass of water, so she got up, took two pills from the bottle and walked to the door.

Slowly, silently, she opened it and peered out into the hall. The nightlight cast its dim yellow glow down the hall. *What else did I expect to see? I've never seen anything.* She walked to the bathroom, making herself move at a reasonable pace instead of running. In the bathroom, she took her pills and splashed her face with cool water. She listened, heard nothing, then left the bathroom and returned to her bed.

The sheets were cool and welcoming and she gratefully slipped between them, turned to lie on her side, then pulled them up to her chin. She turned the lamp off and snuggled, shutting her eyes against the darkness, sighing with pleasure as she relaxed.

After a few minutes, she imagined she felt something gently pressing against her back as she fell back into sleep. It didn't alarm her; she was too close to dreaming to worry. It felt like a lover was spooning with her, a cool lover under the sheets, his body pressed to hers. She could feel the legs, knees bent to knees, hips to hips. He didn't put his arms around her and in the almost-dream, she asked him to. He didn't, but pressed closer and she became aware of breasts, soft and low, pressing like lumps against her back. Still, she went with the dream.

Hold me, darling. It was her old boyfriend, Brad, from high school. He was a football player, handsome and blond. Once, he had held her in this very bed and made quiet love to her while her mother slept down the hall. *Hold me.*

In her mind, she heard an answering voice, old and female, her mother's voice. *I have no arms, you know that dear. Why don't you hold me instead?*

There was no doubt that Doris Tilton, wife of the log-sawing, Colonel Wallis Tilton, Retired, loved her husband of forty years, but the incredibly loud snores, whistles, and lungy sighs, interspersed with Popeye-esque *cha-cha-cha-cha-chas,* and punctuated by loud gulps, were sometimes too much to take. Wallis had always been a noisy sleeper, but age had turned him into the maestro of all snorers. Usually, she wore earplugs, but tonight they'd made her feel claustrophobic, so here she was, in the family room in Wallis's recliner with a crocheted afghan spread over her legs.

Even space and walls between them didn't mum the snores enough for her to ignore them completely—sometimes, tonight for instance, they had the power to drive her crazy—so she reluctantly ended up turning the television back on to drown them out. She had a love-hate relationship with the boob tube. Since retirement, if Wallis wasn't at the golf course or puttering around the garden, he was parked in front of the television watching The History Channel. And now, thanks to the damned cable upgrade, there was a second channel full of old battles for him to watch.

True to form, he'd spent the afternoon flipping back and forth between the two of them.

Maybe I should go in for a checkup. Not since the darkest days of menopause had she been as irritable as she had been today. Wallis was a good man, excellent husband, top-flight father. He had never been a carouser, or forgotten their anniversary or anyone's birthday; even when he was away on active duty, a present and phone call or a letter would appear. And, even now, he remained a tender lover, and even managed to listen to her once in a while. So he snored and watched a lot of television. Why was she so annoyed about that?

Just thinking about it increased her annoyance, and that wasn't like her. Maybe she was simply tired. Maybe the movie drowning out the snores had too many shrill voices in it. She changed stations, finally landing on *Singing in the Rain*, which had just begun. Doris smiled and closed her eyes. *Music to tame the savage beast.*

Maggie Maewood awoke with a start and a grunt as her wire-haired terrier landed squarely on her chest and stomach. "What the hell?" she muttered as the canine tried to lick her face. "Stop it, Anteater! Stop it now."

She sat up in bed, turned on the light. The terrier, eyes glinting, stood on her thighs and watched her intently. He was a cute little creature, white with a brown saddle and, despite his name, a tin can–shaped muzzle.

"Why did you do that?" Her two cats, previously asleep at the foot of the bed, padded up and stared at the dog. "They want to know, too. Why did you do that?"

Anteater threw his head back and howled. The cats hissed. Outside, other dogs took up the call. A flock of birds shrieked overhead. Silence returned. The cats were instantly bored.

"What's wrong?" she asked the dog. "Do you know what time it is?"

Anteater tried to lick her face. His stubby tail wagged madly and he raced from the room, then turned and stared at her from the doorway, still wagging.

"You want to show me something?"

A small bark. *Yes.*

"Okay, but this had better be good."

She dragged herself out of bed, felt around for her slippers, gave up, and followed the dog into the hall and down the stairs, turning on lights as they went. She didn't expect a prowler—the wagging tail reassured her, but she didn't really like being in the dark. She never had.

Downstairs, Anteater led her to the kitchen and barked once, happily, and she heard his claws scrabble across the linoleum.

"I'm not feeding you again," she muttered, and turned on the light. "Crap. I should've known."

An ant trail a quarter inch wide led from the window over the sink, across the counter and down the cabinet. Little black piss ants marched in a purposeful manner across the floor to the dog food bowl, where one nugget of kibble was being excavated and removed, an antload at a time. She looked at the dog, who was joyously lapping up the ant trail. "I should have known. You probably left that kibble there on purpose, you little monster."

One happy bark, lots of wagging. The dog, doing what he was named for, made the trail disappear from the floor until only about six inches was left.

Anteater stopped there and waited. He was a smart dog and didn't want the ants to move the trail.

Maggie wasn't crazy about his predilection for ants, but it didn't really hurt anything. "You have fun, but don't you dare try licking me again!"

Anteater's entire body wagged.

Maggie smiled, and returned to bed.

37

Whispering. Soft, low. Will strained to understand the words, but it was impossible. The soft whisper continued until he became aware of growling next to his ear. Claws woke him as they pressed into his shoulder.

"Freud?" he murmured. "What's wrong?" He tried to push the paw away, but Freud pressed harder and the growl deepened. The other cats tensed on either side of his body.

"Will."

One of the other cats growled along with Freud. Will was awake. But he distinctly heard his name whispered. *Bullshit.*

He became aware that some movie was playing softly on the television. That had to be what he heard; he hated falling asleep with the TV or talk radio on because whatever was said usually incorporated itself into his dreams, turning them into nightmares. *That's what happened.*

Without turning on the light, he found the remote and clicked off the system. "That better, guys?" he muttered.

Freud's claws started to retract. The cat remained tense though, and the other two were shoving themselves tightly against him, definitely not relaxed.

Could somebody be in the house? The sudden thought flipped his stomach. Why else would the cats be acting like this?

"Will, listen . . ." The whisper was distinct for an instant, then it turned into a mutter, just like in the dream. "Will, listen, listen . . ."

The cats, as if of one mind, leapt off the bed. One of them shrieked like a Halloween cat. They thundered down the hall and were gone.

Will sat up in the darkness, began to reach for the light. *What the hell is going on?*

"Will, I'm here, listen . . ."

The whisper was real. It came from within the room.

From beneath the bed.

"Who's there?" he choked. "Who's there?" His hand hovered an inch from the light. *This is hypnogogia. It has to be. It makes no sense. I'm dreaming. The cats are asleep. I'm asleep. This is fascinating. I'm not really sitting up, I just think I am. No wonder people are frightened by this exper—*

From beneath the bed came the whisper. "Will, it's Michael."

"What the hell?" Will slapped on the light and looked around the room. No cats. He jumped out of bed, not knowing if he was asleep or awake, so he pinched himself. It hurt.

"Will, it's me, Michael. Listen . . ."

He dropped to his knees and peered under the bed, saw nothing but darkness and the end of the baseball bat. But from out of the darkness, he heard Michael's voice again, only inches away. He thought he felt his brother's breath against his cheek.

Will scuttled backwards six feet then got up and stared at the bed. "Michael?" His voice cracked. "Michael."

"Will."

That's all he heard, just the one word, just his name, and then it stopped.

He had to be dreaming. He walked to the bathroom and drank a glass of water, splashed his face, and dried it, then walked out to the living room, looking for his cats. They weren't there. He looked in the office next and found them, all three, huddled together under his desk.

"What's wrong, guys?"

They stared at him, eyes wide, and flinched back when he tried to touch them. "Okay. This is some weird dream." So saying, he stood and walked back to the bedroom, climbed into bed and turned off the light. At least he had new understanding of what a hypnogogic hallucination was like. It was horrifying in its realism.

He dreamed he fell asleep, but when the alarm rang in the morning and he found himself alone, not a cat in sight, he shivered. Had it really been a dream?

38

"No, no, no. Go away." Will buried his head in his pillow, trying to drown out the ringing phone. It stopped at four rings then rang four more times. On round three, he looked at the bedside clock. It wasn't quite six A.M. and whoever was calling knew he liked to let the machine pick up. At this hour, it wouldn't be a junk call. At this hour, it was probably important. He answered on the third ring of round four. "Yeah."

"Did I wake you, you grump?"

Maggie's voice. He felt slightly less grumpy. "You woke me."

"It's beautiful out."

He opened his eyes, saw daylight seeping into the room. "Oh? I wouldn't know."

"Want to go for a power walk before work? I'll meet you on the Crescent."

"Oh, Lord. Maggie, I'm still asleep."

"Come on. It'll do you good. I'll bring donuts and a thermos of coffee to offset the healthy part."

"What kind of donuts?"

"Glazed."

"You know me."

"You're easy to please." She laughed.

He smiled and propped himself up in bed. "If you bring donuts, I'll meet you for a walk on the beach. Not a power walk. It's too early to even use that word."

"Okay. Twenty minutes?"

"Yeah, the picnic area parking lot. That's weird," he added, to himself. "Hang on."

"What's wrong?"

He looked around the room. Not a cat to be seen. They should have started climbing on him the moment he answered the phone. "The cats aren't here."

"What do you mean?" She echoed the alarm that he heard in his own voice.

"They spooked sometime last night. Ran out of the room. I thought I dreamed it." *Oh, Lord. Michael. It was a dream. I probably yelled in my sleep and scared the cats.*

"Find them now. Take me with you."

He didn't argue, but got out of bed. "Hang on," he told Maggie, then took the handset away from his face. "Guys? Kitty, kitty, kitties!" he called as he walked into the hall. "Freud! Rorschach! Jung!"

He put the phone to his head. "Nothing so far."

"Do you know how funny it sounds when you call dead psychiatrists like that?"

"You named your dog Anteater, so I don't want to hear about names." He headed straight to his office. Three sets of eyes blinked at him. Morning sunlight haloed their ginger fur.

"This is so strange," he told Maggie as he began

petting the trio. "I dreamed they left the bedroom and hid under my desk. They're on top of it now."

"Are they all right?"

"Slow to warm up," he said as Freud finally gave a tentative purr, Jung made a silent meow, and Rorschach gave a full-tilt trill. "But okay. You guys want breakfast?" Trilling and chirping, the Orange Boys stood and stretched. Breakfast was another special word. "They're hungry."

"They're fine, then. Whatever you thought you dreamed must have been real, though. What was it?"

"I—I can't remember. Some sort of nightmare. I think I yelled and frightened them."

"Bullshit. You can't lie your way out of a paper bag, Will. What did you dream?"

"I don't remember," he repeated.

Maggie, being Maggie, took the hint. "So, six-thirty at the Crescent?"

"Six forty-five. I want to spend a little time with these guys and look around. Make sure nobody tried to break in or anything."

"Okay. See you."

39

"Breakfast is ready. Hurry up and get out here." Kevin plated the cheese and avocado omelets then added a dollop of sour cream and sprinkled each with chopped chives. Hot coffee and sausage scented the air.

"I'm not even dressed yet. Hell, I haven't even showered." Gabe entered the kitchen wearing nothing but a short white terry wrap around his waist. "It smells like heaven in here."

Kevin grinned. "Mr. Smileypants is almost peeking out."

"Nah. You used him up last night, but if you keep staring at him like that, he might raise the drapery."

"Then I won't stare. These eggs can't be allowed to get cold. I worked too hard on them." He placed two sizzling brown sausage links on each plate, then added slices of fresh, fragrant cantaloupe.

"Mmm. Those plates look like photos in a cookbook."

"Thanks." Kevin picked up the plates and took them to the kitchen table.

Gabe filled mugs with coffee and brought them to the table. He slid into the chair opposite Kevin then tilted his head toward the door to the dining and living rooms. "All quiet on the western front?"

"I'd like to tell you I was a brave boy and looked, but you'll notice that the door is closed."

"This food's fantastic," Gabe said. "And I think you were incredibly brave to come into the kitchen by yourself. Man, just looking at that door makes me nervous."

"Shush. Eat. If you say one more word, I'm taking my eggs to eat in the bedroom."

"Sorry."

They made small talk, and quickly forgot their fears until they heard the gunshot. The thud. "What the hell was that?" Gabe whispered. "It was in there. Wasn't it?" He nodded toward the living room.

"They're back."

"I'm going to look."

"Gabe, no—"

"It's *our* house. We can't just stop using half of it." He stood up and went to the door.

Kevin followed, tapped Gabe on the back. "No, let's go through the main hall. That way we can run like hell if we need to."

"Yeah, okay."

Another gunshot echoed hollowly. "Fucking Cockburns," Kevin whispered, trying for levity, failing miserably.

"Come on." Gabe walked into the wide hall that led to the rest of the house. He turned toward the living room.

"Gabe, don't you want to put on some pants first?"

"Why? What are the ghosts gonna do, Kev?"

"I don't know, but I wouldn't take chances with the jewels, you know?"

Gabe turned and looked at him, putting his hands on his shoulders. "It'll be okay. Wait here. I'm just going to take a quick peek around the corner."

"I can't talk you out of it?"

"No."

"Then I'm going with you."

Petrified, scared shitless, and a little excited, Kevin followed, glad he couldn't see through Gabe's broad back.

"Holy shit." Gabe's back stiffened.

"What? What do you see?"

"I see both of them. Carrie's floating around in there near the windows," Gabe said in a low, barely controlled voice, "and old Jason, he's just lying there on the floor over toward the dining room. There's not much head left on that boy. Okay, he's fading out. Want to look?"

"What about Carrie?"

"She's starting to float up into the ceiling like before."

"Tell me when her head's gone."

"Okay." A few seconds passed. "Head's gone."

Kevin steeled himself and peered around Gabe just in time to see the dim image of Jason fade out completely. Carrie's legs and feet disappeared in seconds.

"Man," Gabe whispered. "We've gotta get Will over here. I want to see his face so bad, I'm not even scared."

"Okay, but I think we'd better find an exorcist or something because I'm not going back in that living room. Except to see what Will does."

"We could go in now," Gabe said.

"What if they come back?"

"Don't they have to recharge their batteries or something first?"

"Okay." Kevin rushed in, just like he would jump into a swimming pool in April when he knew the water was too cold, all at once. He took a bow then ran back to the hall.

"Let's get dressed."

They returned to the master bedroom. "Do you think there are any dead babies in the little bedrooms?" Kevin asked.

"No. And don't you think it either."

40

"It was a weird night last night," Maggie said as she and Will sat down at a picnic bench hidden among Monterey pines and shrubs near the Crescent's shore. She had brought two donuts apiece, and the thermos held four cups of coffee, so they'd decided to have a little before their walk. She poured coffee that smelled delicious, and passed him a cup.

"Thanks." He pulled a couple donuts and napkins from the white paper sack, handed one over, then blew on the steaming coffee. "How was last night weird for you?"

"Well, maybe it wasn't exactly weird, but it felt that way for a few minutes. Anteater woke me up, all excited. He just wanted to show me an ant invasion in the kitchen."

"That doesn't sound weird. Ants are caviar to that little guy."

"No accounting for taste." Maggie made a face. "But I think I'd rather eat ants than caviar, too."

"That's what I like about you, Mags. You're a cheap date." Will grinned, then asked, "So nothing was really weird then?" He sounded hopeful.

She hesitated. She hadn't a doubt that he remembered the "dream" that scared his cats, but how could she get him to spill it? Drama, she decided. "You didn't hear the dogs howling last night?"

"No."

"I don't know if they were howling before Anteater woke me up. He jumped on me, a regular body slam, about popped my heart out of my throat. I opened my eyes and he stared at me, then he let out a howl that sounded like it belonged on the English moors."

"Okay. That's pretty weird. What about the cats? Did they run off?"

"No. They looked daggers at Anteater, then freaked a little when all the other dogs started howling nearby, but they were pretty cool. Never left the bed. A flock of birds screeched bloody murder at the height of things and for about five minutes I felt like I was in a horror movie. Then everything went back to normal and Anteater led me to the ants."

"I'm sure the birds were a coincidence."

"Probably."

"The howling probably was, too," Will added, as his brain did its compulsive search for logic. Not that she disapproved, except when he poked holes in scary movies while they were watching them. "He came and woke you up to show you the ants, then heard something out of our hearing range, and howled. Maybe something on a military or police chopper, like Gabe was saying the other night."

"Could be." She studied him, trying to will him to talk. She could see trouble in his eyes. Maybe it was nothing more than what he claimed—that he'd yelled and scared the cats. That would trouble him.

She had given them to him after his last divorce, just after he moved into his ranch house, begging him to kitten-sit for a few days while she found them homes, knowing he'd never let them go, even before he knew. He had never had animals as a child—there was one dog, early on, but something had happened to it and she was almost certain that Pete was what happened. And then there was college, no time for pets, and then he married one harridan after another. No animals allowed. He'd spent his life hanging around her parents' house and then her house, petting animals that didn't belong to him. It was touching, how he would relax and almost purr himself when he had a cat in his lap. After he was married, he continued to retreat to her house or accompany her to the little shelter she oversaw, or even go to her clinic on rounds. Observing the pleasure he took in cradling an ill animal, or playing with a well one, especially if it was feline, she sometimes felt such a rush of conflicting feelings that she could barely stand it. Sometimes seeing the stress go out of him, witnessing the constant watchful stiffness leave his body, made her want to slap him and scream at him to give himself a life, to stop punishing himself for heaven-knew-what by marrying women who were never content, who nit-picked and insulted him, who wouldn't even let him have a damned cat.

She kept her mouth shut and kept shooting down her own incipient relationships. Though she knew the two of them couldn't be romantically involved—they talked about it and decided (mostly Will decided in his logical fashion) that they were too sibling-like for that—she never cared about another human enough to get very involved with him. *Maybe I never gave anyone a chance.* A few times she had wondered if she was even attracted to men, but all she had to do was look to her dreams to know the answer to that.

And Will was right. Up until they were eight or nine, they'd taken baths together. They'd had belching contests and tried lighting farts, and when they reached adolescence, they discussed their crushes and tried to figure out what the "bases" were. Later, they went on to discuss everything from masturbation to differences in female and male orgasms, to the humiliation of intimate medical exams. He said they were like brother and sister, but she felt more like she had a gay best friend who wasn't gay. Sometimes she'd end up crying herself to sleep because she knew he loved women, but didn't seem to think she fit the description. She got over it, watching his torturous marriages. Will had his own problems, but didn't everybody? Especially psychologists?

But with the end of the last marriage, he had at least finally learned what was bad for him. She hoped he'd remember the lessons.

So, while giving him the cats was something she had done out of friendship, she also knew that in giving him companions, he would be less likely to fall for another ice bitch out of loneliness. And there was more—she knew that once Will finally had his own feline companion, he would never give it up for some frostbitten woman who would demand such a thing. It would, he told her once, be the same as giving up part of yourself and how anyone could ask someone they claimed to love to do that was beyond him. She agreed and said no one who loved you could do that. He likened it to asking a parent to give away a child.

Knowing that about him made her feel—well, she didn't know what it made her feel, but giving him those three kittens was the best thing she had ever done. It even brought them closer together, which she'd never considered possible. A new dimension of friendship grew as she helped him raise those little orange furballs. Maggie knew herself well. She had never desired human children, but this feeling she shared with Will was her version of the drive. Gabe and Kevin had joked about them parenting the cats ever since they laid eyes on the kittens, but Maggie had never thought twice about it before, at least not consciously. Now she realized that it was no joke. They really had become parents.

Too bad we can't risk trying more.

"You look like you're going to either cry or throw up, Mags."

"What?"

"What's on your mind?"

"Nothing. Let's walk." She stood and put the cap on the thermos. "You want to leave this stuff in the car or take it with us?"

"Car. Otherwise I'll eat the donut before we get back then I'll try to con you out of yours. You should've bought a half dozen."

"You don't exercise enough for two, let alone three," she said as they put everything in her car. "You have to think of your health for the sake of your furry children." Instantly, she regretted the words, positive he'd know what she'd been thinking moments before.

But he just chuckled. "Okay. You're right. Tell you what. For the sake of my children, we can walk fast."

"Power walk?"

"Almost. Not quite that serious."

"It's a deal. Let's go." She headed for the shore. "I wonder where all the birds are this morning? I don't think I've heard one since we arrived."

Will stopped walking and looked up at the sky. She saw him shiver.

"What's wrong?"

"Nothing. I guess a crow just walked over my grave. Let's go."

41

Up with the sparrows. That's what Pete Banning was, day in and day out, and there were plenty of sparrows in the trees outside his home on Hadrian's Way, the most exclusive street in the Heights, which was what locals called the neighborhood, never mind that it was perched on the eastern inner lip of town. Back when the name was first used, nothing was built on the taller outer lips.

Pete sat locked in his home office surfing through feeds from various cameras he had installed on his goodwill calls to customers' houses the previous day. Simultaneously, he checked the audio bugs. Not too much happening this early, but the scenery was pretty good in Heather Boyd's bedroom.

He bugged her bedroom because he'd had a feeling about young Heather of the full breasts and pouting lips, and he hadn't been wrong. She slept naked. As he watched, she approached the camera and turned on the television. "Back up," he muttered. "I can't see your boobs."

She remained close, doing something. Putting in a cassette, he realized, hearing the characteristic sounds, clear even on the tiny feed. She backed up and stood at attention at the foot of her bed, ten feet from the camera. *Just right.* It was an exercise tape. *It's going to be a good day.*

If he hadn't gotten involved with Miss Boyd's bouncy workout—she really should have worn a sports bra for those jumping jacks, but what the hell, he didn't have to live with those monsters when they started sagging off her chest wall—he might have seen some interesting things in a couple of the other homes. The Flaggs' two kids had turned on the television as accompaniment to their slopping bowls of Sugar Smacks and, unbeknownst to them, a phantom had appeared, a typical "lady in white." It glided back and forth behind the couch, as if disapproving of their breakfast. And in Becky Crachett's apartment, where the television wasn't on, Becky was screaming as she watched what appeared to be blood seeping out of a vaguely man-shaped area of the tan carpet that had been brand-new when she moved in. What neither she nor Pete knew was that the previous tenant had slit his own throat and bled to death on that very spot. The carpet had been installed because the stain couldn't be scrubbed completely from the once beautiful hardwood floor beneath it.

42

Will and Maggie had picked their way over the rocky part of the Crescent and moved onto the narrow hard-packed beach. Behind them, the park and picnic area gave way to quickly rising bluffs, which would, within a few hundred feet, become a warren of shallow, ocean-eroded caverns, where they'd played for hours as kids. Sometimes they even got stuck sitting on a ledge inside one of the bigger ones caves, trapped by the tide. Will smiled, thinking about those accidentally-on-purpose adventures.

"Look up there!" Maggie pointed to her left, at a V of pelicans in the sky over the sea. "They came from the south." The flock fluttered in apparent confusion. As Will watched, it turned and headed rapidly back the way it had come.

"Was that strange? I'm pretty sure it was, but you're the expert."

"Seems a little strange. Something must have alarmed them to turn them so abruptly."

"Maybe they heard hawks?"

"I suppose, but pelicans are too big to be likely prey." She shook her head and smiled. "It's probably nothing. I don't know what's the matter with me. I'm seeing signs and portents everywhere I look."

"Me, too," Will said, spying something not quite right among the rocks at the base of the cliffs.

"You? You don't believe in signs and portents."

"Portents, no. Signs, yes. Come on." He bee-lined for the rocks, Maggie on his heels.

"Dear God," she said, looking at the seal. It was alive, but ill or stunned.

Will passed the seal and rounded an outcropping of cliff that hid a cove and a full half moon of sandy beach. "There are more back here. All alive, I think."

"Don't touch them," she called.

"Don't worry." Half a dozen more seals lay on the half moon of sand, silent, some moving a little, some watching him. The nearest snarled. Will stepped back and turned, startled when the tide sloshed over his heels. As he looked at the water, a school of small silvery fish began leaping above the water like popcorn. "Maggie! Get over here!"

She was there before the words were out, but looking at the seals, not the fish. Will had seen flying fish before, and at first, these seemed to belong in that category. Then they came closer, shimmering in the tide, propelling themselves out of the water with great force.

Shiny silver fish exploded from the foam, pelting Will's legs nearly to his knees. "Maggie!"

"Just a minute."

"Now! Look!"

She arrived as the tide withdrew, leaving flopping little fish at the water line. They just stood there watching the frenzy continue in the water. Within thirty seconds, a low wash of wave brought more fish, pelting both of them.

"Well?"

Maggie looked at him, deadpan. "They aren't supposed to do that."

"Are the seals and the fish connected?"

"Yeah, probably. And the birds, I hope."

"You *hope*?"

"I do. If so, it's some sort of magnetics problem that's affecting them, like we talked about before—something messing up the magnetite in their brains."

"And that's *good*?"

"Sure. It happens sometimes, and it goes away."

"An anomaly of nature?"

"Let's hope so." She toed fish back into the tide. Will followed suit. "They're not jumping as much now."

"They're probably tired." Maggie glanced back at the seals. "They seem disoriented. So do the fish. And we know birds are having problems. Cross your fingers that they're connected."

"If they're not?"

"It could mean that there's something bad in the ocean. A bacterial infection, a virus, something fungal or toxic. I'll take a little disorientation from a geologic or space glitch any day over disease or poisoning."

"Makes sense. What do you mean by space glitch?"

"I don't really know. A peculiar pull of the moon? Sunspots? A ripple effect of electric storms? You probably know more than I do."

"If I do, you don't know much. When you say 'geologic' are you telling me earthquakes are better than illness?"

"Probably. As long as they're far out at sea. Listen, Will, I'm staying here. Will you call my office when you get back and tell Charlie what's up? He'll know who to call. Tell him I'm waiting for help."

"Maggie, maybe you shouldn't stay."

"Nobody's going to attack me. I want to stay and observe."

"I understand. I wasn't thinking about human attackers, though. I was thinking about . . . your being affected by whatever this is. Assuming the birds are part of it."

"I'll move off if I feel peculiar, I promise. But I won't have to. We don't have enough magnetite to be affected much, if at all."

"Okay." Will started to turn to go, then paused. "Mags? What about the cats? And the dogs, for that matter?"

"They'd be far more affected than us. You know, that all fits. Your frightened kitties. The howling dogs. After you call Charlie, check with the US Geologic Survey people and NASA, will you? See if anything's going on."

"I'll put Kevin on it. He hasn't checked the military goings-on yet either."

"He'll love it."

"Ordinarily he would. We've got way too many customers right now."

Her expression changed for a brief instant, uncertainty flashing over her face. A little fear.

Will's stomach dropped.

"You know," she said slowly. "Maybe it *is* affecting people. Or something like it, something related."

"It's got to be coincidence," Will said automatically.

"Why?"

"It's just got to be." He felt helpless.

"No, Will. It doesn't have to be coincidence." She took his hand and squeezed it. "Animals are nervous, people are nervous. There's an explanation for both and it's probably related. Doesn't that sound logical to you?''

"Did I mention to you that Kevin and Gabe believe their house is haunted?'' Dread mounded in Will's gut, even as he tried to deny it. "That doesn't sound very logical to me." He searched her eyes. "They're not the only ones to tell me that.''

She took his other hand and held them both between hers. "Will? Something's wrong, isn't it?''

It's Michael. Listen to me . . . He forced the dream away. "Nothing's wrong.''

"Don't lie. Will, I know you. If something supernatural ever came your way, you wouldn't be able to handle it. Tell the truth. Have *you* seen a ghost?''

"No," he said honestly. "I haven't seen a ghost.''

She studied him. "Okay. I believe you. But I still think you're not telling me everything.''

He made himself smile. "If I told you everything, I wouldn't be interesting." He bent and kissed her cheek. "I'll see you later, and I'll call Charlie right away.''

Before she could reply, he trotted down the beach toward his car. He had wanted to tell her about his too-real dream, his hypnogogic hallucination, but he just couldn't do it. It was ludicrous and although he knew she would never make fun of him or tell anyone else about it, he wouldn't be able to stop putting himself down for repeating such a thing, for giving it any kind of credence.

He got in the car and pulled out of the lot, heading home to change clothes, even though he'd brought a change with him with the intention of going straight to the office. *Why am I doing this?* That was easy. He wanted to double-check on the cats, to see if they were still upset.

And if they were, he wanted to look under the bed. Idiotic fear and silly hope stirred in him and he almost let himself wonder if Michael really had somehow visited him. Almost.

It was stupid and superstitious behavior and he mentally berated himself for it until he turned into his driveway. There, he turned off the engine and sat a moment. Sternly, he reminded himself that he easily accepted, without any derisive reactions, such feelings in other people, in patients and in friends, and that he should do the same for himself.

Damn, but it was a hard thing to do.

43

"Lara Sweethome's on line one," Kevin told Will between morning patients. He stood in the open door of the office Will was using. "She says it's important."

"What does she want? More Valium?" That's what most people wanted this morning.

"Don't be jaded. She just wants to ask you something."

"What?"

"You had sugar for breakfast, didn't you? I can tell."

"What does she want to ask?"

"I don't know. I assumed that was between you and her. It didn't seem polite to ask."

Will shut his eyes briefly. "I'm sorry, Kevin. You're absolutely right about everything. But do you think you could see if she's willing to tell you what she wants? The catering truck just pulled up and if I hurry, I can get an egg burrito to take the edge off the donuts."

"I'll go get it, you take her call, okay? That makes more sense."

"I know it does, but I don't want to hear about ghosts this early in the morning. She's told you about it, so . . . Please take the call? Tell her I'm very busy with patients and will get back to her A.S.A.P."

"Okay. You know, you look exhausted. Didn't you sleep well?"

"I slept fine." Will stood and took off for the back entrance. Kevin went back to his own desk and pressed line one. "Lara?"

"Yes?" She sounded nervous.

"Doctor's with a patient right now, but if you don't mind asking me the question, I'll relay it to him and he'll get back to you sometime today."

"I want to know if he'll come over and see my ghost. He said he would if it didn't go away."

"But I think he meant for you to wait a little longer than this, Lara."

She launched into a frightening tale of her dead mother spooning with her in bed.

"Lara, that's horrible! I'll tell him. I have to warn you dear, that Doctor has a hard time believing in ghosts. I mean, I work for him, and he doesn't believe in mine."

She said she knew and didn't care. He wouldn't have a hard time believing after he experienced hers. Kevin told her that was a ditto, and promised to talk to the doctor, then ended the connection because a small man in a tin foil hat was standing in front of him. He looked familiar.

"May I help you?"

"Yeah." The guy's watery eyes darted back and forth. "I called about the last minute appointment. I'm Mickey Elfbones, and you said I could come in at ten forty-five?"

"Oh, certainly. Doctor will be with you in about twenty minutes. Meanwhile, you're a first-time visitor, right?"

More eye-darting. "Yes."

Kevin handed over a clipboard with a new patient form on it. "While you're waiting, fill this out and bring it back to me, please."

Elfbones looked suspicious. "You give info out? Like to my boss?"

"Everything is confidential."

"I'm paying for this. I don't want it to go through my employer's insurance. That's real important."

"Not a problem."

The man returned to the waiting room. Kevin eyed him. He'd heard of tin foil hats. People who heard voices wore them, so went the story, but this was the first time he'd ever seen one. Kevin watched the man painstakingly fill out the form and it hit him: This was the guy who'd upgraded their cable a week or so ago. No wonder he didn't want his employer to know he was here. Will was going to love this guy.

44

Wallis Tilton was a little concerned about his wife. She'd glared daggers at him all morning and nearly taken his head off when he'd asked if they had any half and half for the coffee. She was behaving totally out of character.

He'd spent the morning weeding, pausing to ask her what he'd done to upset her so much when she hurried out of the house, dressed in neatly tailored navy pants and a white short-sleeved silk blouse. She told him he'd done nothing, she was simply on edge and needed to do the marketing. He watched her go, curious. She hated grocery shopping, always had, and since he'd retired, usually left it to him, since he honestly enjoyed it. She must have wanted to get away awfully bad to take back the job.

There was no ocean breeze at the moment and that let the sun get inland-mean, so he put away his hand tools and went indoors. After washing up, he poured himself a glass of lemonade and settled down in front of the television.

He watched for an hour and as he did, a feeling of unease grew, perhaps pertaining to Doris's behavior, but perhaps not. It was an almost imperceptible feeling, but he'd felt it before, more than once. He couldn't remember where or why or what, maybe never even knew what set off this peculiar uneasiness. But he did know that once he set his mind to it, he'd remember if there was anything specific to recall, and if there was not, his subconscious would work on it and provide him a clue. Maybe two.

45

Officer Eric Hoyle, of Caledonia's finest, returned the icy, brittle stare of icy, brittle Mia Hunt Hartz and briefly wished Kevin were here to say something inappropriate and scathing because if anyone could shatter the façade of this alleged woman, he could.

Putting on his best nice-cop face, he said once again, "I'm sorry, ma'am, but there is no evidence of anyone vandalizing your garden."

"That doesn't matter. Those children were here, running through the flower beds, jumping over the pond, scaring my koi."

"Ma'am, that pond is too wide to jump over unless you've got pole-vaulters invading your privacy."

"I'm going to report you for verbal brutality, young man. Who's your superior?"

Not you. He couldn't believe he was hearing this. If tongues were reclassified, he could arrest this bitch for assault with a deadly weapon. "Sergeant Jeff Thursday, ma'am. You can reach him at the station."

Jeff wasn't really his watch commander this week, but he was often as not, and he'd get a bigger kick out of this than Sergeant Kate Whitt. She had a sense of humor, but she was younger and more gung-ho than Jeff. She'd chuckle to herself and give him a lecture they both knew he didn't need.

"I'll phone him as soon as you leave."

He knew now she wouldn't. She was the type who'd make him stand there while she called if she had any real intention of doing so. "That's fine. Ma'am, if these children show up again, try to detain them until we get here. There's simply no evidence, otherwise, and since you have no idea who they are, I can't do anything."

"They're here."

"What?"

"Are you deaf?" She spat the words and pointed behind him. "Up there in the willow at the back of the yard. Look, damn it!"

He turned and followed her finger to the stately old tree near the back fence. "I see the tree. I don't see or hear any children."

"Cretin!" She glared at him. "They're climbing down. Use your eyes."

There was nothing there.

"You get over here, you little monstrosities!" she shrieked.

Eric watched her eyes jet back and forth as if she were watching something. "Ma'am, there's nothing there. Perhaps you should consider talking to a doctor."

"How dare you!" Her eyes blazed and her hand came up to slap him. He caught it easily and immediately wished he hadn't. He could have taken her in if she'd made contact.

"Hitting an officer of the law will get you thrown in jail."

"You insulted me."

"No, ma'am. I merely made a suggestion based on what I see. I see a woman who imagines she sees children in her yard. Good day."

He started to walk away, then whirled, hearing a distant shriek of childish laughter.

"You heard them. I know you did. Admit it."

The brittle ice was cracking. "I heard children, but very far away."

"You still hear them," she stated.

"No. Not here."

She didn't reply, but turned and let herself into her house. He went out the back gate. As he closed it, he heard one more burst of faraway laugher. It raised his hackles, but only until he was in his unit, where he found out there'd been a break-in at the Marital Aid Museum and Emporium. He snapped up the call.

46

"Please sit down, Mickey." Will had to exert all his willpower not to react to the sight of his brother's lackey entering his office.

The little man in the silver hat nodded nervously and chose to perch himself on the edge of the chair opposite Will. "Th-thanks."

"Would you like some coffee? Water?"

"Water, please."

"Just a second." Will left Mickey in the office and walked up to reception, filled a cup with bottled water. "Kevin," he said softly.

His assistant left his chair facing the waiting room and walked back to Will. "Yes?"

"Did you mean to send me Mr. Elfbones?"

"Yes. He was a phone-in. Oh. I didn't give you the sheet, did I?"

"No."

Kevin snatched it up and handed it over. Will scanned it quickly, glad to see Mickey didn't want

Pete to know he was here. "Thanks. If you're going to read these before giving them to me, try not to let me know about it. I wouldn't want to have to tell you not to do it."

"Sorry, boss." Kevin's apology trailed behind Will, who hurried back to Mickey. Time was far too limited to waste today.

"Here you go." Will handed Mickey the cup.

The man sipped gratefully, hands trembling. "Th-thanks."

"You're welcome." The stutter was new, Will thought. The result of terror. "Nothing leaves this room," he told his patient.

"I wasn't going to take anything."

"No, I'm sorry, Mickey, that's not what I meant. I take it from your chart that you don't want your boss—my brother—to have any idea that you've been here."

"No. He'd kill me." His eyes flickered under the hat. "I mean, he wouldn't like it. I mean—"

"I understand completely. You don't need to worry. Everything you say is confidential."

"If someone, like a patient, tells him they saw me here, can I tell him I was fixing the cable?"

"Of course."

Mickey exhaled noisily and relaxed slightly. "Great. Will, I need help."

"You didn't put the problem on your patient sheet," Will said, smoothly ignoring the foil hat. "What can I help you with?" He sat back, waiting to hear about the voices.

Mickey surprised him. "I'm afraid of animals. I always have been. I mean, I'm not crazy, there's a reason. Do you remember my father's dogs?"

"Yes, vaguely. Big brutes."

Mickey smiled for an instant. "Your assistant said

we only get twenty minutes, so long story short, those dogs are why I'm afraid of them."

"I understand. Go on."

"I was scared shitless of your cat."

"Fear of cats isn't uncommon."

"I don't know why cats and just about everything else scares me. It seems like it should just be dogs."

"Not necessarily. We can talk about that more in the future if you want to. Tell me why you've decided to come here about this now." Will was dying to know how the foil hat fit in, but he knew better than to ask.

"It's worse than usual. I'm afraid of getting fired if Pete finds out. I couldn't even get past this little tail-wagging wiener dog yesterday. It was littler than your cat and it was friendly, I could see that, but I stood out there like an idiot and yelled until the lady came out and got her dog."

They talked for a few minutes, then Will called in prescriptions for Paxil and Xanax; the Xanax would help him until the SSRI kicked in. Normally, he would have had Kevin do it, but Mickey was still very antsy. Will thought it best to do it himself instead of writing anything down. Mickey appeared pleased.

"Tell me about the hat," Will said afterward.

"Oh, it's just a thing my friend's kid made for me."

"Does it do anything?"

"Uh, what do you mean?"

"Nothing. It just looks like it's supposed to do something. It's sort of futuristic."

"Yeah, I guess maybe it's a radio hat or a robot hat or something."

Will stood up. He knew that while the animal phobia was very real, it was the hat that made him come. Mickey would talk about it when he was ready. From the looks of him, Will hoped it wouldn't be long. If he was hearing voices, he needed a different type of drug, but it couldn't be prescribed until he confirmed Will's suspicions. *Poor guy.* "Mickey, make an appointment for two weeks from now when you leave. By then, we should be seeing some results from the Paxil."

He walked Mickey out to reception, where Kevin remembered to hand him the chart for the next patient. Will took it and a fresh cup of coffee back to his office. He read over his notes, but his mind was on Pete. He couldn't help wondering just how many of Mickey's problems had to do with a lifetime spent kissing a bully's ass. *You're not being objective.* But he was. He realized that Pete probably wasn't Mickey's big problem—even Pete couldn't cause what might turn out to be paranoid schizophrenia. But it was fun to blame him, for a moment, at least.

47

Maggie returned to the half moon cove at the Crescent at lunch time, to see how the rescue effort was going. It had taken two hours this morning for a rescue group from San Luis Obispo to arrive, but when they finally did, Maggie was relieved to see Lily Johnson heading the group. Lily wasn't somebody Maggie wanted to socialize with—the very thought made her cringe—but the humorless marine biologist, a professor at Cal Poly SLO, was a tough act to follow. All Lily cared about was contained in the ocean, and she and her grad students had set to work immediately.

Now Maggie, carrying a bottle of water and a bag containing an egg salad sandwich, rounded the outcropping and entered the little cove, hoping to find Lily and talk to her. Instead, she found Pete Banning. *So much for my appetite.*

"Well, hello there, Maggie," he said heartily. He bared big white teeth in a bone-crunching grin. "You just missed your friends. They said you found the seals."

"You saw the seals?"

"Briefly. They took them away. Said they were going to watch them a few days to make sure they weren't sick, then release them. The woman in charge said she'd be in touch."

"She gave *you* a message for me?" Maggie's annoyance grew.

He laughed. "No, I guess not. She just mentioned it. I said I knew you."

"Why would I even be mentioned in the first place?"

"I asked how they found the seals." He looked at the bag. "Having lunch alone today?"

She ignored the question and started to turn. "See you later."

"Wait."

"Why?"

"We haven't talked in ages. Years. How are you?"

"We have nothing to talk about." Anger welled inside her. This man—this creature—had tried to rape her when she was twelve years old. He was sixteen. She was home alone at the time, expecting Will. They were planning on going to the school to shoot some hoops.

When she heard the familiar knock on the door, she'd called, "It's open," without leaving the kitchen where she was finishing washing breakfast dishes. When he'd come up behind her and put his hands on her hips, she felt a little thrill because she still thought he was Will.

But the bastard had copied his knock. Without saying anything, he nuzzled her neck and the feel of his breath, the touch of his lips, aroused her pubescent hormones. She felt delightfully naughty, wonderfully pleased. "Will, what are you doing?"

He kept doing it. His hands moved up to her waist. She let them. She'd been having fantasies about this. But when the hands suddenly shot up and clamped onto her barely-grown-yet breasts, squeezing hard, she panicked. "What are you doing?"

He kept doing it. "Will! Stop it!"

He didn't. She stood there a couple more seconds. Everything she knew about Will conflicted with what was happening. He started sucking on her neck, trying to make a hickey.

"Stop it *now* or I'll hurt you."

He continued.

She hurt him, stomping hard on his foot, then turning and kneed him in the groin. She hadn't meant to do the latter—she still thought he was Will—but her body had a mind of its own. Only when he staggered back, clutching his crotch, did she see who it was. "Get out of here," she growled. "Don't you ever talk to me again! I'll tell!"

"You loved it."

She glared at him. "I *hate* you!" She stepped toward him, seeing red.

Still holding his crotch, he stepped back. "You thought I was my little brother. You want to fuck him, don't you!"

"I'll tell!"

"Tell that you want to fuck him? You'd be better off fucking me. At least I've got something to fuck you with."

That was when she grabbed a butcher knife out of the dish drainer. "Get out."

"You wouldn't cut me."

She moved forward, with every intention of cutting him. "Want to try me?"

He grinned, a lot like he had just now, but back then he didn't know you had to squinch up your eyes to make people think you were really smiling. He had dead eyes. She moved toward him. He turned and ran.

That felt good. Will showed up a few minutes later and she didn't tell him. How could she say she let Pete touch her because she thought he was Will? It was too embarrassing. It still embarrassed her. She should have told him back then. Risked the friend-ship. Maybe Will would have gotten the hint.

"You still holding a grudge, Mags?" Pete walked closer. "We were kids."

She stood her ground. "I was a child and you knew exactly what you were doing."

"Those were sweet little boobies. Ah, come on, don't look like that. I don't mean anything by it. I was inexperienced, too. I hadn't felt many. You were so pretty, I just couldn't control myself."

"Bullshit. The way I looked is no excuse. You would have raped me if you could have."

He held his hands out palms up in a gesture of helplessness. "Boys that age—"

"Don't even say it or I'll crush them for you again."

"I'm sorry. I'm very sorry." He smiled again, like that was all it took. "You and Will ever get it on? You sure wanted him back then. I've seen you two around town together, even when he was married. Always a bridesmaid?"

"You cuckolded him."

"And you weren't fucking him on the side? Come on. Everybody does it."

"No. Some people don't. Believe it or not." She wanted to say more, but he would have enjoyed it too much if she'd gone on the defensive.

"Look, I'm really sorry. For then and for just now. You know what it is?"

"No, I don't."

"My baby brother doesn't like me and I guess I still wonder if you didn't turn him."

"I never told him what you did."

"Why not? Embarrassed that you liked it?" He smiled but forgot to crinkle his eyes. "I'm sorry. I just need to know why he didn't like me. Why he still doesn't."

"Oh, please. Maybe crap like that works on your girlfriends, but don't try it on me. You know why he doesn't like you."

She turned and walked away, almost certain she could hear him laughing behind the roar of the waves.

48

The page fragment shows faint text at the top that is illegible.

"Ghostbusters," Will said, hearing the movie's theme playing as he entered Gabe and Kevin's house. "I thought I was here for dinner."

"Of course you are," said Gabe, holding the door. "Kevin thought you'd enjoy the irony when he saw that the movie was playing on cable. "Hi Maggie."

"Hi, Gabe." Maggie trotted up the walk and entered, paused, and said, "I ain't afraid of no ghosts," along with the music.

Will chastely kissed her cheek hello. "I think we're here to be slimed."

"We wouldn't do that to you guys," Gabe said. "But Kevin did make green Jell-O. Come on in. Kevin's in the kitchen."

All three went directly into the kitchen. Even though Kevin had only been home an hour, he was deep into dinner. "It smells wonderful," Maggie said. "What are you making?"

"It's no biggie," Kevin said, stirring a big pot on the stove. "Just spaghetti and salad, but thank you."

"You made sauce in an hour?" Will stepped up to a covered pot and lifted the lid half an inch. "Ah. I'm officially starving."

"After working like a slave all day for you, you think I made this from scratch? That takes hours, Will. It's bottled sauce, but it was eight bucks a bottle, so it should be almost as good as mine."

"What? You're kidding. Eight dollars? What was it, a gallon bottle?"

"Please. Eight dollars a quart. It's new. Imported from *Patsy's* in New York."

"Patsy's?" Maggie said. "That sounds Irish."

Kevin turned toward them, exposing his Kiss the Cook apron and rolling his eyes. "That would be Paddy's."

"Gotcha."

Gabe tried to poke Maggie in the ribs, but she backed up into Will, who poked her for Gabe.

"You people," Kevin said imperiously. "Out of my kitchen with your childish behavior. I've made a pitcher of raspberry margaritas to keep you amused. Gabe, take them into the haunted room and get them a little sloshed. Pour one for me before you go."

Gabe grabbed the pitcher, filled a glass for Kevin, then led Will and Maggie, who carried three more wide-mouthed stems, back out through the hall and into the living room, which looked utterly normal.

"Why did we go the long way?" Maggie asked.

"So you noticed the pocket door into the dining room was closed?" Gabe asked as he filled glasses.

"Yeah."

"Kevin didn't want to take a chance on seeing any ghosts while he's cooking. Can't say that I blame him. Sit."

He took a chair, leaving Will and Maggie together on the couch. "You're serious?" Will asked. "About why the door is closed?"

"Yep. You want me to turn that off?" He nodded at the TV, where the ghostly librarian was wreaking havoc.

"I don't care," Will said.

"Just turn the sound down a little," Maggie said. "I love this stupid movie. And this margarita."

"It packs a wallop," Gabe told her. "Go easy. He's got a couple different tequilas in there."

"So," Will began, half-smiling. "We get tipsy and the ghost will appear?"

"If *they* appear, they will whether you're tipsy or not."

"They?"

"We saw Jason Cockburn this morning."

"Who?"

"Carrie Cockburn's husband. Our ghosts."

"We haven't had a chance to talk," Will said. "It's not just Kevin? You see this stuff too?"

"Yeah. Plain as day."

"I didn't figure you for believing in ghosts, Gabe."

"Will, I don't know that I do. But I sure as hell saw something. Twice. Kev and I were together both times." He rumbled a short laugh. "Of course, I don't think either one of us has been in here alone since the first time."

"All clear?" Kevin called from the kitchen.

"All clear," Gabe confirmed.

The pocket door opened and Kevin appeared, carrying plates. "Excuse me." Gabe got up to help.

Will looked at Maggie. "What happened with the seals?"

"I talked to Lily, the marine biologist who headed

the rescue team. She says the animals perked right up once they were in the observation area."

"Where's that?"

"A private aquarium and research center down the coast. She thinks they'll release them within seventy-two hours. I talked to her about the birds and fish. She doesn't know what would cause a disruption, but she thinks, at this point, that's probably what happened."

"A disruption—"

"In the animals' senses, especially directional. If we have subs nearby, they're likely culprits."

"Even for the birds?"

"Helicopters with disruptive equipment, maybe. Did Kevin find out anything about that or the geological anomalies?"

"Yes. No quakes out to sea or elsewhere that should have any impact. Nothing in the air either, at least anything natural. We don't know about the military. The more he dug, the more confusing it became. He tried phoning the nearest base and asking about helicopters and so forth, but they denied doing anything that could affect animals."

"Of course they did. They're not going to admit to messing with the wildlife any more than they're going to admit to the existence of U.F.O.s."

"Maggie. U.F.O.s?" Will shook his head. "Not you too?"

"Unidentified flying objects, Will," she said sternly. "Not flying saucers. Just things without a known explanation."

"I think the military is responsible for most U.F.O.s," Will said. "That's why they deny knowledge."

"Or to save face," Maggie argued. "Keep your mind open, Will."

"I saw a U.F.O.," Kevin said from the dining room. "Come on you two. Dinner's ready."

The table was beautifully set, with small summer gardenias and tea lights floating in a low, cobalt glass bowl as a centerpiece. Everyone sat down.

"White or red?" Gabe asked, getting ready to open the wine.

"I shouldn't."

"Me, either," Maggie agreed. "Not on top of the margarita."

"Live a little. Italian food demands wine."

"One glass," Will and Maggie said simultaneously. Kevin and Gabe exchanged glances.

"What?" asked Maggie.

"Nothing," Kevin said. "But I saw a U.F.O. once. It floated overhead like a big Mexican luminaria. Then it just sailed away."

"Hot-air balloon." Will and Maggie said it together, then looked at each other and grinned.

"Why aren't you two sleeping together?" Kevin asked after *tsking* at them. "You do everything else together."

"Mind your own business, Kev," Gabe said, not bothering to hide his amusement.

"Oh, but look at them, Gabe. They need to get laid."

"We're not that kind of friends," Will said.

"That's right," Maggie echoed. "We're like brother and sister."

"Not any brother and sister I ever saw," Kevin goaded. "At least not any normal ones."

"So where are your ghosts?" Will said abruptly. "Shouldn't they be interrupting dinner about now?" He glanced at Maggie and smiled. "That's when unwanted guests always show up."

"I thought you didn't believe us, Will."

"I believe you saw something," he said, not for the first time.

"Don't let him get under your skin," Gabe told Will. "He's messing with you. What he wants—as I do—is for you to see it and tell us what it really is. We'd be grateful for a rational explanation."

"Speaking of not having a rational explanation, let me tell you about what happened on the beach today," Maggie said. Between bites, she launched into the story of the half moon beach.

49

"Eat your peas, Daniel." Lobelia Hatch stared hard at her son, who sat across the kitchen table.

"Mother, I don't like canned peas. I never have, and you know that."

"They're good for you. Eat them."

Shove the can down her throat.

Since walking next door for dinner, Daniel's penis had been getting more and more irritated at Lobelia, urging him to "take care of her." He wasn't positive what that might mean, but had a suspicion that it meant the worst. *Be quiet,* he thought at his dick. "Mother, I'm thirty-four years old. Please don't order me to eat something I detest. Why didn't you make frozen peas instead? I like those."

"I slave over a hot dinner for you, and this is how you repay me, Daniel?"

Fuck her right up the old poop shoot. That'll shut her up. "Be quiet."

"What?" roared Lobelia.

"I wasn't talking to you, Mother."

"Well, I don't see anyone else here, do you?"

"No, Mother. I was talking to myself."

"Oh. Then why did you tell yourself to be quiet? Were you thinking something rude?"

"No." He hesitated. "Yes, Mother, I was."

"What? What were you thinking?"

That you're going to fuck her up the ass.

"No," murmured Daniel.

"No, what?"

Shut up, he thought at his dick. "No, Mother."

"No, Mother, what?" She was getting loud again.

"I don't remember what we were talking about," he lied. "How was your day?"

She looked a little taken aback, then sighed. "How was my day, you ask? Do you really want to know?"

"Yes, Mother." Boy, she was bitchy today. She was never a gem to deal with, but the last week or two, she had been much worse. "How was your day?"

"You don't really want to know."

"Of course I do."

"It was horrible. Mrs. Lavia next door screamed all morning."

"Why?"

"You think I know why? I could care less."

She can't even speak properly, his penis whined. *Get rid of her!*

"It's not like Mrs. Lavia screams on a regular basis, Mother. Maybe I should go knock on her door and make sure she's all right."

Mother sniffed. "I hope she's dead, frankly. Don't go over there. Let nature take its course."

"Mother, what if she's hurt? What if someone broke in and hurt her? What if she's dying?"

"Let the postman find her when she starts stinking."

"That's not nice, Mother." Daniel put down his napkin and rose from the table.

Atta boy, Daniel.

"Daniel!" Lobelia spat out the word. "You sit down, right this minute."

"No."

He pushed his chair in and went to the front door, ignoring his mother's threats. He felt six feet tall instead of a mere five foot six as he left the house and walked next door to the little stucco house belonging to Minnie Lavia. The porch light was off. He knocked, but there was no reply.

Steeling himself, he walked to the back door and knocked some more. Still no answer, but he could see a light on deep inside, and the car was in the driveway. He opened the gate to the backyard and went to a window where a light glowed. There were miniblinds covering the window, but they weren't shut tight. He put his face to the screen and peered in.

Mrs. Lavia sat in a rocking chair by her bed. Next to her was a perch for her parrot, Thoreau. Thoreau wasn't on the perch though, he was on Mrs. Lavia's shoulder, his body angled so that he could reach her face. Daniel knew she liked to feed him peanuts from her mouth. She'd hold them between her teeth and he'd snatch them. It looked like that was what they were doing. Tentatively, Daniel rapped on the window. "Mrs. Lavia?"

Thoreau turned to look at him, a big shiny eyeball hanging from his mouth. Daniel fainted.

50

"William," said Gabe. "William is your real first name?"

"Nope." Will sipped his wine.

"Wilson," tried Kevin. "Wilmer."

"No and no."

"Willem?" Kevin persisted.

"No."

"It must be something awful. Is it awful?"

"I don't think so. Do you think so, Mags?"

"No, I think it's a fine name."

"You know, Maggie?" Kevin asked. "What is it?"

"I'm sworn to secrecy."

"Then it's awful," Gabe decided. "If he swore your silence, then, I'm guessing it's Wilbur."

Maggie giggled.

"Willllburrrr," Kevin intoned in Mr. Ed's voice. "What're you doin' back there, Willllburrrr?"

"It's not Wilbur."

"Wilberforce." Gabe again.

"I love that," Maggie said. "Don't you, Will?"

"It's a name that forces a person to smile, though he doesn't know why. But no, it's not my name."

Kevin scrinched up his face, making a rat face. "Willard. That's it. No wonder you won't tell. Named for a rat."

"Sorry."

"Wilhelm," Gabe said. "That's my final guess."

"That's it," Maggie said solemnly.

"I'm afraid so," Will agreed.

"Oh. My. God." Kevin's eyes widened. "They named you Wilhelm? What's your middle name?"

"Wilhelm."

"You're real name is Wilhelm Wilhelm Banning?" Kevin asked excitedly. He'd gone a little heavy on the wine.

"Actually, I was adopted. My real last name is also Wilhelm. I'm Wilhelm Wilhelm Wilhelm. So where are the ghosts? I have to go home soon."

"Forget the ghosts. Are you *really* named Wilhelm Wilhelm Wilhelm? Really? That's so cool!"

"Kevin, he's messing with your mind," said Gabe.

"He wouldn't do that. He's a psychologist."

"Which means messing with your mind is my life-work." Will pushed back from the table. "None of my names are Wilhelm, Kev."

"Not even one?"

"Nope."

"Why won't you tell us your name? You told Maggie." Kevin poured himself the last of the red wine.

"You're whining," Gabe said. "If he doesn't want to tell us, it's his prerogative."

"Why not? Gabriel Hannibal Rawlins? Doesn't it bother you that you're entirely outed, and we don't know Will's whole first name, let alone his middle one?"

"Will's out. He's openly heterosexual." Gabe grinned.

"That's not what I meant and you know it." He looked at Will and Maggie. "What if I tell you my whole name?"

"Go ahead," Will said.

"Not so fast." Kevin finished the wine. "Any chardonnay left?"

"You don't need more wine," Gabe said. "You'll have a hangover in the morning."

Kevin sniffed. "You're right. I hate headaches. Maggie, what's your whole name? I'll say mine if you say yours."

"I thought it was *my* name you were after," Will said, smiling. He had a slight buzz going himself.

"If we tell, then you have to, too." He giggled in a way that made Will wonder if he'd get to work on time in the morning.

"And, if you jump off a cliff, I will, too?"

"Oh, your mother said that, too?" He giggled again.

"Kevin, everybody's mother said that," Gabe told him.

"Okay, well, my full name is Kevin Damien Bass."

"I knew you were in league with the devil." Maggie laughed.

"What's your name, Maggie?" Kevin, though a little cross-eyed now, gazed intently at her.

"Shall I tell him, Will?"

"Sure. Why not?"

"Margaret—and don't you ever call me that or you'll rue the day you were born, Kevin—Margaret Louise Maewood."

"I like that. It's so old-fashioned and sweet. Can I call you Maggie Lou?" Kevin dimpled up.

"No."

"Okay." He turned his attention to Will. "Spill it, Wilbur."

"I'll give you a clue. My mother loved the movie *High Noon*. I'm named after Gary Cooper's character."

"Will, darling, I'm gay. I don't watch westerns."

"I do," Gabe said. "Cooper was the sheriff who saved the town." He looked at Kevin. "You've never seen it? Really?"

"I like *Wild Wild West* reruns. Well, I like Jim West's pants. And vests." He giggled some more.

"Kevin, if you want to drink as much as I do, you need to gain fifty pounds," Gabe said before returning his attention to Will. "Cooper's character was, uh, Miller?"

"No, that was the chief bad guy. Frank Miller."

"Will Kane." Gabe grinned triumphantly.

"Give that man a cigar." Will grinned back.

"Well, so, what was Will Kane's full name?" Kevin asked. "William, Wilbur, Wil—"

"No! Don't do it again!" Will laughed. "The character's name was 'Will.' My name, therefore, is Will."

"Just Will?"

"Yes. You look disappointed."

"It's like you got cheated out of some syllables. I feel sorry for you. You're a name amputee."

Will cracked up. "It's okay, Kevin. I've learned to live with it. I even like it."

"Really?" Kevin sounded amazed, but his eyes twinkled with merriment.

"Yes. I—What's wrong?"

Kevin's animated face had gone slack and now his color drained away. He swallowed and nodded toward the living room.

Will looked. They all did. Floating slightly above the floor, the specter of Carrie Cockburn held a gun.

The yellow dress was coated down the middle with scarlet gore, and her head, what there was of it, was just as Kevin had described.

Will's stomach tumbled, but he forced himself to stand up and approach the figure. His head swam as he circled the specter, thinking it was probably a hologram. What else could it be? Someone was playing a trick on Gabe and Kevin. A horrible trick. He forced himself to look directly at the head with its hanging jaw and skull shards and blood and brains.

A similar vision reeled through his mind. A memory. His ears started ringing, louder and louder. *Michael! I killed you.* Then black mist swirled into his vision and the world went away.

51

The detached physician part of Gabe Rawlins sat
on his shoulder and told him how interesting it was
to watch people react to something frightening and
incomprehensible. Will had obviously been shocked,
but he practically ran to the apparition, intent on
finding an explanation. Will lived for explanations.
If there was none, he wouldn't rest until he came up
with one that at least satisfied him. Kevin, on the
other hand, stayed glued to his chair, his drunkenness
a thing of the past. He was afraid. Gabe was, too,
and although he'd stood up and gone protectively
to stand by Kevin, his hand hugging his partner's
trembling shoulder, he wasn't about to go any closer
to that *thing* hanging in mid-air. The floating aspect
frightened him far more than the blood and gore.

Maggie had stood up and walked to the wide arch
that demarcated the boundary between the dining
and living rooms. She was fascinated, the calmest of
all of them. She cocked her head and stared and

probably would have joined Will, but the male apparition appeared then, right at her feet. She'd looked down at the mutilated remnants of face, registering only fleeting shock before the captivated look returned. He thought she would arch her eyebrow like Mr. Spock and say, "Fascinating," but at that instant, Will had yelled *Michael!* and fainted dead away. He hoped that was all it was.

"Get a glass of water," Gabe told Kevin.

The ghost still hung in the air, but Maggie paid it no mind. She ran for Will, throwing herself down, covering his body with her own. The little doctor on Gabe's shoulder pointed out that her reptilian brain, the most primitive part of her, made her do that. After a second, maybe less, he saw her rational mind point out that there was no danger from the apparition. She sat up and bent her face down over Will's, checking his breathing, talking to him. For the first time, she looked frightened.

"Water, Kevin. Now!" Gabe pulled his chair back, jolting Kevin back to earth. "Bring water. Bring my bag."

Gabe was beside Maggie in an instant. He took over. Everything pointed to a faint, not a heart attack, and when Kevin appeared with his bag, he checked more carefully, then snapped open an old-fashioned ammonium carbonate cap and wafted it under Will's nose.

After a couple seconds, Will reacted strongly, turning his head away, eyes fluttering, then squinting. Gabe took away the salts. Will tried to sit up, but Gabe put his fingertips against his chest and Maggie positioned herself so that his head ended up in her lap. "Not yet, cowboy," Gabe told him. "Give your circulation a chance to put more blood back in your brain."

"I fainted?"

"Any chest pain? Arm pain? Any pain at all?"

"No. But I fainted, didn't I?"

"Yes. Ever do that before?"

Will looked stricken. "Yeah, a long time ago."

"What caused it? A shock or heat or something else?"

Will closed his eyes. Maggie put a cool hand on his forehead. "What caused it was seeing through my brother's guts when he was shot. Before he fell, I saw daylight through him."

"That explains why you yelled his name," Maggie said gently.

"I did?" Will was fully alert now. "What else did I say?"

"Nothing. Just 'Michael.' Why? What do you think you said?"

Will didn't answer for a long moment. Finally, he said, "I don't even remember saying my brother's name. Kevin, that water looks good."

"Oh, yeah. Here." Shakily, he passed it to Gabe. Maggie helped Will sit up and Gabe held the glass to his lips, but after an instant, Will took it, no less shaky than Kevin, and drank deeply.

Gabe looked at his partner, who hovered a couple feet back. The apparition still hung over them—the willpower Kevin had to have to stand so close was inspiring. Gabe smiled and winked, then said, "How about making up the guest room, Kev? Will can stay here tonight."

"No. I have to go home. I'm fine."

"No, you're staying. Doctor's orders."

"Christ, Gabe, I fainted, what's the big deal? Look, Maggie can drive me home; Kevin, you drive my car into work in the morning. Will that satisfy you?"

Gabe hesitated. It was probably fine, but he really

didn't want him to leave. "No, if anything else happens to you, I should be around."

Will started looking pissed off. He got to his feet, barely touching Maggie's proffered arm. "I have to go home."

"Gabe," Kevin said from the doorway. "He has to feed his cats."

"Maggie can do that."

"I can't leave them alone. Something scared them last night."

"What?"

"How the hell should I know? If you had pets, you might know what I mean. Ask Maggie."

"Animals were not normal last night," she said. "Gabe, come here a minute." She walked into the kitchen. He followed.

She shut the pocket door and spoke softly but firmly. "You're not doing him any good. You're embarrassing him. Do you think he wants to tell you how much he loves those cats? It will humiliate him, but he'll do it if you force him."

"Why?"

"They're his children, and you know it. You joke about it."

"I know. I understand, but Maggie, they're just animals. It's not like they're human."

"How can you be so stupid? They're no different from human children to him. He'd run into a burning building to save them. In case you haven't noticed, they're his main reason for living."

"I noticed. He needs a mate. He needs you, and *you* know that."

"I don't know what else he needs, but he needs to be there for his cats. He needs to protect them. Even if I was his mate, he'd care just as much about them as he does now."

"Come on. How can you think that?"

Her eyes practically burned him. "Because I feel the same way about my pets."

"Then why are you willing to leave them alone and stay with him?"

"You're being a bitch, Gabe, but listen up. My animals were excited. His were terrified. Big difference. I'm taking Will home. I'll stay with him until he's ready to go to bed. Or all night if you think I should."

"Yeah. Okay. Use your own judgment." Gabe took her hand and squeezed it. "I'm sorry, Mags. I deal solely in people. I need to let what you just said sink in. I'm sorry for acting like a shit."

"Apology accepted." She squeezed back. "Thanks, Gabe."

52

"It's going better than I expected," Pete Banning told Nedders. He was standing by his silver SUV on Felsher Hill. Not another living soul was around. *Or dead for that matter,* he thought, as he smirked into the cell phone. "I've been watching the customers, Neddy, just the few I've bugged already, and you know what?"

"What?"

"A whole lot of people think they've got ghosts."

"Ghosts?" Nedders snickered. "What about voices? Anybody talking to themselves?"

"Yeah, we got a little of that. Mickey Elfbones is hearing them, for one. He spent last night making tin foil hats. He's sure I don't know."

"Tell me about the ghosts."

"Well, there's this one woman who I visited today, her mother died a year ago. And now she's back, tromping around the house. Even got in her bed last night, she said. Told me she's going to put salt across her bedroom door tonight. It's ghost repellent."

"Really? Is that some old wives' tale or something?"

"How the shit should I know? Old wives, New Age, whatever. I tested the directional wave from the dish last night. Sent it over the ocean as we planned. Worked like a fucking charm. Bunch of seals got all fucked up. Seal-huggers came and rescued them."

"Nice. What else?"

Pete gave him a few more details, keeping the best for last. "There's one more thing. We're way ahead of schedule."

"How's that?"

"People are hearing things even when their sets aren't on."

"Already? It can't be."

"It sure as hell is."

"In the lab tests it rarely happened, and only after long exposure. Have you double-checked all the wave levels?"

"Everything's right as rain, Neddy. Right as fucking rain."

"I was just thinking about those ghost hallucinations. I'd like to know if you see any evidence of people living in the same residence sharing hallucinations. If you find a shared one, I want to know if one was affected first or if they were both affected and one switched to the other's delusion. Suggestibility. And watch for people who have standing haunt stories about their homes. I'll bet if they already know stories, they will tend to dream up the ghosts."

"Interesting. Gotta go. Felicia's keeping my dinner warm."

"She's patient. What is it, past ten?"

"Just. Felicia understands about working late." He laughed. "I made sure she understood."

"How'd you do that? Beat her up?" Nedders was joking.

"Works for me." Pete wasn't joking. "I got a three-point plan for keeping wives in line. First you love 'em up, bring 'em candy, some bubbly bath, and fuck their brains out. Next point is a little glitter. Diamonds really make 'em behave. Then, if that doesn't work, you have to beat the shit out of them, but never leave a mark. Cover your ass, Neddy, that's what you taught me, and that's what I do."

"You trying a cable box on her?"

"No. We only have a couple TVs, bedroom and den, and I sure don't want to be exposed. Maybe if she pisses me off, I'll buy her a set for her craft room."

"What's a craft room?"

"It's where women keep all that diddly-shit stuff they make things with. Glue and yarn and sewing crap. Felicia has a bunch of flower pots. She likes to paint them. She thinks she's an artist."

"Is she any good?"

Pete laughed, low and lewd. "If she wasn't any good, I wouldn't keep her. The woman can pick up a champagne bottle with her pussy and carry it across the room without dropping it. She does exercises. You oughta see what she can do."

"Maybe you oughta put an eye in your bedroom one night and let me take a look. Recon."

"*Mi casa es su casa, amigo.* I'll let you know when to tune in."

53

The body of Minnie Lavia, neighbor of Lobelia Hatch, had been taken away at last. Her parrot flew the coop in a flash of green when Lobelia unlocked Minnie's door before the police got there. She had gone in, practically dragging a reluctant Daniel with her, but once they entered the room with the body and got a whiff and an up-close look at the face the parrot must have been redesigning for days, it was Lobelia who vomited all over Minnie's poor, dead feet. Daniel had escorted her outside to await the police and had apologized to a nice redheaded sergeant for his mother's vomit. All the while, his penis kept telling him to fuck Minnie in the empty eye socket. Sex was the farthest thing from Daniel's mind, but Dick never stopped thinking about it, and he had absolutely no scruples. Woman, eye socket, the butterscotch pudding cooling in Mother's refrigerator earlier tonight, it was all the same to him. Daniel had let it add a little protein to the pudding, then smoothed it over so Lobelia wouldn't know—the truth was, he allowed it because the image of the old battle-ax eating his jism pleased him tremendously. *Serves her right.*

Daniel helped Mother to her chair by the television, then got her a nice big dish. The pudding was still lukewarm, but nicely thickened. He slathered whipped cream on it because that's what she liked, placed a sleeping pill and a glass of water beside her and went home, pleading a need for sleep. The real need was to get away from Lobelia and her big fat mouth. Ever since she'd recovered from her vomitfest, she'd been yammering on about Minnie Lavia and her messy house. "If she'd known the police were coming over tonight, you can bet she would have vacuumed," Lobelia declared. That was when Daniel decided he either had to leave or take the more drastic measures against her, as suggested by his penis.

54

Eleven o'clock in Caledonia. All over town, people were either in bed, or would be soon. About thirty percent of Caledonia Cable's customers had new systems and in many of those houses, people were feeling a little strange, exhibiting neuroses hitherto unseen, hearing voices, hearing noises, creaks and footsteps, and having nightmares.

There was another death in town that night. Abby Abernathy, a morose woman who lived in the same cheap apartment complex as Mickey Elfbones, had spent the day watching her programs and the late afternoon and evening watching the Soap Channel, taking in rerun after rerun of her favorite serials. Abby, who was in love with at least two men on each show, wrote letters to them during commercials, commiserating and advising them on problems they were having with their wives and lovers.

Abby had a tenuous hold on reality in the first place and now that she had the new cable box—and the wonderful Soap Channel—things deteriorated rapidly. Sitting in front of the television, squinting through little granny glasses perched on her nose, she muttered and sang, called to the people on the shows, trying to get their attention. "Don't talk to her, she cheated on you with your father!" and "Don't touch her! She's a zombie, brought back from the dead!" and "She's carrying Brad's baby, don't marry her!" and on and on. On this day, she proposed to four of the leading men, but none answered, though she was pretty sure one of the females had told her to get lost, that Jeremy was hers and Abby couldn't have him.

Finally, during a late-night rerun, after pleading with Gerald to leave that bitch Chloe and come live with her, she threatened to take sleeping pills. She threatened three times, and he continued to ignore her.

Finally, she went into the bathroom and got the bottle. Then she went to the fridge and took an iced tea tumbler full of white wine from the box she kept next to the orange juice. Topping it with vodka from the freezer, she carried it to the living room and, right in front of Gerald, swallowed the pills one by one. She had to go back twice for more wine and vodka to finish off the bottle.

That bastard Gerald never even noticed when she died.

Lara Sweethome felt better after confiding in that nice Pete Banning, who owned Caledonia Cable. He was her doctor's brother, a fact they both found fascinating. She was sure the doctor would be pleased to know they'd met. Pete was very different from the doctor in some ways. Not as handsome, but far more outgoing. The doctor was sort of an understated type, dignified but very approachable. She loved his shy smile. Pete, on the other hand, had a huge, glowing smile, and was incredibly outgoing. She even asked if he was married. He'd never answered the question, and that gave her hope. Maybe she'd ask him over for coffee.

Like the doctor, he was such a good listener—even better, really, because he seemed to really love hearing about ghosts. He asked questions and hung on her every word. The doctor, good as he was, didn't believe in ghosts, so she knew he thought she was imagining things. Hopefully, he'd call back in a day or two and make a date to come over and meet her mother. He wasn't married either, come to think of it.

She had heard footsteps most of the evening, but the doctor's tranquilizers had helped and they didn't bother her too much. But she didn't want her mother climbing into bed with her again. That was horrible, especially because she'd dreamed it was a man before she felt those cold breasts pressing into her back.

She almost slept in the bathtub, but buoyed by Pete's visit, she poured a thick line of salt across the doorway, closed the door over it, and slept in her own bed. Because of the medication, she didn't wake up, even when the covers moved by themselves and something cool climbed in between the sheets with her.

Doris Tilton wore her earplugs and slept with her husband because sleeping in the recliner had left her sore and cranky. When she'd returned home from her shopping trip, she felt refreshed, and Wallis had quickly whisked her off to an expensive, romantic lunch and a drive up to San Simeon to tour Hearst Castle. She loved to go there, but Wallis could rarely be talked into it, so this seemed extra special to her. Arriving back in town, Wallis had taken her to another exclusive restaurant for a late dinner. When they arrived home, they had gone straight to bed. Wallis didn't even want to watch the news. Instead, they made love, simply and slowly. She snuggled up to him now and in his sleep the old goat reached out and cupped her breast. He hadn't done that in a decade.

In the apartment of the Flagg family, one of the kids finally noticed the lady-in-white phantom pacing back and forth behind the couch. Both kids thought it was pretty cool, Mother Flagg was unnerved, and Father Flagg said it was fog.

Mia Hunt Hartz called the police twice because of noises in her backyard. They came out once, but declined a second trip. Now, lying sleepless in bed, she heard the childish monstrosities again, screeching, running, tramping. The voices seemed very close in the silence of the night and, with a nervous shiver, she got up and closed the window, the blinds, and the curtains. It made no difference. Finally, Mia went to the guest room on the other end of the house and slept there. She could still hear them, but they weren't quite so loud.

Gabe and Kevin were asleep, locked away in their bedroom, which was at the opposite end of the house from the living room. Gabe had let Kevin have another half glass of wine—he didn't want to give him a tranquilizer when he'd been drinking—and the younger man had dropped off quickly, but he remained, after nearly an hour in bed, spooned in against Gabe, curled up as tight as he could, the fingers of one hand twined through Gabe's in a rictus that would probably leave them both with pins and needles.

Gabe couldn't sleep. Instead, he pondered the imponderables, ranging from the existence of ghosts, of God, of good and evil, to the mysteries of Will Banning, his relationship with Maggie, and his dislike of the mere mention of Pete. Then he thought about cats, birds, and seals, and finally, he began to doze off.

On the edge of sleep, he came wide awake, thinking he heard a baby cry. *No,* he told himself, *it was just your imagination.* After a long period of silence, the soft sounds of Kevin's rhythmic breathing finally lulled him to sleep.

Out in the living room, Jason and Carrie Cockburn made several unnoticed appearances. If Pete had a camera in that house, he would have messed his shorts. How could hallucinations appear without the people present? And how could he be seeing them through a camera lens if they really were just simple hallucinations?

Mickey Elfbones built some more hats, this time using tin snips to cut up aluminum pie plates to put inside his hats. That was because the cardboard stiffeners hadn't done a damned thing. Doc Banning's tranks had made work easier—leveling off the panic attacks so that he could function as long as animals couldn't actually touch him, but they didn't do anything for the voices. He'd hoped they would.

The pie-tin hat was uncomfortable, but Pete kept it on in bed. Awaiting sleep, he mentally designed a skullcap style hat in his head. He'd make one of those tomorrow before bedtime. This was just too uncomfortable.

Pete Banning, sitting in his home office, watched Heather Boyd get ready for bed. The young woman with the to-die-for body didn't have the television or pajamas on, but she did spend some time with a large vibrator, relieving stress in the old-fashioned way, the covers neatly folded back so Pete had a front-row seat. Pete saw stress released from her body eight times, then he forgot about counting.

Putting away his own stress-relieving tool, he decided he would have to pay a service call to Miss Boyd at his earliest convenience. Now, it was time for sleep. He stood up, glancing at the clock. An hour remained before his latest broadcasting experiment would begin. It was an experiment Hitchcock would have loved.

55

Will felt like he had been caught masturbating, and he knew it was ridiculous. He hadn't done anything to be ashamed of; after seeing something pretty damn incomprehensible, he had called out Michael's name—*thank heaven that was all I said*—and then fainted. It was nothing to be ashamed of.

"Will?" Maggie said.

She sat next to him on the couch as they pretended to watch the news. Freud had taken over her lap; Rorschach snoozed on the sofa back between them, and Jung was draped across Will's legs. The boys were fine and for that he was grateful.

"Will?" she repeated.

"What?"

"How you doing?"

"I'm good. You should go home now."

"I'll go soon. How do you feel?"

"I'm fine." He heard sharpness in his voice, but

didn't feel like apologizing, just being alone. "The cats are fine. Everything's fine."

"Will," Maggie began, turning her body toward him, "I know there's something wrong. You can tell me anything—you know that. You told me when you came home and found Candy giving your brother a blow job. You told me when Barbara peed in your beer—"

"I have no proof of that. I just think she did."

Maggie took his hand in both of hers. "Who else would have done it? Vomiting on her was the perfect way to say you wanted a divorce."

"I didn't do it on purpose."

"You did it because she peed in your beer. Instant karma."

Will stroked Jung with his free hand. "That was funny in a twisted sort of way. I told you why she did it, didn't I?"

Maggie cocked her head in that way she had that always made Will smile. "No. You just said you were fighting."

"Well, we were, that's true. That's all we ever did."

"It turned her on," Maggie said solemnly. "She'd fuck your brains out after a fight."

Will blushed. "I told you that?"

"Yeah, you did."

"I shouldn't have told you that."

"Why not?"

"I don't know. It's rude."

"I like that you felt comfortable enough to tell me, Will. That makes me feel good. So why were you fighting?"

"If you could sum up Barbara in one word, what word would it be?"

"Sorry, can't do it. I need two words."

Will smiled. "Okay. Two words."

"Domineering bitch."

He chuckled lightly. "That's exactly why she did it. She wanted to dominate me sexually. She wanted me to let her piss on me during sex."

"Oh, yuck! She liked golden showers?"

"I love that expression. Yeah. I mean, I don't know if she'd ever actually done it, but she sure wanted to." He paused. "She also wanted to tie me up."

Maggie cocked an eyebrow. "That's not so odd. Lots of people play that game, don't they?"

"Sure, but *Barbara*? Would you let that woman anywhere near you with a rope?"

"I see your point."

"It would probably be fun with someone you trusted. I mean, I'd let you tie me up without a second thought." Suddenly feeling like a teenager, Will looked down at the cat in his lap.

"You would?"

"I just meant that I'm not a prude. I've never tried it though. Look at the women I married. None of them could be trusted to, you know, uh. . ." *Why did I start that?*

Maggie still held his hand and she gave it a hesitant squeeze. "Not to pee on you while you were helpless. Or leave you like that while they went shopping. Or . . . or hurt you. Slap you or something worse. Will?"

He made himself meet her eyes. "Yeah, you said exactly what I was thinking. They turned sex into this contest of self-control. I never dared goof around, play games. All three of them had fits if I made a joke. Sex was so deadly serious to them."

"You were their prey, Will. They were all bullies."

"I realize that. Now. Took me long enough."

"I wouldn't hurt you."

"I wouldn't hurt you either," Will said softly. "I trust you."

"I trust you, too," Maggie said softly. Now she looked down. "Enough to ask you to tie me up. I know you'd never hurt me."

"You'd like that? Getting tied up?"

"Only with the right person." She met his eyes, flushing madly.

Will was getting aroused. Thank heaven the evidence was hidden beneath Jung. He didn't want to think of Maggie that way. It was wrong. It was dangerous. But he couldn't stop it. He had to break the spell. "Maybe I'd pee on you," he said raggedly.

She laughed. "You probably wouldn't do that even if I asked you to."

"Probably not. Unless you'd been stung by a jellyfish."

She smiled coyly. "You already did that. When we were eight and I stepped on the one that washed up on the beach. That was very heroic of you, relieving the sting like that."

"You're the one who knew about doing it. I only did as you asked."

"Will?"

"What?"

She hesitated. "What if I did ask you to tie me up? What would you do?"

He couldn't make his voice work.

"Well?"

Jung started to stand up, but Will stopped him from jumping off his lap. "Don't I, uh, always try to accommodate you?"

"You—you do." She was sounding pretty odd herself and she wouldn't look at him. "Um, listen, I know you're keeping something from me." She madly scratched Freud's cheeks, her face blazing red. "If we can talk like this—why won't you tell me what happened to you tonight?"

"I don't remember anything that happened more than five minutes ago."

"Me either." She looked at him.

In her eyes, he saw childhood summers and Halloweens; he saw all the tidepools they'd ever explored, all the trails they'd hiked. He inhaled rainstorms and the sulphur of fireworks on the Fourth of July; he smelled the waves they'd splashed in, and the soft clean scent of her shampoo. He tasted mounds of barbequed corn on the cob, buckets of popcorn consumed at matinees, root beer floats, and gingerbread. She held all the good history, none of the bad. *She's my sister,* he thought. Then, *No, she's much more than that.*

Maggie's mouth was barely open. He studied her lower lip, the fullness, the slight tremble. The tip of her tongue shot out and wet it, disappearing again in a flash. Her lips looked darker than usual, but she wore no lipstick. He saw the green of her eyes through the lashes on her lowered lids. She didn't move, but she didn't look away either.

He couldn't breathe, and he couldn't stop his lips from dragging his face toward hers. Their lips met, warm and soft. A heady, sweet dizziness enveloped him. Time stopped. It was a chaste kiss, decades in the making. Seemingly on their own, his arms rose and his hands found Maggie's waist and settled there, began gently drawing her closer.

Suddenly, Freud growled, then all three cats shrieked. Rorschach bounded down over Will's and Maggie's heads, his fur brushing over them. Jung and Freud dug their hind claws painfully into human thighs as they jumped away and fled. Instantly, Will and Maggie pulled apart. "What's happening?" she whispered.

"I don't know."

Something hit the window overlooking the backyard. Will couldn't see anything with the outdoor lights off. "Shit! Get down!" Will pulled Maggie to the floor. "Stay there." He grabbed the remote and turned off the TV then, half-running, half-crawling below window level in case someone had fired a weapon at them, he reached a side-table lamp and flicked it off, then moved on to the main wall switches and shut them down and turned on the patio light.

Something else hit the window, hard.

In the distance, dogs howled.

"Will, be careful!" Maggie called.

He didn't answer, just stayed low and crossed the darkened room, quickly coming to the big window. Carefully, he raised up to peer out, dropped back down without seeing anything when another hit came.

"It was a bird," Maggie called.

"Not again," Will groaned. Still, that was better than a bullet. He stayed to the side of the window, but stood up and looked out, saw a smear of blood. Below, three big birds—*two* gulls and one owl—lay on the ground, two stunned, one gull unmoving, probably dead. "It's okay, Mags. The windows are all reinforced safety glass, and I don't see any flocks coming."

She joined him at the window. "Turn off the outside light so we don't attract them."

"Good idea." He felt for a secondary switch beneath the open drapes and pushed it down. Darkness closed in.

Fifteen minutes passed and no more birds hit. Will closed the heavy drapes, lined to keep the setting sun out, and turned on a table lamp. "Let's find the cats."

He headed for his office. All three were huddled

under his desk again, eyes open so wide that they looked like huge kittens. Will and Maggie squatted down, talking to and petting them. They relaxed a little, but not even Freud would purr.

Finally, Maggie rose, so Will did too. "Whatever it was that mixed up the birds was sensed by other animals, too, don't you think?"

"I do."

"I should get home to my guys. Are you sure you're okay?"

"We'll be fine." He walked her to the front door and out into the driveway where her Forester waited. One bird, on the cement near the Subaru, fluttered to life, tried to fly, then decided to stagger away and recuperate a little first.

Maggie watched it carefully. "He'll be okay. Call me early if those other birds are still there in the morning, and I'll come and get them."

"Okay."

Maggie opened the SUV's door then peered at the sky. "I wonder how widespread this was."

"Good question. You're going back to the beach in the morning?"

"I think I'd better."

"Shall I meet you?"

"No, I'll just trot over to the cove and make sure there aren't any new problems. I'll be quick . . ." She paused. "Uh . . . Nevermind."

"Spit it out."

"Actually, if you don't mind, I think I'd prefer not to go alone. When I went back at lunchtime, I ran into someone there."

"Oh? Do you have something *you're* keeping from *me*?"

"Yes. I was going to tell you, probably, but, you know . . ."

"Who was it?"

"Pete."

Will's gut clenched. "He was on the beach?"

"At the cove. He'd watched the rescuers remove the seals, but he was the only person there when I arrived. He just fries me."

"What did he do?"

"Just said some things I didn't appreciate."

"Like what?"

"He's a letch. Sleazy, you know?"

"I know. Did he make a pass?"

She smiled slowly. "What an old-fashioned expression. I like that, but it sounds so nice compared with what he said. Trash talk is what he did."

Anger ratcheted Will's neck up tight. He tried to hide it. "Did he touch you?"

"Not today."

"What do you mean? He's touched you before?"

"He tried, when we were still kids. That's what he talked about."

"Maggie, why didn't you ever tell me this before?"

"Because it would only upset you. Back then, you couldn't have done anything. I squashed his nuts for him. It was better you didn't know."

"Why are you telling me now?" he asked softly.

"Because I was too embarrassed until now." She looked at the keys in her hand. "I still am, I guess, but maybe something changed a little tonight."

"I don't understand."

"We were twelve. I was expecting you. I was washing dishes. He came up behind me and started nuzzling my neck, touched me, no big deal, but I let him because . . . Crap."

Will put his hands on her shoulders and pulled her close to him. "Because?"

He felt the warmth of her breath through his shirt

when she finally spoke. "Because, Will, I thought he was you."

For the third time tonight, he felt dizzy. "You would have. . . you wanted me to . . ."

"Yes."

He held her for long minutes, neither saying a word. "I'd better check my guys," she said finally. She brushed her lips against his very briefly, then slipped into the Subaru and pulled out without looking at him.

A cool breeze swirled around him, making him aware of dampness on his shirt. *Tears.* He smiled sadly to himself as he went back indoors. He had avoided looking directly at her because of the drops that had rolled from his own eyes. He was sad, joyous, and afraid, all at once. Sad that so many years were wasted, joyous that they could be over, but afraid that pursuing anything might ruin their friendship.

He locked up and stopped in the office to talk to the cats. After a few moments, they let themselves be lured out of hiding, so he rewarded them with slices of leftover chicken breast, staying in the kitchen with them until they were done.

"So are you guys coming to bed tonight?"

They stared at him.

"Bed?"

They didn't respond to the word eagerly like they normally did, so Will went to bed alone. But five minutes after he climbed in, the Orange Boys joined him. Pleased, Will turned off the light and Freud lured him to sleep with his purr.

56

"You're late," Kevin said as Will approached the reception desk.

Will consulted his watch. "Three minutes. And you, Kevin, look like you had too much to drink last night."

"Don't rub it in." Kevin touched the dark shadows beneath his eyes. "If I'd known you were going to be late, I could have used my ice mask and reduced my puffiness."

"I know you have a spare one in the little freezer in the group therapy room. Go ahead and put it on."

"In public?"

"Why not? Tell people you're the Caped Crusader's little buddy."

"Don't be bitchy, Will. I'm bitchy enough for both of us." He looked down at the sign-in sheet, then back up, a grin spreading across his face. "We really rocked your world last night, huh?"

"Yes, I have to admit, I was impressed."

"I guess you believe in ghosts now."

"No."

"How—" Kevin cringed at the sound of his own voice. "Too loud. Sorry. How can you not believe in ghosts after last night? Seeing is believing."

"I saw something. It might have been a holograph someone's tricking you with. It might be a mass hallucination brought on by I don't know what."

"Something in our water?"

"Possibly. You know, Kevin, that's not a bad notion. Caledonia has well water. Maybe it's been contaminated with a hallucinogen. We need to have samples tested. Or maybe it's something in food that's in the local market right now. It would mean it was something we had at dinner since we all saw it. Let's start with the water. How fast can you run to your house and get a sample?"

"If we close for lunch and you go with me, we can get it then. I'm not going there alone."

Will saw the terror in Kevin's eyes. "Okay. Let's do that. We can drive through CharPalace on the way."

Kevin's expression changed. "As long as you don't tell Gabe. I'd love a burger."

"Sure, but why not tell Gabe?"

"Because his cholesterol is too high. I have to set a good example or he'll wolf them down like you do." He paused. "How's your cholesterol, Will?"

"Just fine. Who's up first?"

Kevin handed him a file. "Here you go. You've got five minutes, okay? It's another day of twenty-minute appointments."

"Okay." Will poured himself a coffee and headed for the spare office. Once inside, he sat down and opened the file, relieved to see it was a regular with bipolar disorder. Sipping his coffee, he scanned the file in thirty seconds, then let his thoughts drift to his morning beach meeting with Maggie. They had met in the parking lot. She had picked up two bear-claws and two coffees on her way down, and they sat at the picnic table again, but today, all they talked about was animal behavior. The birds outside the picture window were gone, but Will found several others in the yard, two dead, three that appeared uninjured. Maggie told him about Charlie and Rose's cockatiels. Rose phoned early and said the birds had "gone batty" for about twenty minutes the night before, and that she and Charlie had feared they would kill themselves while trying to escape their large cage. He had thrown a cover over them, and things improved slightly.

Maggie's cats seemed nervous, and her dog was excited, but she thought it might have been due to the marching treats that continued to invade the kitchen. She hadn't seen any birds on her property this morning, but last night, driving home, she'd seen small groups of three to six birds sitting on sidewalks.

After they finished their breakfast, they walked onto the beach and they found a few dead fish washed up on shore and several seagulls that appeared to have dashed themselves against the rocky cliffs, as well as half a dozen pigeons, a little dazed, roosting a foot or two off the sand on the bluffs. Maggie thought they had probably fallen out of their nests high above.

Will had followed Maggie around the outcropping hiding the half moon cove, dreading what he might see. Sure enough there were seals, but only two, and although they seemed a little sluggish, Maggie declared them normal enough for government work. Five minutes later, the animals slipped into the ocean and swam away.

As Will had always feared, he and Maggie, left without animals to talk about, experienced awkward silence for the first time in all the years they'd known one another. Will wanted to touch her, but wasn't sure he should. He wanted to ask her what she was feeling, but Maggie was usually outspoken and if she wanted to tell him, she would. A few minutes after the seals left, they started back down the shore, silence heavy between them. At the cars, they bid one another good morning. Will bent and kissed her cheek like he always did, and then they finally looked at one another, both coloring in embarrassment.

"We have to talk," Will said.

"We do," Maggie agreed. "This is. . . hard. I don't know what I'm supposed to do. We've spent our whole lives as friends. Do you think we can take it to the next level?" Her eyes searched his. "Maybe we should leave things as they are. I mean, last night, it was just a kiss. We'd been drinking."

"We weren't drunk, Maggie. And if that was just a kiss, then why was it ten times better than the best kiss I've ever had before that one?"

Maggie's eyes sparkled with unshed tears. "Really?"

"Yeah, really."

"Without tongue?"

"Either way, ten times better." He nearly pulled her to him then, was pretty sure she would have let him, but he stopped himself. "No matter how good it was, we can't risk our friendship. As it stands, it was a kiss. That's all. We can still back off safely."

"Can we?"

"Probably. If we decide not to let it go any further, memory will fade. We should both think about it long and hard before we. . ." He wanted to kiss her too much to even talk about it. Maggie's lips, slightly parted, looked like they had the night before. He made himself look at the ocean instead.

"You're right," she said, "but Will, I feel like Eve after taking a bite of the forbidden fruit. I want more."

"Kevin would find your calling me 'forbidden fruit' hysterical."

"I know."

"If I look at you, I'm going to kiss you again."

"I know. Don't look at me because I'll kiss you back. Get in your car and go to work. I'll do the same. Do some thinking. We'll talk later."

With that, they had parted. Just thinking about it now caused gave him reason to wish he'd worn loose, pleated pants to work today.

A rap on the door. Kevin's voice. "Doctor, Mr. Hardwick is here to see you."

Will started to stand to open the door then thought better of it and crossed his legs and said, "Come on in."

57

The day raced by for Maggie, who could barely get a moment to breathe. She put a record number of dogs and cats on mild tranquilizers, and frequently, she thought their owners needed them just as badly. Several told her they had seen or heard strange things—two used the word "ghost" without hesitation—in their homes, and that the animals had corroborated the phenomena, keeping their humans from thinking themselves crazy. Maggie believed them.

Each story made her think of the awful visions lurking in Gabe and Kevin's home, and how strongly Will had reacted. She had been the only person near enough to him know he'd said something in addition to his oldest brother's name. The words that followed were strangled, but she was almost sure he'd said *I killed you.* That was why she had tried so hard to get him to talk once they were alone.

Does he even know he said it? Does he know he said it

once before? She doubted he remembered the first time. It was the night of Michael's death, and Maggie had crossed the street to his family's house and gone upstairs to see him at his mother's request. She was worried about him because he had locked himself in as soon as the first tumult had died down, and now refused to speak to anyone or eat any supper.

Once he knew it was her, he undid the little slide bolt Michael had helped him install the summer before. As soon as she was inside, he locked it again. She knew why: He didn't want to deal with Pete, who was downstairs hovering around his parents like a good son. Maggie didn't buy his act because when he'd opened the door for her, she saw the gleam in his eye and realized he was probably happy his big competition was dead. Now he would be the number one son.

Will sat down on his bed and she climbed on next to him. She still remembered how he looked, a youthful version of his adult self, tall, with a cuteness that would mature into handsomeness similar to Michael's, same hair, same half smile. His eyes were red, but he had regained control quickly, as he always did, so his face looked almost normal, not red and swollen from crying. The air in the room, thick and heavy with emotion, hurt her stomach, so she got up and opened a window, hoping the bad vibes would fly away on the breeze. Of course, they wouldn't, not as long as Will's emotions churned, but the breeze felt good anyway.

Sitting on the bed, she watched the curtains flutter like ghosts, and waited for him to show her what he needed. Finally, she saw his hand creep toward hers. Not looking at him, she met his hand and took it. They sat like that for long minutes. Finally, she felt a tremble. Out of the corner of her eye, she saw tears falling from his down-turned face, dropping into his lap like rain. That was her cue to move close to him and pull him to her, holding him against her so he could cry.

That was the thing about Will. He never felt safe because Pete always swooped in at the first sign of weakness. But, locked away in his room, in her arms, he'd cried almost silently for nearly an hour. When the tears were over, but he still had his head buried against her shoulder, she asked softly, "What happened?"

"I think—I think it was my fault. I killed him."

"What?"

"I can't remember exactly," he said, the words coming at halting intervals. "He was climbing the— the fence. I was right there. His shotgun. It went off. There was all this, this blood. I can't remember."

"Why do you think you killed him? Wasn't it an accident? Pete said his gun just went off."

Will pulled away and looked at her, eyes fierce with some emotion she didn't understand. "Maggie, it's like I blacked out or something. I saw *through* him. He stood there for like a millionth of a second, just staring at me, and his stomach was gone. I saw *through* him. Then he fell and I fainted I guess because the next thing I remember was that I was holding his shotgun. Michael let me carry it, you know? I gu-guess it went off. I did it. Kill—killed him."

"But Pete didn't say you did it."

"He said he wouldn't tell."

"Really?"

"Yeah. I gu-guess he felt sorry for me or something. Well, probably sorry for Mom. He said she didn't need to know, then he kept telling me it was just an accident and to picture Michael holding the gun while he climbed the fence and it going off. He said picture it and believe it and it would be true."

"Will—"

He looked at her, his eyes dark pools of sorrow. "What?"

She had been going to tell him she didn't believe Pete would be that nice to him, but looking at Will, seeing and sensing the inutterable sadness, she changed her mind. She didn't really think Pete would be nice to him just because he felt sorry for him, but she did think he might say those things to keep their mother and father from centering their attention on Will. They weren't the kind of people who would hate him for it. They wouldn't blame him, rather, they'd see the hurt and try to comfort him. So, it was better for Pete to be the brave son, the hero who held the family together. "Nothing, Will," she said finally. "It was an accident. Just a horrible accident. Remember it the way Pete said. That's the truth."

Silently, he nodded, and it became the truth. He quickly forgot that he'd held Michael's gun; that detail joined the others in some swamp in his unconscious, and she hoped he'd never remember. Before too long, she forgot, too.

Until last night. She shivered now, knowing the secret was bubbling back up to the surface.

"Maggie?" Annette said from her office door.

"Yes?" Quickly, she wiped a tear away before it could escape her eye.

"Your next patient is here."

58

Officer Eric Hoyle hated dead body calls. This one was almost certainly a suicide. The woman, one Abby Abernathy, had swallowed a bottle of sedatives, downing them with booze. The corpse, in full rigor mortis, lay on the floor in front of the television, which was still on, though he had muted the sound. Abernathy had, at some point in dying, obviously been less than peaceful and had fallen or maybe convulsed out of her chair while her body desperately tried to save itself by expelling everything, from every orifice, that it could. It lay in bitter, sour-booze vomit streaked with metallic-smelling blood. Fecal matter stained the woman's jeans, its odor mixing with the vomit smell and the first hints of decomposition to make Hoyle feel like vomiting himself.

Although most cops claimed you got used to the smell, Eric could still smell it. He always could. Luckily, he rarely encountered such odors. If he had, he would have had to find another line of work.

He watched the police photographer finish up, then a couple of guys wheeled in a gurney and waited while the assistant county coroner and her crew finished their work. He wondered how they did it, day in, day out. How could they go home after a day of slaving over a stinking, mutilated body, and bounce their kids on their knees, eat dinner, make love.

As they began to bag the body, odor bloomed anew and Eric, as casually as he could, hightailed it for the door and stood a moment on the walkway running along outside the second-floor apartments. This place was probably the seediest apartment building in town, but it wasn't bad by other towns' standards. Not bad at all. It was clean, the paint unchipped, the walkway swept. It was an older building though, a simple block of apartments, U-shaped around a clean but dinky oval swimming pool. No frills.

" 'Scuse me, Officer."

He stepped back, allowing a short man in a tin foil hat to walk by. He stopped at the next door.

"Sir?" Eric followed him.

The guy's eyes bugged a little as he looked at the law. Eric was used to that. "Yeah, Officer?"

"You're the cable guy," Eric said. "You installed a new box at my house."

"Hi," the man said, nodding. "Mickey Elfbones. Enjoying your new cable stations?"

"Sure. May I ask you a few questions?"

"What happened next door?"

"Your neighbor is dead. That's what I want to talk to you about."

Alarm flickered over Elfbones's face, gone almost as soon as it came. Eric guessed this was a guy who'd been in petty legal trouble at one time or another—he gave off old guilt.

Or maybe it was just the hat.

"I only got a half hour for lunch," Elfbones said. "You can come in if you want."

"Thanks. Be right back." He went to the Abernathy apartment and checked on timing. They'd be ready to seal the apartment in twenty minutes. He told Dobie, the other cop, where he'd be, and went back to Elfbones, who stood waiting in his open doorway. Politely, he ushered Eric inside.

The little man was guilty of one thing, that was for sure. Illegal mixing of colors. The place was clean, though the paint was dull, the rug threadbare, both much older than those in Abernathy's place, as if Elfbones had lived there a long time and, if he was even offered new carpet or a fresh coat of paint, had turned it down. The furniture clashed in every way, from style to color.

"Want a sandwich?" Elfbones asked. He was already smearing peanut butter on white bread.

"No, thanks."

"Something to drink? I got Coke and Mountain Dew and juice. Not sure what kind," he added, poking around in the refrigerator. "Oh. Forget the juice. It's growing hair."

"I could use a glass of water," Eric said. Generally, he didn't even accept that from someone he spoke to while on the job, but his mouth tasted sour from holding back all the bile.

Mickey took a cold bottle of Arrowhead from the top shelf and handed it to him.

"Thanks."

They sat down at a dinette table and Eric asked the usual questions, quickly coming to the conclusion that Elfbones knew nothing. Mickey freely admitted he didn't like the woman, who got drunk and occasionally came crying at his door. Frequently, she used the cable as an excuse to talk to him, claiming something was wrong. When he'd go over to check it out, it was always an unplugged or cross-wired wire. Abby Abernathy, Eric realized, was so hard up for company that she harassed a little loser like Elfbones. Pretty sad, really.

"Yo, Hoyle." Officer Dobie stuck his head in the open door. "We're closing down next door."

"I'll be right there."

"I'm going down with the coroner," Dobie said. "I'll be right back."

He disappeared and Eric rose, thanking Elfbones for his cooperation.

"Any time."

He saw him to the door then walked outside with him.

"Mr. Elfbones?"

"Yes, Officer?"

"What's the hat for?"

Elfbones looked embarrassed. "My nephew made it. I forgot I had it on—shit!" He pointed at Abernathy's place.

Eric turned in time to see a woman peering at him from the front window. It looked like the deceased. She disappeared almost instantly. He trotted to the door, goosebumps rising on his neck, his hand on his .38. He was vaguely aware of Mickey Elfbones beside him as he watched the dead woman, who was in a body bag getting put in the wagon and apparently simultaneously cruising her living room.

"I thought you said she was dead," said Mickey.

"She is. They just took her downstairs." He looked at Elfbones. "You see her?"

"Of course I see her. She sees us, too."

Dobie appeared at the end of the upstairs walkway. "What are you looking at, Hoyle?"

"We're looking at a ghost," he said.

"Ha. Real funny." Dobie peered inside and promptly passed out.

Mickey Elfbones murmured something as Eric turned and bent over the other cop.

"What?"

"This hat is a rip," he said. "It doesn't even keep ghosts from appearing. No wonder it doesn't stop the voices."

59

Kevin sighed and looked at the clock. It was nearly six, which meant the last patient of the day would be gone in mere minutes. Despite the clamor for appointments, Kevin had taken it upon himself to cut off the flow a little earlier than usual. He was prepared to tell Will he'd done it because of his fainting spell, to help him recover, but Will hadn't asked any questions, just thanked him.

The trip back to the house for a water sample had been hairy at first. Well, maybe not the trip itself, but the morning had been hairy because Kevin had fixated on it, worrying and fretting. But at the house, Will accompanied him inside without being asked and showed absolutely no interest in looking in the living room. In fact, he seemed to share Kevin's interest in completely avoiding it. They were in and out in a moment, then they drove to CharPalace, grabbed sinfully delicious burgers, and took them back to the office. While they ate, they grilled one another about what each had seen the night before. Both he and Will were fascinated that they'd apparently seen exactly the same thing. Will seemed surprised, but Kevin wasn't in the least.

The final patient broke his reverie when she approached the desk to make her next appointment. They were done in two minutes and Kevin walked her to the front door, then started to lock up, pausing when a police cruiser pulled into the lot. *What now?* he thought, then relaxed, recognizing Eric behind the wheel.

"What brings you here, fella?" Kevin held the door for him, then locked them in.

"I need to ask your boss a couple questions. Is he still here?"

"I'm still here," Will called from the hall. "Come on back."

They went into Will's office and Kevin put on his beggar's face. "May I stay for the inquisition?"

Eric looked at Will. "That's up to you."

"Why not?" He looked at Eric. "You realize I can't answer any questions about patients."

"How about a dead one?"

Will sat forward. "Who died?"

"We had two deaths last night. One was one of your patients. Abigail Abernathy."

"Abby was killed?"

"Suicide, we're pretty sure."

Will looked troubled. "She had responded very well to the meds we had her on. I have to admit I'm surprised, although a bi-polar can have sudden swings." He took a notepad and wrote something down, gave it to Eric. "Here are a few questions for the coroner about drug levels I'd like answered. It's safe to say Dr. Rawlins will want the same information."

"Yeah," Kevin said. "He will."

Eric glanced at the note, then folded it and put it in his breast pocket. "I have no idea what that said, but I'm assuming doctors take a class in reading each other's handwriting."

Will faked a quarter-second smile. "Was she drinking?"

"She washed the pills down with a lot of liquor, judging by what I saw."

Will nodded. "She was an abuser." He looked troubled. "I'm usually pretty good at knowing when a patient is backsliding."

"You haven't seen her for nearly a month," Kevin said. "She was due back in next week. A lot could have happened."

"True."

Kevin could see the wheels turning. He was wondering if Abby's death was connected to all the other patient strangeness that was going on. "Eric?"

The young cop had been about to say something, but he put it on hold. "Yeah?"

"Can you tell us who else died?"

"An older woman over on Mockingbird Lane. Mrs. Minnie Lavia. A widow. They don't know the cause of death yet, probably a heart attack. The neighbors that found her said that her parrot had one of her eyeballs in its beak when they entered." He paused. "Don't repeat that."

"Of course not," Will said. "A parrot?"

"It worked on her face. Jeff, the cop who took the call, said she'd been dead for a couple days. Maybe the parrot was hungry, huh?"

"Maybe," Will agreed. "I don't know much about birds."

Eric cleared his throat and looked at Kevin. "Can I ask you something?"

"Sure."

"Have you seen your ghost again?"

"Have we ever. Will's seen it too, haven't you Will? Tell him."

"I saw something that could be described as ghostly," Will said carefully. "Why?"

"Your patient? The one that died?"

"Abby?"

"Yes."

"I was talking to her neighbor while they took the body down. Her apartment was empty. But I saw her. At first I thought I imagined a woman looking at me, but I walked over and looked inside. She was walking around in there. The neighbor saw her, too."

"Did you tell anyone?"

"No. Just you two. I'll tell Barry, but none of the guys I work with would believe me. They'd laugh me off the force."

"You're lucky Will saw our ghost," Kevin said. "Otherwise, he'd tell you you'd imagined it."

Will lifted his eyebrows and shrugged. "I might. Can you get a water sample from the apartment? And from your home, and from Abby's neighbor? I can supply containers."

"You think there's something in the water?"

"It would explain a lot. These incidents—sightings, people hearing things—are increasing."

"Your other patient, Mia Hartz, has been calling regularly," Kevin said. "She insists there are children in her yard. I suggested she consult her mental health care professional." He half smiled. "But when I was leaving her place yesterday, I'd swear I heard kids laughing and yelling for about three seconds." He paused. "I realize it must have been a sound that carried from elsewhere, but it made my hair stand on end."

"Curious," Will said slowly.

"And the animals," Kevin said. "They could be affected by something in the water around here, too."

"Animals?"

Kevin explained, adding, "That's why the parrot is so interesting."

"Maggie told me her partner's cockatiels went nuts for a little while last night," Will supplied, then told them about the birds that had thrown themselves against his window. He mentioned his cats, and told them about the radio interference theory. "I'm inclined to think," he concluded, "that we're dealing with separate causes."

"Coincidences?" Eric asked.

"Separate, but related," Will said. "There's too much coincidence for it to be coincidence."

"Spoken like a true headshrinker." Kevin smiled at Eric. "That's how they talk, you know."

"I know," Eric said, and looked at from Kevin to Will. "And I agree. One of you guys, Jung, I think, said, 'There's no such thing as coincidence.' It's true."

"I agree for the most part," Will said. "Sometimes a coincidence is just a coincidence, but most of the time it's not. Especially if there are a whole lot of them."

Kevin looked from Eric to Will. "What are you implying? That somebody's raising the dead, zapping animals with radio waves, and poisoning the water?"

"Something like that," Will said. "Though I'd limit it to zapping animals and drugging people. The ghosts are the result of the drugs."

Eric nodded. "That's logical."

Kevin rolled his eyes. "I should have known you'd be on his side, Eric. We have ghosts."

"Someone wants us to think we do," Eric said softly.

Will nodded. "I wonder if people can be affected by radio waves."

"You just got in way over my head," Kevin said.

"The neighbor of Ms. Abernathy was wearing a tin foil hat," Eric said. "He said his nephew made it, but aren't those things used to keep voices out of your head?"

"Her neighbor is Mickey Elfbones?" Will asked, eyes bright.

"You know him?"

"He works for my brother." He shot a warning glance to Kevin, who'd been about to reveal he was a patient. Sometimes, Will could read minds.

"What street was the other victim on?" Kevin asked.

"Mockingbird Lane."

"That's what I thought. We have a patient on that street."

"He's right," Will said, "But we can't tell you who. Can you tell me who found her?"

Eric hesitated then said, "Why not? A mother and son name of Hatch. If you want to know first names, I'd have to check."

Kevin and Will traded glances, then Will said, "No, that's okay."

Eric stood up and dug in his pocket, drawing out his wallet. "My shift's over and Barry's waiting." He took a business card from the wallet and wrote another number on it. "Here's my office and cell phone numbers." He handed it to Will. "Can we keep one another informed?"

"How far is the information going?"

"Just to me. Like I said, nobody on the force would believe it, but I can work on it on my own."

"Okay." Will took his own card from a holder and added his beeper number, then gave it to Eric.

Kevin stood up. "I'll get the containers for the

water samples. They're really for urine, but they haven't been used," he added quickly. "I'll put labels on them for you."

"Thanks." He turned to Will. "I can probably drop them by tomorrow."

"I'd appreciate it. Just give them to Kevin or take them directly to Gabe."

"Will do. Good night, Doc."

"Night."

60

Will spent a quiet evening at home, sharing warmed-up pizza with the cats in front of the television, then flipping through magazines with one eye on the TV, trying to distract himself from thoughts of Maggie.

He wanted to call her. He wanted her to call him. Neither happened.

Maggie, in her own home, mirrored Will's actions and thoughts. She shared leftover oven-fried chicken with her pets, topping it off with a green salad dressed in red wine vinagrette. Zoltan, a fat black-and-white short-hair, licked the dressing out of the empty bowl—why he liked it, she couldn't fathom—then had a sneezing fit. He always did after licking vinegar and oil dressing, so Maggie foresaw it and managed to snag the plate of chicken and hold it above sneeze-level until the cat got over the fit.

Like Will, she watched a *Simpsons* rerun while dining, and after, scanned a magazine—*Entertainment Weekly,* she was done thinking for the day—and half-watched the television, multi-tasking to get her mind off Will. *Why doesn't he call?*

Kevin and Gabe ate in the kitchen with the pocket door closed, busily telling each other that they knew the ghosts couldn't hurt them, but who needed to deal with those awful images. They went to bed early, put in a porno tape, and wore each other out. Gabe told Kevin at some point that it was nice that the gruesome twosome in the living room at least improved their sex life.

61

Pete Banning ate dinner at home with his wife—give her a little thrill, he figured—then called Jennifer Labouche and told her to meet him on Felsher Hill for a dose of breast enlargement medicine.

She was waiting for him when he arrived, and she was eager as hell, especially after he locked them in the dish enclosure and he examined her bazongas in the shadows and declared that he was sure they had grown a tiny, tiny bit. Reliving old times, he had her turn around so he could fondle and squeeze them while planting hickeys on her neck. Her boobs were much bigger than young Maggie's bee-stings were so long ago, but that was all right, because he was imagining Jennifer as a grown-up Maggie—after all, he was no child pervert.

On the beach, Maggie's had looked adequate, but definitely in need of some growth medicine. In the cove, he'd become incredibly turned on, could barely keep from jumping her on the sand. She wasn't his type, exactly. It was knowing that she and Baby Brother wanted each other that made him fantasize that Jennifer's breasts were hers. Possessed by lust, he wanted to do Maggie, squeeze her tits, fuck her mouth and maybe make her take it up the ass, taping the whole thing so he could send it to Will. Then he'd watch Will watch the tape and that would be even better.

She doesn't know how lucky she is that Jennifer's standing in for her. It was true. Over the years, especially while in black ops programs, Pete had raped dozens of women, always getting off best by humiliating them. That's why he choked himself down their throats, pinning their heads against his crotch. Eventually, they all stopped gagging and gave in. Sometimes he'd sodomize them first, just to hear them scream and then watch their faces as he squeezed their noses shut to make them open their mouths and swallow his dick while gasping for air.

"Ouch," Jennifer moaned. "You're hurting my boobs. Stop it! Pete!"

"Shut up, bitch. Take off your panties. I want your ass."

She turned, upset. "What about my medicine, Pete? I want my boobs to grow."

"Oh, don't worry, you'll get your medicine. We're just gonna take a little detour first."

Obediently, she slipped off her panties and handed them over. He shoved them in her mouth in case she screamed, because when he said ass, he meant *ass,* whether she realized it or not. He hoped she didn't. Forcing her down on all fours on the hard-packed earth, he took her dry. She went rigid with shock then her body began shaking hard, and she whimpered around the panties. It was fantastic. When he couldn't hold off any longer, he shoved her over and sat on her precious boobs, knocking the wind out of her. Without looking at her face—that would ruin the fantasy—he yanked the panties from her mouth and as she gulped oxygen, he drove in, as far and fast as he could. Her throat constricted around him. He started coming and, through gritted teeth, cried a name. When he was done, he stood, leaving Jennifer on the ground to clean herself up.

A loyal assistant, she didn't complain, but as she put her underwear back on, she asked, "Who's Maggie?"

"Just some bitch I fucked when I was a kid. You remind me of her," he lied.

He waited until she drove off then called in a report to Nedders. Finally, he drove down the hill and, before going home, cruised past Maggie Maewood's isolated home. Labouche had tamed the monster for the moment, but Maggie was going to stay on his mind. He wondered idly what he should do about it.

62

Will awoke suddenly from a sleep so deep that his body panicked and his mind did the same, tripping back and forth, trying to figure out where he was, *when* he was.

Then he became aware of the whispers coming from beneath the bed, and knew that he was in his own house, in his own bed, at the blackest time of night, and that Michael was with him. Michael, dead and gone so many years, was back.

"You're dead," Will whispered. "You're dead."

"Will, I'm here. Will, can you hear me? It's Michael."

Dreaming, Will told himself, *I'm only dreaming. I can wake myself up.*

Michael's voice continued to whisper, but he couldn't understand most of the words. He concentrated instead on bringing himself to consciousness by picturing himself taking over the dream and moving his arm to the nightstand and turning on the lamp. As soon as he was in control, he could do anything he wanted, from simply banishing the nightmare to creating a dream he wanted to experience to making himself wake up. That was the theory, anyway. He'd only done it a few times, years ago. It took practice, but he had no time. He had to stop the nightmare before he went mad from the whispers of his dead brother.

This is hypnogogia, he told himself. *The voluntary muscles are paralyzed in this stage of sleep. This is when the boogeyman scares children and people see aliens coming to experiment on them. My boogeyman is Michael, and he's under the bed. I am taking charge by moving my dream arm and clicking on the light. The light will make the whispering stop. Michael will go away. He will rest in peace.*

Will continued the litany of the lucid dream, refusing to listen to the constant whispers, paying attention only to his own voice as he visualized his dreaming body obeying his command to turn on the light.

It wasn't working. He heard Michael whisper, "You're already awake, Will. You're awake. I'm here. Listen to me." The voice softened, returning to murmurs Will couldn't understand.

Maybe I'm imagining him because of what I remembered. Because I killed him. How could I have forgotten that? How? He still couldn't make his dream body obey his orders. *Whisper, whisper, whisper, whisper, whisper.* It was unbearable. *Stop it! Be quiet! Go away!*

The clinical part of Will's mind clicked in and he realized he had probably created the whispering ghost to make peace with it. The clinical part was amused at what the human mind could do to itself, but the rest of him took the advice, knowing it would work.

"Michael?" he whispered. "Michael?"

"Will. Will. Will. Listen to me, it's Michael."

"I know it's you," he murmured. The skeptic in him was having difficulty playing along. *I can't believe you're doing this,* it told him. He thought back, *Shut up!*

"Michael?"

"Will, I have to show you something."

"Michael, I know what I did. I know I killed you. It was an accident. I'm sorry. I'm so sorry."

"Will, listen to me."

"Listen to *me!*" Will countered. "I'm sorry for shooting you. I never meant to. If I could trade places with you, I would. I'm so sorry. So sorry. Please forgive me, Michael. Please forgive me!"

Whispers surrounded him, many whispers, all Michael's, filling the room, urgent and undecipherable.

"Michael!" Will shouted. "I love you. I'm sorry. Please forgive me!"

The bed began to shake, and the air seemed to change, growing thick and heavy in a syrup of urgent whispers.

"Stop it!" Will cried. "Stop it!"

He sat up and grabbed for the lamp, found it. Light bloomed in the room. The whispering ceased, the air thinned. The cats weren't there, and he could feel tears sliding down his cheeks. The alarm clock claimed it was nearly five A.M.

"I'm awake," he said, looking around the room. He pinched himself. It hurt, but some people, he knew felt pain in their dreams. Some people even died in their dreams.

The disorientation he felt now was nearly as fierce as that he'd experienced when he first became aware of the dream. *Was I awake the whole time? I couldn't have been.*

But he remembered everything from the time he

first awoke. He remembered it straight through, as if it had all happened. *Did it happen? No. You're fully aware of how powerful hypnogogic experiences can be. You've done research. Don't fall for it. Go check on your cats. You scared them. Only you.*

He climbed from bed, still not completely sure he was awake. After turning on the overhead, he got down on his hands and knees and looked under the bed. Except for a couple of Ping-Pong balls, the bat, and three fur mice, there was nothing under there.

He wondered if a ghost would notice the cat toys, then stood up.

And saw what lay on the bed, on the sheet where he'd slept only moments before.

The world reeled in and out of focus, but he barely noticed because all he could see was Michael's battered old baseball. He recognized the ancient smudges and stains, the missing stitches. Will reached down and touched it.

It was ice cold.

63

For Will and Maggie, Gabe and Kevin, the rest of the weekdays passed in a frantic haze of patients, most of them new. For Gabe and Kevin, the nights weren't so bad; though they avoided the living and dining rooms studiously, they were happy together in their bedroom. In an odd way, the second honeymoon they were experiencing more than made up for staying out of half their house. Though they had a TV set in the bedroom, they used it only to run an occasional video; they were enjoying life without sitcoms.

For Will, nights were hell. He had put the baseball back in the car trunk and it had not reappeared a second time, but every night was filled with whispers now. The cats refused to enter the bedroom, and were spending less and less time in the living room, preferring his office or the kitchen or small dining room to all else. Will, in the habit of leaving doors to the other bedrooms closed, tried leaving them open, but while the cats would enter if he was in one, they were uninterested otherwise. The last few evenings, he'd spent mainly in his office after eating at the dining room table—the felines had stared balefully at him from the doorway when he'd eaten at the coffee table.

He still slept in the bedroom, even though he wanted to blow up the air mattress and toss a few blankets on it and sleep in the office with the Orange Boys. He could also sleep in the guest bedroom, which contained a comfortable bed, ready for use.

Refusal to give in to his fears, to admit that the whispers—the ghost—was real, made him return every night to the bedroom. Each night, when he awoke to the whispers of a dead boy, he considered, in the darkest hour, that Michael might be real, but he always ended up discounting the idea in favor of his own guilt over Michael's death being the cause of the sounds. If so, it was another reason to continue to spend nights in the bedroom. Until he could find forgiveness within himself—in the guise of Michael— the voice would continue to haunt him.

Now, at quarter to eleven on Friday night, he considered facing the voice again. He was exhausted, though, and thought it might be a good idea to attempt to give himself a night off, to try for an entire night's sleep. He could laze in the morning, having given permission to Kevin to refuse Saturday appointments this week, for the sake of his own health.

Rorschach slept in his lap, Jung was draped on the catpost at eye-level, and Freud was stretched out behind the laptop on the desk, one eye on him. They didn't want him to leave the room. "Okay, another hour. Then maybe I'll sleep in here with you guys."

Freud's rumbling purr filled the room so suddenly that Will almost believed he understood what he'd said. "Mysterious little creatures, aren't you?" he murmured as he reached over and turned on the radio. He'd unwind by surfing the Net and listening to Coastal Eddie, who tended to yammer on about government conspiracies and other things that might be highly amusing at this point in time.

"Join us in ten minutes for a special hour-long interview with our own bestselling horror novelist David Masters on the Coastal Eddie show!" an overly excited announcer cried. Rorschach dug his claws into Will's legs in alarm, and the other two glared at him, furious at the disturbance.

Will quickly turned the sound down to a reasonable level. "Sorry, guys, but one of you must have turned up the volume—and I'm talking to you, Freud— when you stretched."

The disturbingly smart cat stretched again and let his right front paw rest on the volume knob as if to prove Will's point. "What's next, buster? Going to start making prank phone calls?"

Freud purred madly, eyes inscrutable, and as if to prove his point again, the phone began to ring. Will gave the cat another look, thinking about coincidences and picked up.

64

The nights, for Maggie, were not haunted, but merely lonely and filled with questions about Will—all unanswerable—and about the strange behavior of the wildlife and domestic pets. Research yielded little that she didn't know already; no one knew a hell of a lot, but theories, logical and ridiculous, littered the Internet.

By week's end, having seen no more upsets in the wildlife, she concentrated on the problems of cats and dogs, leaving the peculiarities of the avians to Charlie. As far as the four-legged pets went, from what she saw, both canines and felines were equally affected. But she could find no unifying factor to work from.

Thursday afternoon, the lab reports on the water samples gathered by Will had come back. The water was untainted, shooting down what had become the favorite theory. Gabe, Will, and Maggie had given up on the water and were trying to find something else that might be ingested by all affected humans and animals, but so far there was nothing.

By Friday, Maggie was back to favoring theories about glitches in the earth's electromagnetic field, or disruptions from a man-made source. Late in the afternoon, she spoke to experts at the U.S. Geologic Survey and several other organizations, but all they could do was continue to rule out natural anomalies in the Caledonia region. She phoned fellow veterinarians to the south in Candle Bay, Red Cay, San Luis Obispo and to the north in San Simeon and even Santa Cruz. No one else was experiencing anything out of the ordinary. Finally, she tried tackling the closest military bases, asking about sonar disruptions from subs, even though that would only affect sea life. She was hesitant to ask more, probably because of all the conspiracy crap she'd been reading, so she only went as far as asking if equipment in helicopters, theirs or police choppers, might be detected by animals. She found a friendly tech at the base near Avila Beach, a flirtatious young man who told her that perhaps if a chopper were directly overhead and using equipment with certain microwave frequencies, it might upset particularly sensitive animals. He assured her that only a few animals could possibly be bothered, and only while directly in the waves' field, likening the rarity of affected pets to that of people who could hear dog whistles or detect the sound of an electronic alarm system in a department store. When she asked what type of equipment might affect animals, he pleaded ignorance. *Quel surprise.* She let it drop, not wanting to draw any more attention to herself than she had to.

Now, late Friday night, steeped in nutty conspiracy theories about military experiments, she began to put aside hope of ever knowing what was causing the upsets. That was when she saw the first unifying factor, one so obvious that it could have reached out and bit her nose off. "Hot damn," she said, and picked up the phone to call Will.

He answered on the first ring, and that was a real surprise. "Hey there, it's me. Why are you answering your phone?"

"It just seemed like the thing to do," Will said. His voice was fairly relaxed but she could hear the exhaustion in it. "I've been meaning to call you. It's been days since we did more than trade information on what's in the local water."

"I know. It's been busier and busier at the clinic."

"Mine, too. You're up late. Don't you usually do early office hours on Saturday?"

"Yeah, usually. Charlie's covering tomorrow by himself. I need a little time off."

"I'm taking off tomorrow, too. You want to have lunch or dinner or something? Take a walk?"

"I'd love it." His invitation, one extended almost every weekend and some weeknights, now took on new meaning. She felt a little thrill, like a teenager being asked out on a date. *It's not a date!* "Hey, let's do something special," she heard herself blurt.

"Like what?"

At least he sounds interested. "Why don't we leave town? Maybe have lunch at Satyrelli's in the Candle Bay Hotel?" *Then we could get a room.*

He paused so long, she was afraid she'd said the last part out loud, but then he spoke. "Okay, but I'm buying. It'll be our first date."

Two minds, one thought. She smiled for the first time all day.

"Maggie?" Will said. "Did I say something wrong?"

"No. It's just that it took you over thirty years to ask me."

He chuckled. "Hey, take a decade off that. We were only four when we met. I should have asked you out when we were freshmen in high school, not in kindergarten."

"Okay. It only took you twenty years to ask me out."

"You could have asked me," he said softly.

"I was afraid to."

"We were both afraid," he agreed. "So are we going to do this?"

"Let's do lunch, maybe poke around a couple of towns, do a little bird-and-people watching."

"Walk out the pier at Red Cay and tell each other ghost stories about Body House and the lighthouse?"

"Why, Will Banning, I thought you weren't impressed with ghost stories."

"I am if it means a girl will get scared and hang on to me."

Butterflies flew giddily behind her breastbone. She heard the same giddiness in his voice. "What else do you want to do?"

"It's a first date," he said slowly, finishing what she'd started. "Let's just have fun. No expectations, except to remain bosom buddies." He paused. "Except since it's a date, I guess you get to slap me if I get too close to your bosom."

Never in her life had she been so turned on so quickly. Heat rose in her face and her groin. "Maybe I'm a slut," she said coyly. "I might let you cop a feel on the first date." She blushed harder, embarrassed. "Of course, I'd probably knock your block off. You know that, right?"

"Right." In the background, she heard Rorschach start trilling loudly. Will was petting his pussycat. Even that thought went straight to her crotch. "So did you call me up in the middle of the night to tease me, Maggie?"

"No. I figured something out about our behavior problems."

"Ours in particular? I thought we just worked on them."

"You know what I mean. Do you want me to tell you or not?"

"Tell me."

"The domestic animals I've been seeing? Every one of them spends most of their time indoors. They all sleep in their owner's homes at night. In the house, not in the yard."

"Wow."

"Hey, don't knock it—"

"I'm not. That was a serious wow. You're sure?"

"I need to access my files to be certain, but I don't think I've seen many outdoor animals, especially since Wednesday or so. That's when the wildlife incidents dropped off, too."

"I think you're onto something, too. Let's brainstorm a little tomorrow, while we're out of town. Maybe we can elaborate on your theory." He paused. "It fits. All my patients sleep indoors at night."

"Will, I ought to slap you upside the head for saying that."

"You should. Maybe tomorrow, after I cop a feel, you can take care of two birds with one stone and slap me silly."

"You're already silly."

"I know. I can't believe what I'm about to do."

"What's that?"

"Listen to Coastal Eddie interview David Masters."

"When?"

"Starts in about two minutes."

"Ghost stories," she said. "I'll listen, too. Maybe we'll get a clue."

"Maybe. He's a good writer, but I don't buy all that crap about ghost hunting."

"Of course you don't, but try to keep an open mind, will you? Remember what we saw at Gabe and Kevin's."

"It had to be a trick. Ghosts don't exist."

"Will, maybe you're putting too fine an edge on the definition of 'ghost.' It doesn't have to mean a boogedy-boogedy earthbound spirit. It means an afterimage by all nonsupernatural definitions. Why couldn't that apply to what we saw the other night? An afterimage that somehow got stronger. You know, like when a cat craps in the house, but you don't find it when it happens because you don't go in the room and smell it? Then, six months later, you go in the room on a hot day and you smell a ghost of the crap?"

"That's charming, Mags, just charming. But I see what you mean. I guess it's possible. I'll try to keep an open mind, I promise. What time do you want me to pick you up in the morning?"

"I'll pick you up. If we want to go off-road we need my Forester."

"Off-road? What are you thinking of doing?"

"Nothing. Come on, Will, I've only had it three months. I want to drive, okay?"

"You only had to say so. What time are you picking me up?"

"Eleven?"

"That's not very early."

"It's twelve hours from now. We'll have the rest of the day. Now, hang up and listen to the ghost expert so you can tell me a really good story tomorrow. I don't scare easily, so if you want me to cling to you in terror, you have to work for it."

"Okay. See you in the morning."

She put the phone down, her head buzzing, her crotch aching as much as any pubescent boy's with his first *Victoria's Secret* catalog. The cats and dog were still downstairs, so she sneaked up and shut the bedroom door before they could follow. She'd let them in a little later. She turned on her radio just as the interview started, and turned on the vibrator a moment later, knowing she wouldn't remember a word of the interview if she didn't relieve her tension.

65

"Good evening to you, friends and neighbors, from me, Coastal Eddie, at KNDL on the cool California Coast. It's eleven-oh-five in the P.M. and here in Candle Bay it's a perfect sixty-eight degrees. Down in Red Cay, home of tonight's special guest, it's sixty-nine degrees, and up in Caledonia, it's a warm seventy-one. Greenbriar College calls in with a very warm seventy-eight degrees."

Eddie prattled on in his folksy way while Will tried to settle down and concentrate, which was none too easy after talking to Maggie. He couldn't believe he'd asked her for a date. It had just popped out. And the flirting. They'd always flirted, but it was different. Tonight, it aroused him. There had been a new tone to it, though the silliness that they'd always indulged in remained. Tonight, there was something serious lurking in the background. Maybe it had always been there, but neither of them had ever dared to stir it up before, to even acknowledge it.

He wished his pants weren't so tight, thought briefly about doing something about it, but then Eddie was leading into the interview and Freud was staring at him reproachfully. Mastering one's domain wasn't something that could be done when cats were watching, especially a cat possessing the gravity of a Supreme Court judge and a name automatically associated with sexual obsessions.

"David Masters is the bestselling author of many horror novels and he'll be signing his newest, *The Portal,* tomorrow from two to four at Deliciously Dark Booksellers in Red Cay. David, the reviews on your new book are terrific. Congratulations."

"Thanks, Eddie. And I'm a big fan of your show."

They continued to pat each other on the back for several minutes, went on to talk about the contents of the new book, notable to Will because it was supposed to be based on a "real" haunting a few miles inland at Greenbriar, a pricey private college. Will had given a few guest lectures at the tweedy old school, but hadn't known the walls held any ghosts. Of course, looking at the Georgian architecture, well over a century old, it was obvious the place *had* to have a ghost or two. And if it didn't, David Masters was just the man to plant some there.

Finally, after a set of commercials, Eddie asked, "What is your definition of the word 'ghost'?"

Will sat up and waited to hear about wailing spirits waiting to be freed from earthly chains, to be led into the light by tiny eccentric mediums. And all the rest of the usual rot.

Masters cleared his throat. "Essentially a ghost is an afterimage, and when I say that, I don't mean it's always a visual image; generally, it's not. It's an imprint, a recording hidden in the walls of buildings, particularly those with plenty of rock in their makeup. Silica holds imprints well and many homes have it. Early phonograph records used to have silica in them, in fact.

"In my experience, most ghosts are aural rather than visual. Perhaps that has something to do with the ease of recording on materials that make up the building. These ghosts are usually repetitious. Footsteps and slamming doors are very common. If a ghost manifests as a minor poltergeist, rocking chairs often move, and hanging lights and fans will sway. It takes very little energy for these things to happen."

"When you have a ghost that, for instance, stomps around your house, why does it do it?"

"Well, Eddie, there are many theories. While I don't commit to any of them, I'm inclined to think that certain personalities—living ones, I mean—give off an energy that somehow activates a ghost."

"Does a ghost walk when no one is there to hear it?"

"That's a good question. I'm going to take a chance on disappointing a lot of people and tell you my opinion."

"Before your answer: Why will it disappoint people?"

"Many readers assume that because I write about the paranormal, that I'm a believer. I'm not. Frauds abound in parapsychology, intentional and unintentional. I'm a skeptic. A true skeptic. Do you know what that is?"

"Yes, but tell our listeners, since many won't be as familiar with your nonfiction and your essays as I am."

"A skeptic is not the opposite of a believer. A disbeliever is the opposite of the believer. They are at two ends of the spectrum. The skeptic lies dead center with a fairly neutral attitude best summed up with two words: 'Prove it.' This attitude is vital to the study of things which are currently inexplicable. Facts must not be twisted to suit the beliefs or disbeliefs of the investigator. They must be examined scientifically, and with an open mind, with the understanding that there truly are things we cannot explain at this point. A skeptic can easily become a disbeliever, and that's as bad as a believer, in my book." Masters chuckled lightly. "A skeptic is a *non*believer."

"What about people whom you say activate hauntings. Are they believers?"

"Not necessarily. They're personality types. Maybe they give off an abundance of some type of brain wave that can be used by a ghost. Eddie, you've been around people who leave you exhausted, haven't you? All you have to do is be in their presence, and they seem to be able to suck all your energy away. Many people call them 'psychic vampires.' Psychologists call them passive-aggressives. Some doctors refuse to treat them because they're too draining."

"Maybe this guy isn't a charlatan after all," Will told Freud.

"Another type of haunting might be a sense of profound unease, sort of a thickness in the atmosphere that feels depressing or ominous. You may have had a similar sensation around living people, not just bad people, but good people in bad moods. Not everyone senses this, but many do."

"I know exactly what you're talking about, David."

Will nodded agreement, sitting forward now, hanging on every word.

"A ghost can be that emotional imprint. You walk into a room and seem to be drowning in gloom. That is a type of ghost."

"So there aren't any ghosts that communicate with people?"

"Generally, they don't communicate. They are shadows, recordings. They may seem to be interacting, but it's very rare."

"But didn't you have lots of run-ins with these kinds of spirits in your home, Baudey House, when you first moved in? You recounted your experiences in *Mephisto Palace*, a book that scared me half to death."

"Thanks. That was a fictionalized account, but yes, I've had interactions with what seem to be spirits. Usually, if there is interaction, it's because a living human is, typically without knowledge, fueling a ghost. This often happens when a marriage is bad. 'Often' being a very relative word."

"But in your home, weren't you actually attacked by spirits?"

"I dislike the word 'spirit,' because it implies an intelligence that I've rarely experienced. With that caveat, yes, I was attacked. My family and other people in the house were all attacked. At least three ghosts—two would fall in the 'good' category and one in the 'evil'—were physically attacked without any indication of a living human directing the attacks. I have no explanation for these incidents. They simply happened."

The interview went on for some time in the same vein before it wound down. When it was over, Will turned off the radio, wondering what Maggie's take on it was. He'd know soon enough, he decided as he opened the closet and took out the air mattress. He pumped it up in a jiffy then went to the linen closet and dressed it. Ten minutes later, he'd brushed his teeth and stripped to his shorts. Usually, he showered and shaved at night, but tomorrow was special. He'd bathe in the morning.

The cats, all three, watched him closely as he got between the sheets on the floor. After a moment, he got back up and went to his bedroom, allowing himself to turn on the overhead while he grabbed his pillow. He didn't stay long enough to hear anything. He closed that door behind him, then shut the office door most of the way. He wanted to lock it—*face it, Masters spooked you*—but if a cat had to use the facilities, that was more important.

All three stared down at him. He patted the top blanket. "Come on, guys."

Trills and grunts, and then heavy purring ensued as the cats settled into their accustomed positions.

66

There was a dead woman—the ghost of a dead woman—next door and Mickey Elfbones was far more concerned about the noises she made than about the voices plotting against him in his head.

Every night since they took her body away, he'd been aware of her. She was growing stronger and louder. A little while ago, he'd heard her sing one of the songs she'd crooned while alive. It was "Help!," the classic Beatles tune. Hearing it come from a ghost, gave it new meaning that frightened him.

Alive, when Abby Abernathy was in a good mood, she was nutty-happy as often as not, and then she'd sing. Mickey hadn't minded; her voice wasn't bad, and if he didn't want to hear it, his television or stereo easily drowned her out. Most of the time, she sang folk songs, sometimes the oldest Beatles tunes, and occasionally, when she was extra nutty-happy, she belted out commercial jingles. Hearing a fifty-year-old woman sing "I wish I were an Oscar Meyer wiener" was very disturbing.

Hearing a dead woman sing anything was incredibly worse.

Although he couldn't see her from his apartment, he could hear her often, not just when she sang. The television would be turned on, channels changed, turned off again, and sometimes she banged on the wall separating them. He wasn't sure, but he suspected it was drumming, a part of the nutty-happy side of her. He hated it.

"Go away," he muttered. "Go to your grave."

She banged louder and began singing the wiener song, as if she'd heard his thoughts. Maybe she had. *Why not?*

Mickey curled up on his sofa, which was against the wall farthest from her apartment, and tried to get to sleep. Sometime after three in the morning, she finally stopped making noise, and Mickey wondered if maybe he should tell the shrink about it, or better, talk to the young cop who'd seen the ghost, too. It couldn't hurt. The cop was nice. He'd never met a nice cop before.

67

Lara Sweethome was having ghostly problems of her own, but at least she could sleep in her own bed, alone, as long as the thick ribbon of salt was unbroken. She had listened intently to the David Masters interview, wishing the entire time that she'd taped it for Dr. Banning. The doctor would respond well to Mr. Masters, she thought, and maybe he'd better understand what she was going through.

While he had briefly called her back, he hadn't had time to come over and experience her mother for himself. He had apologized and told her he would as soon as he could. He made it sound like he never had a minute to himself, and maybe that was true since he didn't have the part-time partner anymore. No matter, she decided. She had an appointment Monday or Tuesday—she needed to double-check— and would try to talk about her ghost the way David Masters had.

Her mother was walking the upstairs hallway and

stopped at her locked bedroom door each time she came to it to scratch on the door with her toes. Lara silently cursed herself for not putting salt outside the door as well. That would have kept her from touching the door.

Tomorrow, Lara promised herself, she would have a day to herself and drive her little Toyota down to Red Cay to meet David Masters and have him sign a copy of his new book for her. It would be an adventure; she hadn't left the confines of Caledonia for well over a year. Thinking about doing so frightened her a little, but it would be well worth it, especially if she could talk David Masters into visiting her home and maybe exorcising her mother. If anyone could do it, he could.

68

Daniel Hatch's dick wouldn't stop talking about Mother and it was driving him to distraction. Dick wanted to "get rid of her," and Daniel figured that was polite penis language for murder.

Not that he blamed Dick, whose name he'd finally accepted because it was easier now that they were having so many conversations. Dick was a relentless talker, but he was also rather cruel and selfish. He didn't think much about other people's feelings, not even giving a flying fart about Daniel's well-being.

But then, what else could you expect from a penis?

Daniel and Dick were in bed at Mother's house and it was well past midnight. All Daniel wanted was to go to sleep, but Dick wasn't having any of it. He was incensed because Mother had dominated their time every night since they found poor old Mrs. Lavia with her eyes pecked out. Mother wanted Daniel with her from the time he got home from work until bedtime, and every night she tried to talk him into staying at her house in his old room instead of going home. She claimed she was afraid to be left alone. Dick had insisted he leave and Daniel acquiesced to him until tonight, when Mother seemed to be truly frightened.

It's all an act, Dick said. *She's acting afraid to get you to stay with her. She wants you, Daniel, you know that. She's always wanted you. She wants me too, the sick old broad. We have to do something about her.*

"Shhhh. Go to sleep."

How could you stay here? How could you lower yourself to sleep in this old twin bed right next to her room? You know what she used to do, don't you?

"Nothing," he muttered.

You know better. She'd listen to see if you were whacking me off, and then she'd barge in here to catch you in the act.

"She just happened to come in a couple of times. You have to admit, we did it a lot."

It's only natural, Daniel. Tell you what, you stroke me now, and she'll hear you and come in. It turns her on. What she really wants is for you to stick me in her, but you'd never do that, would you? It would kill me to be a plunger stuck in that stinking old cesspool.

"Shut up, Dick. You're twisted."

(Laughter.) Let's hope not, that would ruin all my plans in the future. We're going on a fucking holiday, Daniel, as soon as Mother kicks off. We'll do every babe on Catalina Island, you and me.

"Grow up," he muttered. "Besides, we can go to Catalina even if she's alive."

But think of the hassle. She'll want to go too and when you come back, she'll never stop going on about how you didn't take her.

"Look, I'll just tell her I'm going to a convention. There's one coming up in Sacramento. We'll go to Catalina and say we're at the state capital. She'll never know. We'll call her from my cell phone so she can't figure anything out."

Daniel, Daniel, Daniel. How can you put up with having to call your mommy every night, no matter where you go? You have to stop aiding her. Remember your shrink telling you she's a co-dependent type? You are too, buddy boy, but you need to be co-dependent on me, not your mommy.

"I'm not co-dependent. Dr. Banning said she was. He didn't say I was."

He was being polite. He assumed you'd figure it out on your own, buddy boy. Now, why don't you give us a little stroke?

"No! Not here. She's probably listening!"

(Laughter, more laughter.) See? You just admitted to what I told you about her. She listens. Now here's what we're going to do. You always hated that old swordfish mounted up there on the wall. Look at it.

Dick was right. It was three feet long, counting the sword-beak, and old and creepy, a gift given to him by his uncle Horace, when Daniel was only in first grade. Dick began to talk again. Finally, Daniel nodded and took the fish down. It didn't take long to remove the fish from the wooden plaque that was holding it.

For a couple of moments, he sparred with his shadow, then he took the fish and climbed back into bed.

Set it down. Yeah, let the cover fall over it. Now, let me loose and wet me down.

Silently, Daniel did as he was told. In a few moments, he was breathing hard and stroking harder. His breath came in withering sighs. He forgot about Mother until she barreled into the room, opening the door without bothering to knock.

"Daniel Boone Hatch, just what do you think you're doing?" she demanded. "Are you abusing yourself? In *my* house? Answer me!"

Say yes.

"Yes."

"Put it away!"

No.

"No."

"Do as I say, young man."

Let me go, but don't put me away. I want to watch.

Daniel let Dick flop into the shadows as Mother approached. "Show me your hands, Daniel. Let me see what's on them."

"No."

Do it. Get her closer, then grab the fish Daniel. Run her through.

"I can't."

"You can't what?" demanded Mother, now standing over him. "Show me your hands."

Do it! Do it now!

"I can't kill her."

"Wha—what?" squawked Mother. "Kill me? Who do you think you're talking to young man! I think it's time for a high colonic. Your body's obviously poisoned. Get out of bed and march to the bathroom right now!"

Are you really going to let her run cold water up your rectum until you faint from the cramps when she makes you hold it for an hour? Do you get off on that?

"No!"

Then pick up that fish and run her through.

Daniel's hands moved fast. Not letting himself think, he grabbed the fish and rammed the sword into her gut. It made a horrible squishing sound and before he even withdrew it, Daniel could smell the stink of guts and shit. His mother stared at him in disbelief. She looked at her stomach, at the spreading blood, then back at him again.

"You're in big trouble, young man!" she intoned, then fell across him, 225 pounds of maternal lard.

Get her off me! I'm suffocating!

Daniel slid out from under her, thinking he shouldn't have let dick talk him into this because he was as bad a nag as she was, but she could cook.

Forget food. You and I can play all we want. I'll make sure you have women to fuck all the time. You'll love it. Now, you have plenty of dark left. Go out to the workshed and get the shovel. You can bury her in that spot you have all primed for planting that weeping willow. She'll be great fertilizer, and she'll never nag you again. When the tree is bigger, you can carve your initials on the trunk and it'll be just like carving your initials on her face.

"Yeah, yeah, yeah." Daniel dressed in old clothes, blue jeans and a black T-shirt. "For a penis, you sure have anger management problems."

Forget the shrink shit, buddy boy, it's just you and me and a world of sweet tail to fuck now.

Right before dawn, Daniel finished tamping down the earth that covered Mother. "We have to wait a couple of days for the earth to settle before we put the tree in, Dick."

That's fine and dandy. Now, let's go in and have a shower. Bring the lotion because I need a rub down.

"Now?"

Can you think of a better time for a celebration?

"Yes. I'm not interested in jacking you right now. I just buried my mother, thanks to you."

I know, I know, but jacking's the thing we're going to do. I have a mind of my own and I've led you around by the short hairs since you were thirteen years old, remember? You just let me do the thinking for you and we'll be fine and dandy!

69

"When David Masters compared a ghost with years-old scent on a handkerchief in an attic trunk, he had me," Will told Maggie between bites of cannelloni. He grinned. "It reminded me of what you said, only the ghost of aging perfume on a hanky sounded much nicer than your ghost of old cat crap in a warm room."

"Am I going to have to poke you with my fork?"

"Nope. I'm done."

Maggie smiled as she pushed her empty plate back. "That was wonderful. I'm so full I could pop."

"You really put it away. I don't know how you ate all that." Will put his silverware across his mostly empty plate. "If I ate all those different pasta dishes, I'd sleep for a week."

"Hey, watch it. If this is a date, you can't make remarks about how much I can shovel down."

"And still keep your girlish figure."

"Well, okay. In that case, you can say what you want."

"Coffee? Dessert?"

She glanced at her watch. "It's getting late. Do you still want to go to visit St. Martin's before we go down to Red Cay to meet your new favorite author?"

"He's not my favorite author. He simply has expertise in an area that currently has an impact on my own interests."

"Gee, do you think you could say that any more stiltedly?"

"I could try." He motioned for the check and a waiter appeared almost instantly. Will handed him a credit card without looking at the bill. "We're in a hurry," he said. The waiter nodded and glided off.

"This is a beautiful old place," Maggie said. "Have you ever looked around?"

"Not really. It was closed so much of the time when we were young. You've been here?"

"A few times. For meals. The indoor pool is amazing."

"How about the theme rooms? Ever see one of those?"

"No." She eyed him. "Have you?"

"No. They probably have a list of them at the front desk to pick from. Kevin and Gabe like the Caveman room."

"Prehistoric Paradise," Maggie corrected. She added dryly, "I've read the list."

"What else do they have?"

"Arabian Nights. King Arthur's room. An Elvis room. A circus room, I think."

"Anything kinky?"

"Well, I don't know about you, but I think a circus room might be kinky."

"Does it have a trapeze?" Will felt butterflies try

to dance despite the cannelloni, minestrone, and salad they were swimming in.

She looked him straight in the eye, so hard and fast that he felt like he hadn't a stitch on. "I don't know, Will. We could come back sometime and ask."

"O—okay." He poured water down his suddenly dry throat.

She wasn't done with him yet. "They have a dungeon room. More than one, I think."

"How do you know that?"

"Kevin told me. The dungeons are very popular."

"Do they have trapezes?"

"You like those, huh? What if they do? What can you do while you're hanging by your knees?" She finished her water in one gulp, her eyes never leaving his.

"I can probably do all sorts of things while hanging by my knees if the trapeze is in the right spot."

The waiter came back with the receipt, which was either a relief or a disappointment. Will looked it over, signed off, and put his card away.

"Shall we?" Maggie started to rise.

"Let's sit here for just a minute or two and talk about baseball scores or something."

She cocked her head, then understanding lit up her face. "You have a—"

"*Shhhh.* Baseball scores."

70

"Miss Boyd?" Pete Banning put on his biggest, whitest smile.

"Yes. Oh, hi, um, you're Mr. Ah . . ." Even though it was past noon, Heather Boyd appeared to be wearing nothing but an ass-high pink cotton robe. The cotton-candy polish on her fingernails and toenails matched her lipstick. Her dark hair was in two pigtails. All she needed to complete the look was a lollipop and crotchless panties.

"Banning. Call me Pete. I'm the owner of Caledonia Cable. I came by the other day?"

"Yes, yes, sure. I remember. You adjusted my sets. Is there anything wrong?"

"No—well, yes. Would it be convenient if I just came in for a moment and tweaked a couple things?"

"Yes, now's fine. I mean, I was just going to take a shower. You can tweak first. It'll only take a moment, right?" She stepped back to let him pass.

"Miss Boyd, it will take just as long as you want it to."

"Okay." She shut the door. "You want to do the family room or the bedroom first."

"Let's get the family room out of the way first."

She nodded, and led him into the downstairs room where a boy of nine or ten sprawled on the floor in front of the tube, glued to cartoons.

"Hello, young man. What's your name?"

The kid didn't look away from the screen.

"Rudy."

"Get out of the way, Rudy. He's gotta fix the television."

"Isn't broken."

"I'll be out of your hair in a flash, Sport." Pete fiddled with the cable box, making it go off and on repeatedly, enjoying the sound of the kid letting off steam like a teapot. "This your little brother?" he asked Heather.

"Yeah."

"Where're your parents this morning?"

"They're in Bermuda."

"Yeah," said Rudy. "Maybe they'll get lost in the triangle."

"They leave you two alone?" he asked, putting his screwdriver in his back pocket and smiling at her from hair to toenail polish.

"Oh, please, I'm a sophomore at Greenbriar. I'm not a high-school kid. You ready to go upstairs?"

"I sure am."

"Follow me."

"Bye, Rudy."

Rudy, absorbed in the TV, grunted. *Good.*

Pete stayed four steps below Heather on the stairs, but couldn't catch sight of any bush. Probably, she was wearing a thong.

"So, are you a cheerleader?" he asked as they entered her room.

"Me?" she laughed. "Why would you think I was a cheerleader?"

"You have the personality for it. And you look like a cheerleader, you know . . ." He feigned unease. "You're very vivacious."

He walked to the set.

"Hey," she said, behind him.

"Yes?" He kept his eyes on the cable box. Turn too soon and all would be lost.

"Thanks."

"You're welcome, Miss."

"I got implants last year. Want to see?"

71

Felicia Banning loved her house in the Heights. She loved her furniture, her vehicles, her jewelry, her clothes . . . why she loved just about everything in her life, except for her rutting, rotten husband, Peter Banning.

But since he was rarely home and didn't even make that many demands on her physically, he was a small price to pay for such happiness. Every towel was Egyptian cotton, her everyday dishes were fine hand-painted china, her water glasses were crystal, and she had a housekeeper to handwash those things that required such care. She wasn't a snob; she just liked owning things. In fact, most of the time, she used simple Fiestaware dishes and Mexican blown glass—she had several sets of everyday dishes and glasses.

Her sheets were pima cotton with staggering thread counts that made them feel like the softest down. She loved sheets and had them in every color of the rainbow, along with a dozen different comforters, which were kept stacked in their own closet on shelves that rotated. Sachets of lavender, of rose, of cinnamon, fragrance tarts to melt over tea lights in porcelain holders, scented candles, bath salts, skin creams, handmade glycerine soap, everything with a fragrance, were kept in a small cabinet Pete had specially built just to hold such delicacies a few Christmases ago.

How could she complain? She couldn't, she didn't. Felicia finished her workout in her own exercise room—keeping her body nice for Pete was, as she saw it, part of the deal—and headed for the shower, stripping off her shorts and sports bra as she walked. Pete was long gone; she doubted he'd turn up again before evening, and the maid wouldn't be in until three o'clock. The only person who would be visiting her before then would be her lover, and that would be soon.

Walking naked down the hall, wiping sweat from her blond brow, she noticed that the door to Pete's office, the one that was always locked, was ajar. "Pete?" she called. "Petey, darling, are you here?"

He wasn't. She looked at the door. *Bluebeard's Closet.* Or did it belong to Blackbeard, or maybe the king who chopped off Anne Boleyn's head? Who cared? She smiled slightly, wondering if he had dead women's heads in there, if she would join them if she looked, like in that old story about the guy with the beard. "Nah," she said.

But just to be safe, she bounced and jiggled downstairs and looked out the window. No vehicles. She went into the kitchen and opened the door to the garage. The silver SUV was gone.

Grinning now, she ran back up the stairs and tiptoed into the office without turning on any lights. She knew him well enough to look for cameras, but didn't see anything, and he was such a freak about keeping the door locked, he wasn't likely to bother with them. Besides, he trusted his little Cunnikins. And she was trustworthy; he probably wouldn't even mind her having a lover if he knew who it was.

Just a quick peek. She tiptoed farther into the room, around a screen, and found a bank of mini-TVs. Surveliance equipment. There were six TVs and four were on. One showed some kids watching television and a weird white ghosty-looking thing walking back and forth behind them. Another showed Mickey Elfbones sprawled in front of his television—*shouldn't he be working?*—wearing a metal hat. The third was an empty living room, and the fourth was a real hoot. She concentrated on it. All she could see was a bed, a girl spreadeagled under a man who was pumping away like there was no tomorrow. Curious, she turned the volume up slightly. Just a lot of grunting. Then the man pulled out and sat up. She could only see his back, damn it, and she didn't recognize the girl, but she could tell she was young.

The man pushed the girl's crotch up, legs over his neck and started munching. "Mmmm-mmmmff," he said, muffled. "That's good eatin'!" He sounded like *Slingblade.*

"Pete!" Felicia turned the sound down. "Pete, you bastard! You're only supposed to say that to *me!*"

Furious, she stared harder at the screen, finally making out the blur of the Navy insignia tattooed on his ass. "You son of a bitch!" she muttered. "You dirty rotten son of a bitch!"

The doorbell rang.

Her lover.

She turned and left the room, raced downstairs and peeped out the window then opened the door wide.

Her lover's eyes opened just as wide at the sight of Felicia's naked body. "Well, hello, Felicia! You're looking good."

"Get in here!" She grabbed Jennifer Labouche by the arm, yanked her in, then closed and locked the door before kissing Jenny.

"Wow. You're wet," Jen said, running her hands down her belly and over her sex.

"I haven't showered yet. I'm just sweaty."

"Then let's go shower together."

"In a minute."

Jenny smiled. "You need a quickie first?"

"No."

"Well, why are you so excited?"

"Come upstairs. You have to see this. It's Pete. He's cheating on us!"

72

Mia Hunt Hartz watched the young cop, Officer Hoyle, as he prowled through her house.

"I'm sorry, ma'am, but there is no sign that children broke in."

She closed her eyes. "I heard them. They were in the yard, and then they were in here. Ask my housekeeper."

Jamie, the plump little housekeeper, nodded. "I heard them too, Officer."

"I'm sorry. There's no one he—"

Distant laughter echoed down a hall upstairs.

"I told you," intoned Hartz.

"Stay here."

Eric raced up the stairs, hearing the laughter twice more, louder. He stopped at the top of the stairs. "This is the police. No one will hurt you. Come out now so that I can see you. You're trespassing and need to leave this house."

Whoooosh. He felt something pass through him,

something that giggled in several voices and left a slight smell of dirt and shampoo in its wake. He thought of the movie *Poltergeist*, where the mother feels and smells her missing daughter pass through her. It was like that, only not so nice.

Eric, with Abby Abernathy's ghost still fresh in his head, took no chances on the phantom children returning. He took the stairs down two at a time, slowing only when he knew he'd encounter Mia Hartz. He caught his breath.

"Well?" demanded Mia Hunt Hartz, all imperious and foul, her voice as thin as her equine face. "Well, I told you, didn't I?"

"I saw nothing, Ms. Hartz," Eric said. He didn't know what he would have said had he liked the woman, but he couldn't stand her, and he wasn't lying: He saw nothing.

"You heard something. I know you did."

"Something far away. There's nothing here. I think you ought to talk to your therapist about this, Ma'am. Now, have a good day."

Nurse Boobies always had Saturdays off, so Kevin had gone in with Gabe, who was working a half day. Ordinarily, Gabe would have had to con him into it with sex, food, or presents, but not this time, and they both knew it.

Now, having had lunch at the Gables Inn, they were done for the day. Arriving home, they went into their bedroom and called Maggie and Will, with no luck, then Eric and Barry. Eric was working and Barry had rented a roto-tiller and was about to tear up his garden. They declined their invitation to come over and weed.

Now, here they were, in the bedroom again, too

full to do anything but watch television. "Even my eyes are full," Kevin said when Gabe suggested reading.

Gabe nodded. "Maybe we ought to go for a walk or a run."

"In a little while," Kevin agreed. "It's time for *The Christopher Lowell Show,*" he said, turning on the tube.

"You hate him," Gabe said, flopping down on the bed next to Kevin.

"I know. Let's make fun of him."

"You go ahead. I'll listen."

The show was half over when Kevin realized he'd been asleep. He nudged Gabe, who snored softly beside him.

"What?"

"Wake up."

"Why?"

"It's time for your sleeping pill."

Gabe groaned and tried to wrap a pillow around his head, but stopped cold. "What the hell was that?"

"Uh, Christopher Lowell?" Kevin asked.

Gabe muted the television. "God, I hope so."

Then they heard it again, just a little ways down the hall; a hair-raising cry of distress.

"Gabe?"

"Uh-huh?"

"I sure hope that was a peacock."

"Why's that?"

"Because if it isn't, we've got dead babies!"

"Kev?"

"Yeah?"

"Let's go to the Crescent and take a nice long walk on the beach."

"We need the exercise," Kevin agreed, up and changing into shorts and a polo shirt.

"Turn off that damned fairy," Gabe said, dressing as fast as he could.

"You got it." Kevin turned off the set then waited for Gabe. "Age before beauty."

Sex. Sex, sex, sex. Dick wouldn't leave Daniel alone. After Mother was buried and Daniel had been allowed a couple hours of sleep, Dick was up and at 'em, standing tall, at attention, on red alert. And bitching. Dick didn't care if he'd just orgasmed, he wanted another one. He didn't care if Daniel's hand was ready to have a stroke—not the good kind, either—he just wanted to be serviced.

That was when the Jehovah's Witness showed up at the door. Daniel answered it warily, and there she was, an attractive sixtyish woman extending a flyer to him. "Do you want to go to a better place?" she asked.

Dick said yes. Daniel invited her in.

And the old lady talked about the Rapture, but not very well, not like the Witnesses whom Mother had allowed to ramble on. This one was distracted and, sure enough, she changed subjects suddenly, asking him if he'd ever seen a ghost. She blushed and said one was visiting her at night. A gentleman caller, an old boyfriend. He was interesting, she said, *very* interesting, did Daniel know what she meant.

Daniel didn't. Dick did though. It was time to harvest the winter wheat.

73

"This is a beautiful place, Will," Maggie said, looking across the acres and acres of grave markers. Michael's stone was partially shaded by a majestic live oak and they sat at the edge, just out of the bright hot sun. "Somebody left a baseball here. It doesn't look like it's even been used. That's kind of nice, don't you think? I realize it's a coincidence, but since Michael loved to play . . ." Her voice drifted off.

"Peaceful," said Will.

"Do you still come here on his birthday?"

"Yes. And the baseball's no coincidence. I brought it. I do every year."

"That's nice. Better than flowers."

"Michael'd like it better." Will smiled, then looked at Maggie, suddenly serious. "I still have *his* baseball. I keep it in wrapped in tissue in the trunk of the car just in case I decide I'm ready to leave that one."

"Is that why you wanted to come here today?"

"No. I came here today to tell you a story about the ball—it appeared in my bedroom the other night."

"What?"

"I can't explain it. Michael has been visiting me. He whispers to me at night. He says he wants to tell me something or sometimes that he wants to show me something. And the other night, I got up and looked under the bed—he whispers from beneath the bed—and then I stood up—and the ball was there, the one I keep in the car. It was right where I'd been sleeping."

"Will! Michael is haunting you?"

"Well, in a sense. I realize that I must have been sleep-walking and brought the ball in. Either that or Pete's gaslighting me."

"Wait. Don't explain it away. What about the whisper? Do the cats hear it?"

"That's what scares them. Last night I slept in the office with them. First good night's sleep all week for me."

"Michael is back. . ." she said, wonder in her voice.

"Maggie, I don't mean literally. It feels literal when it happens." He went into a recitation of how hypnogogic states work. "So you see, it's really me. I'm using a ghost to force myself to confront what I did that day."

"What you did? What do you mean?"

"I'd forgotten this, Maggie, in self-defense. It's horrible, horrible." He shook his head, close to tears. "I was the one, Mags. I killed Michael."

"I know."

"You *know?*" How can you know?"

"You told me the night it happened. And then you forgot. It's good that you did."

He nodded. "Got me through childhood, but I

wish I hadn't forgotten so well. I must've really been a basket case for Pete to go along with it."

"Will, don't give him any credit. He doesn't do anything for nothing. Think about it."

"About what?"

"After I ran into him the other day, I thought about it. I think he hid it because it made him look good. He took care of you, he comforted everyone. If you'd told your parents you shot Michael accidentally—"

"They would've hated me."

"Will!" Maggie snapped at him, made him look at her. "Don't feel sorry for yourself. Be honest. You know they wouldn't have hated you."

"Pete said they would."

"Fuck Pete! Fuck him! You might've believed him when you were a kid, but you know better now. What would your parents have done?"

Will knew, but couldn't say. He looked at the gravestone instead.

"They would have loved you and tried to make sure you felt no guilt."

He nodded. "Yeah. That's true."

"Pete wouldn't have had any attention then."

"Oh, please, Mags, even he's not that shallow."

"Oh, please, yourself. He's that shallow and more! You see things about people so easily, why are you so blind about him and about yourself?"

Will shrugged. "It's human nature, actually. Ego takes a beating about things like this and it's hard to get through it."

"But you know, right?"

"I know. I think. I still have trouble wrapping my mind around the idea that he's that bad."

"Don't worry about it for now. Tell me how Michael coming back ties in with your memory returning."

"Your people skills are a little raw," Will said lightly.

"Good thing I'm a vet. Will, this is me. Tell me."

"It's pretty simple. I remembered I killed him. I need forgiveness. I keep apologizing to my made-up ghost, but it hasn't been laid to rest yet. I have to continue to confess, to apologize, until my subconscious accepts it and the ghost is exorcised."

"Will?"

"What?"

"You said the ghost says something."

"Yes. I can't understand most of it. It wants to show me something, to tell me something."

"And you're not listening. You're too busy apologizing."

"There's nothing to listen to."

"You don't know that. Whether it's really Michael—don't make that face—or whether it's your own subconscious, something wants to tell you something. Until you hear it, it's not going away."

"I don't know."

"Look, let's assume it's your subconscious, since you won't allow it to be anything else."

"Maggie—"

"Hush. Your subconscious is still holding back a detail of some sort that you need to remember. Doesn't that make sense? Don't you think you should relax and listen?"

"I guess you think you're pretty smart."

"You bet."

Colonel Wallis Tilton had been doing a lot of thinking during the week. He had watched Doris get more and more irritated, had seen her mood improve whenever they were away from the house and seen her crumble into annoyance and anxiety when she was home. The more she was there, the worse it was, and vice versa.

And he himself had felt an unease like termites slowly burrowing into the very foundation of his home, into his walls, and, damn it, into him.

And he knew. He *knew.*

Goddamned Project Tingler is active.

Disgusted, he stood up and unhooked the cable box then started yanking cable out of his house. He should have put it together already. Pete Banning was one of the Tingler ops. His civilian status—*apparent* status—changed nothing.

The Goddamned thing of it was, Tilton couldn't do shit about it. He was lucky to be alive—the others in his camp were dead or sent far, far away. Tilton pulled half a string, got a discharge, gave it up. Looking back, the only reason he was alive now was probably because Doris was a cousin of the president.

Outside, he removed the cable entirely from his house, following it to the back of the yard where it attached to a small phone pole. There, he cut it off as high as he could, then coiled up the cut part and put it in the back of the tool shed.

Back inside, he took the cable box apart and swept the house for bugs. Clean.

"Wally, what are you doing?" Doris asked, coming in from the market.

"We just gave up cable television."

Her eyes widened. "You're kidding. What about our shows?"

"We're getting a satellite. I'll call in a little while."

Doris smiled. "Good. I never liked giving Caledonia Cable our business. That Banning character, wasn't he a problem for you years ago in the service?"

"He was." He hugged his wife. Banning was still a problem, but he didn't dare say so. All he could do was try to get rid of the new cable in town. If he was too overt, he'd be dead. Who could he talk to safely? Who would believe him?

"What was Pete Banning's brother's name, Doris?"

"Will? The psychologist? Such a nice man. Those two are like night and day."

75

The Deliciously Dark Bookshop in Red Cay was a marvelous little store stuffed full of specialty books, mostly horror, fiction and otherwise. Every bit of wall space was covered with posters or with strange *things* ranging from body parts from movies to gargoyles for sale. There were greeting cards with Dracula on them and jewelry in the shapes of skulls and snakes and bats, and Will was extremely surprised to find that he liked the place. Despite all the strange things—and a few very unusual people, mostly kids in black clothes and goth makeup—the store had a nice feel.

The signing was winding down when they got there, but there was still a line to see David Masters, who sat in a throne-like chair before a table in an alcove created by removing a set of bookshelves on the right hand side of the store. Will and Maggie grabbed a book and got in line. When other people came along, they let them go ahead.

"This is strange," Will whispered to Maggie.

"I know. I've never done it before. I feel like a fan. I'm a little embarrassed."

"Just don't ask him to sign your breasts, and I'm fine with it."

Maggie elbowed him in the ribs. "Watch it."

"Have you read any of his books?" he asked her.

"A couple. He gives me nightmares. I kind of like Dean Koontz."

"He's good. I've read a couple."

"I like the dogs."

Will raised his eyebrows.

"You know, lots of times he writes about golden retrievers. Sometimes they're regular dogs, sometimes they're preternaturally smart." She grinned. "You should take up writing thrillers, Will. You could do for ginger cats what he did for ginger dogs."

Will opened his mouth to reply and shut it again as he spotted Lara Sweethome enter the store. "Oh no," he muttered.

"What?"

"Quietly. One of my patients just walked in."

"Dr. Banning?" Lara called. "Dr. Banning, is that you?"

"That must be her."

Will nodded, then smiled and introduced Maggie. Lara started telling her all about her armless mother's ghost.

It went on forever.

Finally, it was their turn. Will almost put Lara ahead of them, but considering her penchant for talking, and his lack of desire to hear the same story yet again, he held his place.

David Masters looked up and smiled. A pleasant man—Maggie probably thought he was downright good-looking—he smiled at them then stared at the book Will held.

"How would you like that signed?"

"Oh, I don't—"

Maggie stepped on his foot and took the book. "Make it to Will and Maggie."

"Okay."

Masters began writing.

"This is embarrassing," Will said.

"Oh, don't be embarrassed, Dr. Banning," piped up Lara. "Mr. Masters, this is Dr. Banning, he's my psychologist, and that lady is Dr. Maewood, she was my veterinarian until my little Scottie dog passed away in 1993. Dr. Banning, are you going to ask Mr. Masters about my ghost?"

Masters looked as confused as Will felt, but after a moment, everything started to gel in various minds and Will was glad of Lara's introduction.

"A psychologist?"

"Yes."

Masters glanced at Lara, who was obviously going to stick like glue. "I'm writing a book with a psychologist protagonist, Doctor. If you're not in a huge hurry, would you let me buy you a cup of coffee when I'm done here? If I could ask you a question or two, it would really help me. I'm in a little bit of a bind for an answer." He took a business card from his shirt pocket, wrote on it, then put it in the book and handed it to Maggie.

"My pleasure." Will accepted the book from Maggie and smiled at Lara. "I'll see you next week."

She started to protest, then forgot about him when Masters addressed her. Will paid for the book and they stepped outside and away from the window before checking the card.

"Lara is a nice person, but I can't talk to him with her breathing down my neck," he said.

"Of course not. So, what's it say?"

"Miss Scarlett in the pantry with the dagger."

"Wiseass."

"He wants to meet at the coffee shop on the pier in twenty minutes."

"Let's start walking."

76

The Pigskin Sports Bar's parking lot was less than half full but it sure as hell looked inviting to Pete Banning when he pulled in for a cold one. He had worked hard and the brew would be a richly deserved reward. After fucking Heather Boyd until her eyes were ready to pop out—the girl was insatiable and had damn near worn him out—he'd made six house calls to install various bugs and cameras. It was time for a break.

He walked into the cool, dark bar, and was instantly hit by a barrage of sports noise from the eight televisions scattered around the place, all of which had been equipped with new cables by Mickey earlier in the week. Live baseball was the big thing at the moment, Angels versus Padres, though at least one TV was running an old Super Bowl game.

"Miller Draft," he told the bartender, sliding onto a stool. "How's business?"

"Fair." The bartender looked at him. "You're the cable guy. Banning?"

"Pete. Owner/manager."

"Nice picture. Funny thing, though."

"What's that?"

"Ever since you installed the new cable, something funny's been going on over there." He pointed to an empty group of tables where a TV was being ignored. "Some sort of double picture or something. Puts people off. They say it's a ghost."

"Ghost?"

"Oh, well, you know how it goes. There's an old ghost story about this place. Former owner hung himself. That's true, but the ghost part. . . I dunno." He shook his head. "A few people like to blame broken glasses and so forth on the ghost, but nothing spooky's ever happened here before. It's all been talk. Go have a look. Some of the customers say they can see a dead guy hanging there, sort of superimposed over the screen."

Pete snorted, then walked over and looked.

And saw it. "Holy shit." Shimmering transparently before the screen, which was playing the Angels/Padres game, was a dim image of a man, hanging by a noose. Pete shuddered slightly, glad he couldn't see it better; the tongue lolled, the eyes bulged, he could even see that the face was purple with trapped blood. "Incredible," he muttered, walking from side to side. The form seemed to be almost in front of the television, though some of it went through the set itself. Looking up, Pete saw that a dark-stained open beam lay in precisely the right spot to hold the spectral rope. "I'll be damned. I'll be Goddamned!" He reached up and snapped off the set, then looked away, clearing his vision. When he turned his gaze upward again, the hanging man was still there, even with the set off. "I'll be fucked six ways to Sunday. This isn't supposed to. . ."

"What?"

"Nothing." He waved off the bartender, who had followed him. The Tingler microwaves were meant to disrupt thought, to bring out and prey upon the frailties of an individual human mind. The waves piped into places like this via the new cable held no subliminal messages, they were simply a tweaked-up frequency that messed with brain function.

These particular extra low frequency waves rarely, in earlier Tingler experiments, produced anything in the shared-hallucination camp, and although it was possible that a person could, after a long enough exposure, be plagued by hallucinations when the set wasn't transmitting, it wasn't expected.

In fact, it was fucking rare as hell.

And here I am, seeing somebody else's hallucination and the goddamned set isn't even on.

He and the bartender returned to the bar. "A lot of people see it?"

"Yeah. Most people." The guy used a remote to turn the set back on. "It's less noticeable when the TV's on. So what is it? You're the expert."

"You got me. Get me another beer, will you?"

The bartender nodded, filled a fresh glass and set it before Pete, who asked, "You can see it?"

"Yeah, but I don't like to admit it, not unless somebody else says they do and they're not soused, you know? I sure never saw anything like it before. It's like one of those Disneyland things—like in the Haunted Mansion, you know, where the ghost gets in the cart with you at the end?"

"Hologram. Yeah."

Somebody called the bartender away, which was good because Pete wanted to stare at the alleged ghost while he finished his beer. The phantom was sort of in the television, but sort of outside of it. Damndest thing he'd ever seen. The barkeep was right; the thing looked like a faint hologram.

He drained his glass, then went out to the SUV and phoned Nedders.

"Got a mass sighting of an apparition."

"Where?"

"In a bar."

"Real funny," Nedders said. "Pink elephant, is it?"

"No. Something's hinky. I saw it, too. Evidently, it's been there for days, appeared right after we installed. It's a dead guy, hung himself on a rafter. It's a ghost. And it doesn't go away when the tube is off."

"Well, fuck me," Nedders said. "I didn't really think that would happen. Shouldn't happen. The boys at the top haven't figured out how to make a ghost appear." He barked a dry laugh.

"Well, one did. You sure there's nothing subliminal programmed in?"

"As sure as possible. No. It's just the Tingler wavelength. Subliminals belong to the other guys. Project Sybil's subliminal messaging. Project Medusa is visual hallucinations."

"Right. Any crossovers from Medusa on the Tingler team?"

"No."

"By the way, we installed at Colonel Tilton's house last week. Remember that old bastard?"

"Sure do. You have him bugged?"

"No. Not yet. Is the old silver eagle knowledgeable about anything anymore?"

"No. Completely out of the circuit since retirement. Old boy never really wanted in in the first place." Nedders cleared his throat and spoke tersely, "Nevertheless, something has happened."

"What?"

"You've been breached."

"*What?*"

"You left your home office open, Chief."

"I did? How do you know?"

"Because your wife walked in. She didn't see the camera that watches the room, that's for sure."

"Felicia went in there?"

"She sure did. How much did those boobs set you back? What a looker."

"What are you talking about?"

"She walked in naked. Looked like she'd been working out. I'd say it looked like she'd been fucking but that came later."

"She's cheating on me?"

"Yeah. With your secretary. She brought her in and showed her your screens. Your secretary—calls herself Labouche?"

"Yeah."

"Labouche was all over her. I couldn't see the screens, but they were watching you do some woman and they were grooving on it."

"Felicia's no lezzie. Neither's Labouche."

"Then you better smell their breath, Pete, because you are wrong, wrong, wrong. And you didn't background check Labouche, did you?"

"With that mouth?"

"With that mouth. You let your dick do too much of your thinking for you. That'll get you in trouble every time, Bucko. I checked her out. Can't be sure yet, but she might be a spy in your ointment."

"Spy? What do you mean, spy?"

"Military. Anti-Tingler people. Same ones Tilton used to be friendly with. Can't be sure yet, in fact, it's mostly a hunch—she was in the Air Force for one tour—but I think she was handpicked to keep an eye on you."

"Shit. I better take care of her."

"No. They're going to take care of you. They're pissed at you for cheating on them."

Pete suddenly got a hard-on, wondering if they'd go for a three-way.

"Don't even think about it," Nedders said, knowing how he thought. "Don't go home. Don't go to the office. Go blow yourself or something. Just don't be where they could find you for now."

"My wife is no killer."

"You didn't know she liked pussy, either. But you're right, she probably isn't a killer. But Labouche is a cipher. I had a lipreader look at the video. They want revenge." That dry laugh again. "From what we could tell reading lips, it's too bad you went and shoved it up Labouche's ass."

"Jennifer Labouche is a dumb blonde, Captain. She seriously thinks that swallowing sperm will make her boobs grow."

"Pete, you're an ass if you believe that. Put your goddamned dick away and give those women some credit. Male chauvinists are a dying breed, Chief. Smart women are killing them. We have three women on Tingler and I wouldn't want to cross them any more than you."

Emotions roiled up. Nedders was saying he was as harmless as a woman, and he didn't like that. But he was right about everything else, so he was probably right about the women—Jennifer, Felicia, and the gender in general. "Shit." He dug in his glove box for Rolaids.

"Don't do anything until your Uncle Neddy says so. Just stay low. Wouldn't hurt if you got out of town until the intelligence boys find out what we need to know."

"I'll stay low."

"Pete?"

"Yeah."

"I know you like to masturbate on that satellite receiver."

"How do you—"

"You think I don't keep an eye on you? I'm your Charlie, you're my Angel."

"Fuck you."

"Hey, cool off. You can spew on that dish all you want, what do I care? But not until I give the go-ahead. Stay away from Felsher Hill."

77

"So you live in Baudey House?" Maggie said as she, Will, and David Masters held on to their coffee cups. They sat at a small round table on the windy pier just outside the little white frame shack of a fish and chips stand toward the end of the pier. Baudey House and the lighthouse were visible on Byron's Finger, cliffs jutting out into the ocean as far or farther than the pier. It was hard to tell.

Masters smiled a little shyly. "That's home."

"Is it haunted?" Will asked.

"Residually, yes."

"Residually? That's like the old perfume on a handkerchief example you gave?"

Will's eyes slid briefly toward Maggie, a half smile on his lips. The man was telling her he'd beat her to the punch—if he'd paused for an instant, she would have piped up with the cat crap simile.

"That's what I mean," Masters said. "Once quantum physics gets involved in these things, parapsychology will lose some of the onus that surrounds it. I say that because of the look on your face, Doctor."

"Will. It's true, I'm a skeptic."

Maggie rolled her eyes for Masters. The writer grinned. "I'm a skeptic myself."

Will nodded. "I have to admit, I was very impressed with what you said in your interview. But I'm more skeptical than you are."

"Only because you haven't seen as much as I have."

Will smiled. "That remains to be seen. The thing is, Mr. Masters—"

"David."

"David," Will continued. "I've seen things that I can't explain. I'm sure there's a logical explanation for them, something rational."

Masters sipped his coffee. "Have you ever thought about this: What we consider rational today was irrational a century ago. Go to the moon in 1900? Totally irrational. Now? Been there, done that. I believe there's a rational explanation for everything, Will. Absolutely everything. The problem is we don't have a rationale for some things yet. Like ghosts. That's what you're talking about, right?"

"Right. And you make a very valid point. It's easy for me to fall out of a neutral state about such things."

"Same here. It's easy for a skeptic to slip into a state of disbelief that causes him to think everything paranormal is fraudulent. Some magicians who specialize in debunking call themselves skeptics, but they're way to the right of that. Because they can do a trick—make a ghost appear, for example—they assume that the appearance of an apparition is *always* a trick.

"A magician who performs that trick has proven one thing, and one thing only. That he can mechanically make us see a false apparition. He has not proven that there is no such thing as an apparition. Unfortunately, if the magician has become narrow-minded, he asserts that his trick is proof there are no real apparitions. And you know what?"

"What?" Maggie asked, pushing hair out of her face.

"Somebody who bends the facts to suit his personal beliefs can't be open-minded, can't be a skeptic. The debunker has a set of beliefs that are as strong and solid as those of the believer. Each must sway everything to fit in with his or her own personal world view." He looked at Will. "So, do you feel you can still call yourself a skeptic?"

Will didn't answer for a long moment. Seeing strain in his face, Maggie took his hand under the table and held it.

"We're having problems with apparitions and other phenomena in Caledonia."

"As your patient mentioned."

"Yes. I haven't experienced her, uh, ghost, but we," he glanced at Maggie, eyes hopeful, "have experienced a couple of them—apparitions—at our friends' home. A few other patients have mentioned the same kind of thing. And I'm having a huge upsurge in my practice. People are exhibiting schizoidal symptoms from hearing voices in their heads to, well, you name it."

David nodded and sat forward, arms on the table, coffee forgotten. "Any ideas about what's going on?"

"Animals were affected," Maggie said when Will glanced at her. "At first, it was wildlife, but that's tapered off over the last few days. Pets are still affected. I was thinking about geomagnetic anomalies, but from what I could find out, nothing strange is going on."

"Holograms," Will said. "But why would someone beam holograms into a few peoples' houses?"

"It's possible," Masters said, "but it doesn't explain the other phenomena."

Will nodded. "There's an idea about schizophrenics that I've never given credence to that maybe deserves some attention. A few of my collegues believe that schizophrenics are ultra-sensitive— which they do tend to be, to be fair. They believe they pick up on things that are normally beyond the five senses."

"Like ghosts?"

Will studied David. "Ghosts, yes. Schizophrenics are people who are overloaded with input, whether it's real or imagined. They lack the filters most of us rely on."

"Filters," Masters repeated. "Your filters are being damaged by something."

Will and Maggie traded glances. "That makes sense," Will said. "How'd you do that?"

"Because I'm not living in it and because coming up with stuff is how I earn my keep."

Beneath the table, Will's hand tightened around Maggie's, almost squeezing too hard. "My brother died when I was ten. He was sixteen. It was a shooting accident. I only recently remembered that I caused it to happen. It was my fault. For the last few nights, he's been whispering to me from under my bed." His hand squashed hers. "If that doesn't sound like a case for a psychologist, nothing does. I've assumed it's all due to dealing with the memory, and I've tried to apologize to him even though I have believed it's my own subconscious that is acting as my brother. I'm telling you this for three reasons. The first is that I'm desperate. The second is that I've been insisting

I'm dreaming the voice, but when I try lucid dreaming, it doesn't work because I'm not asleep."

He paused, letting up on Maggie's hand. She stroked the back of his with her thumb.

"And what's the third reason?" the writer asked.

"My cats won't sleep in the bedroom anymore."

"Well, whatever it is, I don't think you arguing with your subconscious in the privacy of your own mind would scare your cats." David Masters finished his coffee. "Okay if I come by?"

"Just say when."

78

Pete Banning, his feet on Mickey Elfbone's coffee table, sucked on a bottle of Bud he'd helped himself to and watched a snowy picture from a shitty little local station that almost came in without cable. Mickey was out on the job, and Pete had let himself in the same way he'd let himself into his brother's house after leaving the Pigskin. A little sleight of hand and—*voila*—locks opened up for him like Heather Boyd's legs.

He'd earned the Bud by staying in Will's house long enough to install a camera and bug in the living room and another in the bedroom, just for fun.

The fucking place gave him the heebie jeebies from the moment he broke in. It looked okay, downright homey in fact. Will had two fucking cat posts, so kitty was probably the only kind of pussy he was getting, but Pete didn't catch sight of a whisker. That was normal; animals usually took off when he was around.

He'd started to chuckle over that then stopped, his laugh swallowed instantly by the house.

For the life of him, he didn't know why he felt like the house was watching him. It was the same feeling he had back on some of his missions, squatting in a jungle, hoping the enemy wasn't watching him take a shit. It was like that; it wasn't just the being watched, it was feeling helpless while being watched, the sensation that something was going to shoot at him while he was squeezing out a loaf. He hated it.

First thing he did to fight back was check the house. Cable was off. No security cams. Maybe it was just the fucking cat watching him from some hiding place. Goddamn cats would stare down anybody. They had no respect for authority. *Fucking cats.* He didn't much like dogs either, except for the well-trained ones, but at least they did what you told them.

Pete belched long and deep then got off the couch to grab another beer. Will's entire house creeped him out, but it was when he was in the master bedroom that Pete practically turned tail. It was when he thought he heard something.

His name.

Pete. Michael's voice.

Pete had whirled from the television and looked around the room. The place was empty. Hurrying through the job, he told himself it was something outside or maybe the mystery cat hissing, something. He even started thinking that maybe, although Will's set was off, something was going on like it was at the Pigskin. Whatever it was, he didn't like it. And he couldn't stop thinking about Michael. Michael the golden boy. Michael, who was taller, handsomer, excelled in school and at sports. Michael with girls coming out of his ass. God, he'd hated that bastard. The only thing he ever did for Pete was die.

Back on Mickey's couch, he flipped off the cap off the beer and chugged half the bottle. If he'd lived, what would Michael say now? Pete had the money, the business, the charm, the women. "Fuck you, Michael," he muttered, and finished the beer. "I piss on your grave, big man."

Bored, but not quite enough to risk effects of the new cable, Pete got up and started going through Mickey's racks of DVDs. "Christ, fucking goddamn pussy." Everything was in order, almost prissy, and there were a hell of a lot of musicals in there. "Goddamn faggot? Mickey? Are you a faggot?" He chuckled, thinking about the ribbing he would give the guy when he came home. He knew Mickey wasn't a fag, but he thought maybe he could make him wonder about himself. That would be fun.

He finally found a DVD of Gladiator and stuck that in the machine. It started playing, but Pete wasn't through exercising. He got the last beer out of the fridge and walked outside, standing against the railing to get a little wind and sun. He looked around the apartment courtyard. Nothing with tits by the pool. No tits anywhere. Some guy lifting weights in an apartment across the yard. Window shiny clean, no curtains in sight. Fucker was showing off his precious pecs. He'd rib Mick about that too. Ask if he liked to watch.

Movement in the apartment next door caught his eye. The curtains were half closed, the lights off. In fact, there was a big lock over the doorknob that meant the place was empty. But it wasn't. There was a skinny broad pacing around in there. He watched her for a moment as she moved around, a big cat in a cage. It was weird.

"Shit!"

He could've sworn that the woman was far back in

the apartment, but suddenly her long pale face was in the window staring at him with dead eyes. "You fucking bitch!"

He beat it back into Mickey's and slammed the door. "Crazy fucking bitch."

"Hi Pete," Mickey said as he came through the door an hour later.

" 'Hi Pete?' That's all? Aren't you surprised to see me?" Pete sat up straighter, fighting off the beer-drowsiness that had set in.

"You parked your SUV in my garage slot," Mickey explained. "It's okay," he added, afraid of the wrath of Pete. "It's just how I knew you were here."

"What the fuck is that on your head?"

"Like it? A kid from downstairs gave it to me."

Pete knew he was lying, but didn't give a shit. "Who's the crazy bitch that lives next door? Fucking nutcase."

"What?"

"The bitch next door. She plastered her face against her window and stared at me like a god-damned zombie. What is she? A crack whore?"

Mickey stared at him a moment then spoke flatly. "She's dead."

"She looked dead, fucking fish face."

"She *is* dead. Suicide. They took her away a couple days ago."

Pete sat up. "No shit?"

"No shit."

"You're telling me that was a ghost?"

"Yeah."

"You see it?"

"Me, and a cop, too. He saw her."

"What'd he say?"

"Not much."

"He tell anybody?"

"Doubt it. Who'd believe him? And nobody's been snooping around."

In covert ops, Pete had seen amazing things, some of which he couldn't quite understand. This had to be something to do with Project Tingler, but. . . He thought back to other projects he'd heard a little about. The ones involving remote viewing, attempts to increase psychic powers in humans. *Maybe Tingler's the magic bullet.* He smiled. "Mick, my man, you're out of beer. Why don't you run down and buy us some."

"Sure, Pete. Arc you staying?"

"You got plans?"

"Nope."

"I'm staying, but if anybody asks, even if you run into Jennifer or my wife, you haven't seen me. Got it?"

79

Wallis Tilton got Will Banning's answering machine all afternoon, and he'd hung up every time. This wasn't something you could leave a message about. Frustrated, he tried again.

It wasn't bad that Will Banning was unavailable; it had given Tilton time to think back. Memories he'd locked away had returned; memories of seeing companions laid low by Project Tingler. He was supposed to be driven nuts or killed—whatever—in the early days too, but he was a resister. His mind had some kind of built-in defense mechanism that kept anything more than uneasiness from getting through when those bastards played with their microwave machines. He knew with certainty now that what he'd felt before he yanked the cable and the presence of Pete Banning were no coincidence. Tingler had gone into a full-scale experiment phase. Caledonia was isolated. It was perfect.

Will Banning's phone began to ring.

Tilton thought back to earlier times. Experimenting on the public was nothing new, and only slightly less common than experimenting on service men and women. Decades ago, when the Soviets and the Americans were just beginning to zap each other with electromagnetic radiation, the Navy released bacterial fogs in San Francisco Bay and other major cities. Harmless forms of pneumonia. Only a slight upsurge in cases reported in the areas. They did that and lots more. It all reeked, harmless or not, and the military even admitted to doing a lot of it. In these days of "for your own good" militia might, it was even acceptable. People were willing to sacrifice freedom for their country, for their own safety. What they didn't get was that, no matter how good the intentions, too much power always led to corruption. Hell of a situation. Now here it was, Power Incarnate, stinking up his own hometown.

"Hello. Will Banning."

"Hello, Dr. Banning," he began. He explained just enough to convince Will to meet him in the park on the Crescent, where they wouldn't be overheard, then hung up and told Doris, who was her own sweet self, that he'd be back soon.

80

Daniel Hatch had finally lost his virginity, but as he said good-bye to the seventy-year-old Jehovah's Witness, leaning down to plant a pristine kiss on her withered cheek, Dick started nagging him again.

He closed the door. "You made me have intercourse with a woman as old as my mother," Daniel said. "Older."

And you liked it!

"*You* liked it. I thought it was disgusting."

Let's go cruise the bars for some young stuff. You'll like that, too. If we can't find anything around here, we'll go down to the Candle Bay boardwalk and pick up a hooker.

"No!" Daniel nearly yelled the word as he turned on the shower and began undressing, anxious to get the smell of ancient sex off him. He felt dirty. Filthy dirty, like he'd broken a taboo.

You're such a sissy, Daniel. Enjoy the smell. Dick started laughing.

Daniel opened his razor and put a new blade in it

for a nice, close shave, then set it on the shower shelf next to his shaving cream. Dick kept laughing, but Daniel paid no attention as he climbed in the shower and let the hot water beat over him.

When are you going to wash me?

Silently, Daniel shampooed his hair.

I want sex. Hurry up. We've got to go find a good looking babe who'll give me a blow job.

"Shut up!" Daniel yanked on Dick, lathering him so roughly it hurt.

Harder. I like it.

Dick grew and spoke of women in pornographic poses, of huge breasts, of bush and tush. He spoke in the most obscene language possible and was almost in total control when Daniel realized he was still holding on to his penis. *To Dick.* "No," he said, removing his hand. "You can't control me."

Of course I can. You know I can. Say it. Say, I am your slave, Mr. Dick.

"Shut up." Daniel smoothed shaving cream over his cheeks then picked up the razor and began to shave. Using an old-fashioned safety razor was trickier than the new kinds, but this one had been his father's and he just couldn't give it up. Carefully, he ran it along his jawline.

Dick throbbed between his legs, demanding attention in a strident voice. *Put that thing down and finish me off! Can't you finish what you started, Daniel? Sure you can. Give me your hand. Just for a minute. Then you can shave and we'll go find a girl.*

"No." His hand jerked as he spoke. Blood welled from a sharp stinging cut. "Damn it, Dick. Just shut up."

Dick throbbed harder. *I'm the one in charge, Daniel. You shut up and get to work.*

Something twinged in his head. He saw red. He

really did. He didn't know that "seeing red" was more than an expression. But it was.

Come on, Daniel. Finish what you started!

"You're not the boss of me," he murmured, taking the blade out of the razor, careful not to touch the sharp edges. "You can't tell me what to do." Calmly, he placed the empty razor back on the shelf.

You wouldn't! Dick screeched as Daniel took him in hand.

"Yes, I would."

Dick shrank in fear, but Daniel stretched him out taut and put the sharp blade against the pink skin.

It barely hurt at all.

81

David Masters arrived at Will's house just before six P.M., five minutes ahead of Maggie, who had wanted to stop by the clinic and then her home to change clothes and feed Anteater and the cats.

The cats stood sentry under the table while they ate fish and chips from a little place on Main Street. Will spent most of the meal telling them both about his meeting with Colonel Tilton. Masters, slightly familiar with military antics, held that Tilton made a lot of sense. They finished eating and Masters rose. "Have you unhooked your cable yet?"

"No. I thought I'd let you check out the place first."

"Good. Let's see what happens."

Will led them to the living room. "See how the cats stopped at the entrance to the room? I wonder if they'll come in when we unplug."

"We'll know soon."

Will turned on the system. "Don't expect much."

"Unless you have the senses of a feline," Maggie added.

They let the news run for nearly ten minutes before David spoke. "I don't feel a thing."

"I don't either," Maggie said.

Will agreed. "Let's try the bedroom." He led them in, feeling stranger and stranger, not in an eerie way, but more along the lines of humiliation.

"Okay." He turned on the set. "The only experiences I've had have been after three A.M."

"With or without the TV on?"

"With and without. One night nothing happened and that was the only nights the cats followed me in."

"They must have sensed the absence of whatever is bothering them," Masters said.

"That's the best explanation I've heard."

"It's not much of an explanation. Look, I've been thinking about what you told me this afternoon and this evening. I think maybe the signal the Colonel says is being sent via the cable boxes is meant to cause symptoms of schizophrenia. But maybe it can do more. Maybe it opens the floodgates."

"You mean it's sensitizing people to hauntings?"

"Why not? If there's validity to schizophrenics being bombarded with input, that could certainly be part of it. Or maybe it energizes haunts on its own. Brings them to life." He paused. "Bad choice of words."

"I understand," Will said. "So what if there aren't any ghosts around?"

"Then maybe it just gives you other symptoms depending on the person under attack. It could do both."

"The mind boggles," Maggie said, covering for

Will, who was fighting to be a skeptic instead of a debunker.

"It does," Will agreed.

Minutes passed without anything happening. "Nothing," Will said, relieved but embarrassed.

"Let's unplug and at least see if the cats are happier before we take off," Maggie said.

They unplugged the cable box in the bedroom then did the same in the living room. Almost immediately, all three cats walked cautiously into the room. Will undid the cable and held the box down to them to sniff. Freud hissed, but then that wasn't too unusual.

After thoroughly sniffing the room, the Orange Boys jumped into Will's recliner and started an old-fashioned grooming fest like nothing had ever been wrong.

"Should we see what they think of the bedroom?" David asked, stroking Jung's luxurious fur.

"We should, but no, let's not," Will said. "Just in case."

"I agree," Maggie said. "We don't want to freak them out when we're leaving."

"You'll see something a lot more interesting at Gabe and Kevin's house anyway," Will said, grabbing his keys. "Let's go. We're late."

82

"Did you see the look on his face when the Cock-burns materialized?" Maggie tipped her flute of champagne against Will's, all smiles as she sat back on Will's sofa.

Will laughed. "That was not the reaction I expected, not even from a ghost hunter. Not a trace of fear."

"He looked like a kid set loose in a candy store." She sipped champagne. "I think the idea that the ghosts will disappear with the cable boxes is devastating to him."

"Yeah. His loss, but not ours." Rorschach leapt into his lap, sloshing the champagne all over his pants.

"I'll get that." Maggie leaned forward and used her napkin to soak up the drops of sparkling wine. Her movements were brisk at first, then she slowed down as she moved higher up his thighs. She looked into his eyes. "Okay?"

"You missed a spot," he said.

"Where?"

"There." He pointed at a tiny water spot a little higher up.

She blotted it. "Okay?"

"Uh, there's one more on this leg. Here."

Her eyes were bright, her lips parted and damp. She gave him a funny little quirk of a smile then dabbed the napkin in the vicinity of the spot without looking. "How's that?"

"Fine," Will managed to stammer. He sat up a little, embarrassed by the sudden growth in the groin area. "I need a refill. How about you?"

She picked up her glass and drained it, then held it out while he poured. They toasted again and drank.

"So," Will said. "Is this the part of the date where we make out?"

"I'm not that easy," Maggie told him. Then she slowly licked her lips with the tip of her tongue. "You'll have to convince me."

"How?"

She smiled slowly, then tilted her glass until champagne trickled down into the hollow at the base of her neck then drizzled lower, disappearing beneath her pink silk blouse. "Oops." She undid the top two buttons, exposing cleavage and the top of a lacy push-up bra the same color as her shirt. Not taking her eyes off Will, she let a little more wine spill on her breasts. "I wish somebody had a napkin I could use before my bra gets all wet. I don't want to have to take it off."

Turned on as hell, Will looked at her in wonder, as well as lust. This was a side of Maggie's personality he'd never seen before. He'd never dreamed a coquette lurked behind that self-possessed exterior. "Uh, I think the napkin is used up. I could get another."

He started to rise, but she reached out and pressed his leg. He sat. "What do you want me to do?" He was sixteen again, fumbling and nervous. He loved it.

"I guess you'll just have to make do." Her voice trembled as much as his hands.

"With?"

She poured the last of the champagne down her neck. "Oh, darn." Setting the glass aside, she slowly reached toward him, hand curled gently but for one finger. She touched his lip. Slowly. Gently. Withdrew. "Any ideas?"

"Give me another hint."

A tiny smile trembled as she put her finger to her lips and wet it with the tip of her tongue. She put it back to Will's lips again, a little firmer, and ran it over his lower lip, slowly pressing down until she was touching the sensitive inner flesh.

His mouth closed around her finger and he laved it with his tongue.

"That's it," she said huskily. She kept her finger in his mouth but slowly pulled back.

Will let her finger go when he was inches from her neck. He bent to her flesh, smelling her warm heady fragrance despite the champagne. Slowly, he pressed his lips to her skin, just between the swell of her breasts. After a moment of stillness, he tasted her. She shuddered and moaned softly as she wrapped her fingers in his hair and urged him on.

83

Jennifer Labouche smiled into the dark night from the window of Felicia Banning's bedroom. She was in love for the first time in her life. When she'd begun her assignment keeping track of Project Tingler, that's all it was, an assignment with some very distasteful aspects, number one being Pete Banning and his goddamned prick. Getting close to his wife, Felicia, was part of the plan, though only as a friend.

Who could know that when they met, sparks would fly? Certainly not Jennifer, hardboiled military operative. She'd always preferred women, so her attraction wasn't a surprise, but she was a professional soldier. She never got involved. But Felicia was something special.

Tonight, after Felicia proposed they dump Pete and move in together, Jenny had told her lover everything she could. Felicia was alarmed and asked enough questions to understand that Jennifer's line of work was similar to Pete's military days. Secret stuff. She accepted it and in turn told Jennifer everything she could about herself, which turned out to be pretty vanilla. Jennifer found she loved that. She'd had enough of the games. She was thirty-one, and more than ready to settle down.

And so they agreed to get rid of Pete. And to become a couple. Although Jennifer hadn't told her yet, she was seriously thinking of retiring after the job was finished. Felicia would own Caledonia Cable and she'd need someone to help her run it.

She glanced at the glowing hands of the alarm clock. Three A.M. No sign of Pete. Felicia slept peacefully in the bed. And Jennifer, her Glock 9mm snug beside her, kept watch.

84

"Will. It's me. Michael. Listen!"

Will sat up in bed, disoriented. Three fifteen. The cats were in their usual spots, but he could feel the tension in their bodies. *Maggie?* he thought suddenly, then remembered she had gone home to her own brood sometime after midnight.

"Will. It's Michael. I have a message for you." Whispers from under his bed.

There was no cable box in the house. *I'm imagining things.* He lay back down. His subconscious must still be playing with him.

"It's me, Will. I'm real. It's Michael. You're not making me up."

Will wondered if he'd see anything if he looked under the bed. Michael, dead, gutshot. He shuddered and made himself close his eyes. He'd had enough ghost stories to last a lifetime.

"Will. Listen. Let me show you something. Will. It's Michael."

He thought about Masters's suggestion that the devices in the cable could actually allow you to sense things. Like ghosts.

Nah. The cats are here. They wouldn't be if he was really hearing a ghost. But maybe they weren't afraid of Michael. *Maybe they were just afraid of whatever the cable box was giving off.*

"Will! Please. It's Michael. Listen to me."

"Michael?" he asked softly. "Is that really you? Or have I lost my mind?"

"It's me. Listen to me."

"I'm sorry I killed you."

"You didn't."

"Yes, I did. It was an accident."

"Will, let me show you something."

The whisper grew louder, seeming to fill the room. It was all around him, in the air, in his mattress, his clothes, his body. As it enveloped him, he began to see a summer's day long ago.

Heat shimmered on the golden grass on Crackle Hill where Michael, Will, and Pete had gone to target shoot. It was a mile and a half bike ride to get there, then a half-hour hike on foot to reach the backside of the hill where there was an old log to set up tin cans to shoot. It was Will's first summer as a shooter and he loved it. Michael said he had a knack.

Pete hated that Will was a better shot than he was. Michael was, too. Pete hated, hated, hated it.

Today, like other days this summer, they had hiked the rolling meadows and set to shooting with a purpose. The only bad thing, in Will's opinion—and Michael's he knew now—was that Pete was with them. He was so sour he drained the happy right out of people, but when Will was with Michael, Pete didn't bother him much. He felt safe.

As far as Will was concerned, Michael was royalty. He was going into his senior year in high school. He was lighthearted, outgoing, excelled in both sports and academics, and had a smile that could light up a pavilion. He was growing into a handsome man with wide-open features, a square jaw, and broad shoulders.

Pete was something altogether different. He always looked sullen, always felt sullen. Even then, Will understood that Pete hated Michael for the same reasons Will loved him. Pete oozed jealousy.

Slighter of build and his face was narrower than Michael's but similar in features. He could have been almost as attractive as Michael but he tended to scowl, holding his lips in a grim line. He hated team sports, primarily because he wasn't much good at them, and while he wasn't a loner, he wasn't popular like Michael. His friends, like Mickey Elfbones, were as sullen and unfriendly as he was.

The one thing Pete did love was a practical joke, usually at Will's expense.

These were all things that Will didn't think about much consciously, and when they were plinking cans, he never thought about them unless he felt Pete's eyes boring holes through him. Michael was an excellent shot and he seemed to hit his targets effortlessly. He taught Will how to shoot and he caught on quickly. Pete wasn't a really bad shot, and Michael never crowed about it, but it drove Pete nuts anyway.

That day, they finished shooting and began heading back across the mile of meadowland. Pete had made a couple of dead-on hits, but Michael made three times that. Will had made two, as well, and, safe with Michael, he did a little teasing as they hiked home. Michael chuckled and Pete seethed as his older brother pointed out that little Will and Pete made the same number of dead-on hits.

Pete fell behind as they walked, but Will barely noticed because Michael was telling him stories about outer space and stuff. The two came to a delapidated old wooden rail ranch fence. Will bent to go between the two rails while Michael started to swing his leg over them. A shotgun blast rent the air.

Time stopped. Something hot spattered over Will and he couldn't figure out what it was. It was red. At the same time, he heard Pete laughing and screeching, "Ha ha! I scared you!"

Will stood staring at Michael, at the hole in his middle, at the daylight he could see beyond it. He couldn't comprehend what he saw even as time sped up and Michael crumpled to the ground.

"Scared you!" Pete repeated, running up. He saw the blood on Will, then looked down and saw Michael. Saw what was left of him. He looked from Michael to Will, back again, his facing draining of color. Finally, stilted, he said, "Oh my God. You killed him!"

Will stared up at him, at his shotgun. "You shot him."

Pete fell on his knees in front of his little brother. He laid his weapon on the ground by Michael's and took hold of Will's shoulders. "No, Will. I didn't shoot him. I was just walking along slow, looking for arrowheads. Your gun must have gone off when you went under the fence."

Will looked at the shotgun. It was Michael's. He'd let him carry the 12-gauge while he toted Will's smaller piece. Will loved carrying the big gun. "But it wasn't loaded," he said, voice breaking.

"Sorry. It must have been." As he spoke he finally

looked away from Michael and into Will's eyes. "I'll fix it for you, little brother."

Pete had never called him that before. Only Michael called him that.

Will didn't reply.

"Nobody but you and I need to know what you did. I'll tell Mom and Dad that his gun went off by accident while he was climbing the fence. Nobody will ever know that you shot him."

Numb, Will nodded. "Thank you."

"You're welcome. Remember, now. Michael carried the gun and it went off when he climbed the fence. Remember that. Forget that you shot him."

And Will did. For a long, long time.

Will came out of the vision, tears on his face. "Michael."

"Do you understand now?"

"Pete killed you. Why?"

"Because he hated me. It was a practical joke, Will. He didn't mean to kill me, but he did."

"I miss you, Michael. I love you."

"Be good, baby brother. Go live your life now."

Something rolled onto his chest. *The baseball.* He picked it up and smelled it, breathing in nostalgia. Silent tears rolled from the corners of his eyes. Tears of loss, tears of relief, tears of joy.

He slept peacefully among his felines, his dreams full of Michael, full of mostly repressed childhood memories. Not bad memories, but good ones he'd forgotten existed. Memories too painful until now to allow, memories that he had to suppress to be free of guilt. Days playing catch, nights camping out in the backyard. Going on the merry-go-round when he was too young for school, Michael standing by the tall white horse, one hand resting on Will's leg, making sure he wouldn't fall off. Playing tag, listening to Michael tell ghost stories or tales about Davy Crockett or a million other things.

The night was full of beautiful dreams. Only when he woke up did he feel the anger.

85

Pete Banning had some dreams of his own. They were all about Maggie Maewood and what he wanted to do to her.

Dressed in his skivvies after a night on the couch—Mickey offered him his bed, but Pete knew he slept in the nude and he wasn't about to lie where some other guy's dick and ass had rolled around—Pete ate a big breakfast. Mickey was a decent cook, a little heavy on the grease, but who fucking cared. He made bacon and eggs and hash browns. The coffee sucked, but Pete didn't complain.

After breakfast, he put his clothes back on and checked in with Nedders, who told him that if he wanted fresh clothes, he should go buy them rather than go home and change. So, he had time to kill and decided to spend it with the lady veterinarian.

He gave Mickey the day off and took his van, parked right in front of Maggie's house, went up and knocked on the door. And knocked some more. A dog barked upstairs.

Finally, he heard the dog bark again, behind the front door. Footsteps approached and the door opened. "Yes?" Maggie looked young and sleepy.

"I'm sorry. Did I wake you?"

"Yes." Her eyes had hardened. "What do you want?"

"To offer up an apology."

The dog growled, sensing its mistress's mood. "Fine," she said. "You offered. Now go away."

"I have something for you. A peace offering."

She eyed him warily. "Oh?"

"Free cable. I'm here to run the line and install however many boxes you want. See? I have the work truck and everything."

"Not interested."

"I know you have a satellite company, but this is free. Absolutely free. All the stations you get now and more."

"No. Go away."

"Sorry," he said, pulling his little .38 from his waistband. "Gotta come in or I gotta shoot you." He leveled the gun. "Or I could shoot your dog."

"Anteater. Hide."

The dog looked at her stupidly, then took off. Bat out of hell time.

"What kind of name is Anteater for a dog?"

She started to close the door so he pulled off a shot that whizzed past so close that it ruffled her hair. He glanced around. "Nice living out in the sticks all by yourself, huh, Maggie? I wish my neighbors weren't so close to my place. Have to watch the noise, you know? Now let me in or I'll get you before you can try to shut the door again. Get you right in the face. Let me in, I won't hurt you."

He was a little surprised when she stepped back and allowed him to enter. The surprise put him on guard or she might have managed to hit him with the tire iron she'd kept behind her back. Instead, he twisted her arm, but she wouldn't drop the damn thing until he heard a bone snap. The iron clattered to the floor.

Tears welled in her eyes as she cradled the arm. "Who the hell do you think you are?"

Holding the gun on her, he yanked her by the good arm. "You know who I am, and you know what I'm here for. Let's go. Upstairs." He poked her with the gun.

They marched up the stairs and at the top, Maggie yelled "Hide! Downstairs!" at the top of her lungs. Two cats and the dog he'd seen before all tore out of a room and raced down the stairs, nearly knocking Pete off his feet. He didn't quite get a shot off. "Bitch," he said, pushing her forward. "Get moving."

In the bedroom, he held the gun on her and rifled through her dresser. He pulled out panty hose, forced her down onto the four-poster bed, and started tying her down. The cunt screamed bloody murder when he grabbed the broken arm, so he took pity. She couldn't use it against him anyway.

Finished, he surveyed his work. In his haste, he hadn't made her strip, but cutting off the clothes would be more fun anyway. Her face, though tear-streaked was stone cold. He knew the look. "Bitch," he said. "I can have your body, but I can't have you, is that it?"

She didn't reply.

"I guess that's it, then. So guess what, bitch? I don't want you. I just want your body."

She wouldn't answer.

He put the gun on her dresser and undressed. "Look at me," he ordered.

She stared at the ceiling.

"Look at me, bitch. Look what I got for you. Gonna ram it up every hole in your body."

No response. He took his pocket knife from his pants pocket and opened it, holding it over her face. "Maybe I'll make some new holes to ram it up. Think you're tough, don't you? Not sobbing over the broken wing makes you a tough broad. Well, you don't know shit about tough. I'm gonna rip you in two, you goddamned whore."

The phone shrilled and she showed signs of life, but it stopped after four rings. "Where's your machine?" he demanded, taking the broken arm in his hand.

"Broken," she muttered.

"Good. Probably just somebody wanting to sell you something anyway. Now, let's do something about all those clothes."

86

When Maggie, who always answered her phone if she was home, didn't answer her phone, Will felt unreasonable worry. Silly, probably. He knew it was most likely born of excitement and anger at what he learned during the night, but it didn't matter. He almost tried the phone again, but decided to just go on over.

He pulled on his clothes and put food down for the cats, then drove toward Maggie's, pausing only to drive through CharPalace for a couple of Sunny Sandwiches and coffees. As he drove, he imagined how annoyed she'd be at his showing up, relatively unannounced. They planned on getting together, but they hadn't set an exact time, though it definitely involved some kind of morning meal.

He turned onto her street, too pleased about seeing her to think about Pete, but as he approached and saw the Caledonia Cable van out front, his gut tightened. *Pete.* But Pete didn't drive this old van. He had a nice new one. And he rarely used that—at least Will always saw him driving his own vehicle. No, this had to be Mickey or some other employee.

But why here? She doesn't have cable. Why so early? Shit.

He didn't knock on her door. Instead, he found his key to her house and unlocked the door, stepping quietly inside. It was quiet, empty. Then Anteater's muzzle and button black eyes came around the corner. The dog smiled and took a step forward. Will made a quiet signal and then one to stay. Thank heaven Maggie was so into communicating with animals. He was glad it rubbed off.

He tiptoed across the room to the little spare bedroom the dog was in. The dog trembled. "Hide," Will said softly. After the briefest hesitation, Anteater got down on his belly and crawled under the bed. Will saw the cats' eyes watching him as the spread raised. "Stay," he told the animals. "Hide."

He left the room, looked around the living room again. Behind the door, a big crowbar lay on the floor. He picked it up and started up the stairs, hoping to avoid the creaks.

Barely started, he could hear a voice above him. *Pete.* He was talking in that low nasty voice he used when he didn't think anybody who mattered could hear him. It was a steady stream of talk. Not a peep out of Maggie, but she was up there. He had no doubt.

Keep talking, you sonofabitch. Keep talking. Will took the stairs as quickly as he dared. He paused at the top, listening.

"There we go, Maggie, you didn't need that robe anyway, did you? Goodness, I'm going to have to sharpen my knife after cutting through all that terry cloth. Now, let's have a look at you. Pajamas with little dog drawings all over them. Isn't that cute. Is that what the well-dressed virgin vet wears these days? Okay, now you just stay real still and we'll have those buttons off in a jif. Are you one of those women who wears a bra to bed?

"Didn't think so. You don't have much up there, do you? But what you have, it's damned nice. Now, if you promise not to struggle while I cut off your bottoms and your panties—do you wear panties to bed, Maggie?—I'll let you keep your top on, just open so I can bite your titties. If you struggle, I'll take it off you and not worry about hurting your arm. It's already broken, anyway, right?"

His laugh filled Will with fury. He had crossed to the doorway while Pete tormented Maggie. Now, hefting the crowbar, he peered in. Pete, naked, stood over Maggie, a knife flashing in his hand. Hunks of cloth lay on the floor around his feet. As he began pulling down her pajama bottoms, Will sprung, the iron aimed at the back of his brother's head.

Pete heard him and moved like a snake—the blow got him across the back and upper arm. Barely wavering, he grinned at Will as he ran at him. Will whipped up the iron, but Pete was trained in martial arts and he deflected it easily. It slid under the bed.

Pete grinned, bouncing back and forth on his feet like a fighter getting warmed up. Like a gorilla getting ready to kill.

"What's the matter, Willy? Don't know how to fight?"

"You killed Michael. You told me I killed him. How can you live with yourself, you son of a bitch?"

"You're the shrink. You tell me."

"Let Maggie go. The police are on the way."

"The police are on the way," Pete repeated, singsong. "The police are on the way. Bullshit. You wouldn't have known to call them. Now, I think we'd better get you all tied up. Then you can watch me do your girly friend."

"Get away from her."

"Hands behind your head, baby brother. Do that or I cut her. Like this."

Quick as a flash, he slashed Maggie's leg. She uttered a strangled cry. Will responded instantly, tackling Pete.

They rolled on the floor, Pete still holding the knife, trying to stab Will. Will fought through sheer willpower, but Pete was getting the upper hand. Somewhere in the background, Will heard Maggie yell, "Up here!"

Pete jabbed him in the neck and Will nearly blacked out, but he heard footsteps and so did Pete because the iron fingers backed off for an instant. Will got both his hands up to Pete's face and went for his eyes, then Pete was yanked up and off him. He saw Pete's wife untying Maggie and another woman holding a gun on him.

"Will?" said the strange woman.

"Yeah."

"Move your ass."

He crawled to the other side of the bed, dragged himself up as Felicia helped Maggie sit up and cover herself. She looked at him, agony in her eyes. "You're bleeding."

He glanced down, saw a few slashes on his arms. "I'm fine."

"Pete Banning, you're a dead man walking," said the other woman. "Drop the knife."

"Blow me, you fucking bitch!"

"Okay, if you say so."

She fired. Pete's back straightened then he bent, hands to his groin. "You fucking bitch. You goddamned fucking bitch!"

"Sorry, Petey," said the woman. "I was going to make it a head shot until you told me to blow you. That was just one time too many."

Pete dropped to the floor.

"Call the police," said Maggie.

"No," said the woman. She flashed credentials. "Military's after him. We'll take care of it." She looked at Felicia. "He probably won't die from that wound, but he's not going to be raping any more women, either."

Maggie stood up, steadied on Will's arm. "What the hell?"

"Don't worry," said the government woman. "Will, you take her to the doctor. When you come back, you won't know anyone's been here. People are waiting to come in and help. They'll get him out of here and clean up like it never happened. You stay quiet. Got it?"

Will looked at Maggie. "I can live without all the legal hassles. Can you?"

"Yes. My animals will be locked in a room downstairs. Make sure no one bothers them."

"Will do."

"Do you want me to help you dress?" Felicia asked.

Maggie gazed at Will, almost looking pain-free. "He can help me."

Epilogue

Fall flirted with the late-summer sun as Will and Maggie stood over Michael's grave. Maggie bent and laid a bunch of yellow daisies before the stone. "I'm so glad you found out the truth," she murmured.

Will hugged her, careful to avoid the arm in a sling. "He hasn't been back since," he said, looking at the old baseball cradled in his hand. "In a strange way, I miss him."

"Gabe and Kevin sure won't miss the Cockburns."

He chuckled. "No, they won't." Two weeks after Pete disappeared, leaving his wife and her gun-toting friend to run the cable company with Mickey as the manager, all of the new cable boxes had disappeared. Strange behaviors, like Mickey's tin foil hat paranoia dissipated quickly, but many of the ghosts remained, though the ones Will knew of were weakening fast. Or, more likely, people's brains were restoring their wiring. Kevin was a quick healer; he barely saw the ghosts now, but Gabe was still unnerved once or twice a day. It would pass, much to David Masters's sorrow.

The writer was spending most of his time in town visiting haunts, still the kid in the candy store.

"I wonder what happened to Pete."

"Maggie, he's gone. That's all that matters. I don't want to know what happened to him—I've seen too many *X-Files* reruns."

She laughed. "You're right." Studying the grave, she said, "I'm sorry Michael died so young."

"Me, too." He looked at the baseball, his throat tight. "It's time to say good-bye. He doesn't need to hang around here anymore now that I know the truth."

"Bye, Michael," Maggie said. She stepped back, into the shade of the old live oak.

Will knelt. "Thanks, big brother. Thanks for everything." He placed the old baseball over the flower cup, like he had so many times before, but those were all fake good-byes. This was the real ball. This was the real thing. Sorrow welled up and hot tears fell silently onto the grave.

I love you, little brother.

The words floated around him, through him. Never even wondering how real they were, he smiled. "I love you, too. Good-bye, Michael."

See you later, Will.

Will swiped his hand under his eyes then rose and turned to see Maggie smiling as if her heart would break. "I heard him," she said as he bent to kiss her. "He said 'See you later,' and it was his voice. It was *his* voice." She looked at him. "I mean, I saw Gabe and Kevin's ghosts, but this was different. This was *real.* Do you know what I mean?"

"Yes. The Cockburns were residuals."

"Old cat crap." She grinned. "But Michael . . ."

"The real deal," Will said, taking her hand. "The real deal."

Author's Note

It's true. E.L.F. waves have been used covertly (and overtly) since the mid-twentieth century. With slight variations of degree, these microwaves can cook your dinner, transmit a phone call, subliminally suggest that you refrain from shoplifting, or fry your brain. Hauntings, particularly poltergeist activity, occur at a higher than normal rate near electrical currents.

The Navy recently showed off a microwave gun that cooks the enemy. They have H.A.A.R.P. and other big projects. Mind-altering microwaves have been used in riot control for years. Technology exists that allows a satellite to send suggestions or feelings of unease or illness to a mass of people or zero in on just one. The mention within this book of the Cold War antics between the U.S. and the Soviet Union is based solidly in fact. You can look it up.

Ever read a conspiracy-oriented book about mind control? I found them highly amusing and imaginative until I delved into books geared toward consumer awareness and the nuts and bolts of electromagnetics. For good basic information, I suggest *Electromagnetic Fields* by B. Blake Levitt. After you have the facts, try one of Jim Keith's books on conspiracies, and see what you think.

For more reading suggestions, visit my website, www.tamarathorne.com.

Dear Readers,

Ivy-covered halls. Tweedy professors. Homecoming. Football. Quarterbacks. Cheerleaders. Fraternities. Animal House and Skull and Bones. Keggers and cramming. These are the things we associate with college life.

But don't forget the sororities, especially Gamma Eta Pi, a very special one at expensive, isolated Greenbriar University, just a stone's throw from Caledonia. Only very special young women are considered for this elite group, and only a few of those are invited into the inner circle, a secret society known as Fata Morgana, where pledge initiations are taken to new highs, problems are solved with magic and murder, and mysteries are waiting to be solved by the right initiates.

Sorority sisters are sisters for life . . . and for death in Fata Morgana. These girls don't just have school spirit, they have school spirits!

Watch for THE SORORITY trilogy, coming to bookstores everywhere in June, July, and August, 2003. And if you or a loved one is thinking of joining a college sisterhood, you might want to think twice before even attending a rush party at Gamma. They can be murder. Watch for updates and background goodies on THE SORORITY, THE FORGOTTEN, and my other books at www.tamarathorne.com.

As always, thanks for inviting me into your home. If you do again, I promise not to steal any silverware. . . .

Tamara